From The library of girlean Chase
Ap 29, 1946 - Dec 05

D0208445

Love ruins everything

Love ruins everything

A Novel by

Karen X. Tulchinsky

To Gillean
Hope you enjoy the
book.
Karen X Tulchinsky

Press Gang Publishers
Vancouver

Copyright ©1998 Karen X. Tulchinsky
1 2   3 4   00 99 98

All rights reserved. This book may not be reproduced in part or in whole by any means without written permission from the Publisher, except for the use of short passages for review purposes. All correspondence should be addressed to Press Gang Publishers.

The Publisher acknowledges financial assistance from the Book Publishing Industry Development Program of the Department of Canadian Heritage, the Cultural Services Branch, Province of British Columbia, and the Canada Council for the Arts.

CANADIAN CATALOGUING IN PUBLICATION DATA

Tulchinsky, Karen X.
  Love ruins everything

  ISBN 0-88974-082-8

  I. Title.
  PS8589.U603L68 1998   C813'.54   C97-911076-9
  PR9199.3.T75L68 1998

An earlier version of Chapters 1 and 2 appeared in *HeatWave: Women in Love and Lust*, edited by Lucy Jane Bledsoe (Los Angeles: Alyson Publications, 1995).

"That's Amore" was written by Brooks and Warren, copyright Warner Chappel Music Canada.

Material on the origin of AIDS was paraphrased from the following sources: *AIDS and the Doctors of Death: An Inquiry into the Origin of the AIDS Epidemic*, by Alan Cantwell, Jr., M.D. (Los Angeles: Aries Rising Press, 1993); *Queer Blood: The Secret AIDS Genocide Plot*, by Alan Cantwell, Jr., M.D. (Los Angeles: Aries Rising Press, 1993); and *Emerging Viruses: AIDS and Ebola—Nature, Accident or Genocide?* by Leonard G. Horowitz, D.M.D., M.A., M.P.H. (Rockport, Massachusetts: Tetrahedron, Inc., 1996).

Edited by Ann Decter
Copy edited by Robin Van Heck
Design by Val Speidel
Cover art: detail from "The Dark City of My Heart Keeps Its Secrets Still,"
  watercolour and ink on paper, © 1997 by Sheila Norgate
Printed by Best Book Manufacturers
Printed on acid-free paper ∞
Printed and bound in Canada

Press Gang Publishers
225 East 17th Avenue, Suite 101
Vancouver, B.C. V5V 1A6 Canada
Tel: 604 876-7787 Fax: 604 876-7892

Dedicated to the 30 million people worldwide
who have been infected with HIV

Part

Life *is what happens while you're making other plans*

Chapter One

The last rays of the setting sun reflect off the Castro Theater marquee, shining brilliantly through the window onto the table at our favourite Thai restaurant in San Francisco. We come here every Tuesday night for their special on seafood curry. I squint at my lover through the glare. Sapphire smiles, reaches for her glass of white wine.

"I think we should become non-monogamous," she announces, taking a sip.

"*What?*" A chunk of curried prawn lodges in my throat.

Sapphire sets her wine glass down. Sucks in a deep breath. "I've wanted to talk to you about this all day."

I swallow hard, try to force the prawn down. "You have?"

"I've been thinking about it."

"Since when?"

She picks up her fork, plays with a piece of sautéed eggplant. "Since yesterday."

"Yesterday? What happened yesterday? I thought you went for groceries."

"I did."

"At Safeway."

"I did."

"And then you came home."

"Right." She stabs mercilessly at the eggplant. At the next table, a mere three inches away, a forty-something gay white couple are talking about a new software program that will revolutionize the banking industry. Both have short grey hair, balding on top. One has a mustache, the other a goatee. Their sweaters are in matching chartreuse.

"And while you were shopping you decided we should be non-monogamous?"

"Yes. No. Well . . . not while I was shopping. I don't know when. I just did."

I fold my arms across my chest. "Who is she?" I blurt, a little on the loud side.

"Nomi." Sapphire glances nervously at the sweater fags. There's a lull in their scintillating conversation. Forks scrape against plates. "Lower your voice."

"Why?" I shout. "I've got nothing to hide." Sapphire hates "a scene in public." Her WASP upbringing is deeply ingrained.

"Nomi, I won't discuss this if you keep shouting." Someone's cell phone rings.

"Who's shouting?" I yell. The fags raise their eyebrows in our direction.

"Hello?" A man behind me answers his phone.

Sapphire tosses her napkin on the table and stands. "I'm leaving," she whispers, glancing furtively about the room. Everyone around us is listening, half-hoping she'll throw wine in my face or slap me. Better story for their friends.

"Sapphire," I whine. "Come on. Sit down. You haven't finished yet." She shakes her head, silently fumes across the restaurant and out the door. I signal for the waiter. An instrumental version of "Have You Ever Loved a Woman?" is playing softly in the background.

I pay and run up the hill to our flat on States Street, the home I've shared with Sapphire for two and a half years. Jody, Sapphire's grey tabby, and The Twins—Martina and Whitney, two all-black kittens she recently brought home from the animal shelter—scamper over. Sapphire is lying on the couch in a knee-length Gay Freedom Day 1993 T-shirt, watching "The Simpsons." I stand beside the TV and watch her.

"Are you going to sit down?" She's still angry.

It occurs to me that *I* should be the angry one. "Are you going to talk to me? No one can hear us now," I say icily. It drives me crazy that she's so uptight. My family screams and carries on in public all the time. It's as natural as breathing.

Sapphire shuts off the television and makes room for me on the sofa. I sit cross-legged, facing her. She takes my hands and gazes at me with a sweet, loving expression, the very look I fell in love with in the first place. "I don't want to hurt your feelings, Nomi. I love you. It's just that . . . I've always gone right from one relationship to the next, with no space in between. I've never really been single, and I don't know how to date."

"It's not all it's cracked up to be."

She sighs. "Maybe so, but I need to find out for myself. I don't want to break up with you to do it. I just want to try my hand at dating. Can you understand that?"

"Sure, I understand. You're bored with me and you're looking for someone new." I sulk, turning away from her.

She leans forward to gaze into my eyes. "Nomi. I'm not bored with you."

I face her. "If you dump me for someone else I'll kill you."

She touches my cheek tenderly. "I'm not dumping you."

"I'll shoot you. I don't care if I spend the rest of my life in jail. I'll do it."

"Come here." Her hands draw me to her for a kiss.

The next day, I'm strolling down Castro, a warm sunny afternoon in early November. The morning fog has lifted, revealing a pure blue sky. I'm carrying a bag of groceries, a box of croissants and cut flowers for Sapphire, all of which slip from my grasp and slide to the dirty sidewalk when a huge muscular man with a buzz cut, baggy pants and a baseball cap bends forward and French kisses my girlfriend. I stare at them. Everyone else stares at me.

"Hey lady," an adolescent boy shouts. "You dropped your stuff."

The lovebirds break apart. Sapphire's eyes are soft and dreamy. She enjoyed being mauled by this Rambo. I stand, transfixed. The guy shifts to one side and Sapphire's eyes connect with mine. She freezes, like a kid caught smoking cigarettes or stealing candy. I glare pure contempt at her. She rushes toward me. Every muscle in my body flinches and I turn away, leaving everything on the ground.

"Nomi," she yells. "Stop!"

I stomp up the street.

"Nomi! Wait! Let's talk about this."

"What's to say?" I yell over my shoulder. It's uphill and I start to breathe heavily.

"Nomi. What about your stuff? You can't just leave it here."

"The hell I can't."

Then I don't feel her behind me anymore. She's stopped to pick up the groceries. I march right past our street and keep walking. And walking.

"I knew it," my mother says, when I call her in Toronto later that evening. Sapphire is out. We had a huge fight when I finally came home. She bolted, slamming the door behind her. I'm sipping a glass of Sapphire's fifteen-year-old port. A present from her father she's never opened.

"What? What did you know, Ma?"

"I knew she wasn't a real lesbian." There is smug satisfaction in my mother's voice, like she's just solved the bonus phrase on "Wheel of Fortune."

"Ma. What do you mean, a 'real lesbian'?"

"I always thought she was very feminine."

"Yeah? She was—is. So?"

"So? So, she probably really likes men."

"Ma, that makes no sense. Feminine doesn't have anything to do with it. Anyway, since when are you such an expert on lesbians?"

"I learned everything I know from you and a little from Phil Donahue too. Did you see the show about lesbian serial killers?"

"Ma, don't start with me. Please. Are you listening? Me and Sapphire are breaking up. It's just like a divorce, Ma. I'm a wreck. I want sympathy. I don't want Phil Donahue."

Silence. I can picture my mother nodding her head. I glance at the photo taken last December on our second anniversary, framed on Sapphire's fake-oak entertainment centre. We look happy and in love. I flip it face down. Hard. Unfortunately, the glass doesn't break. "You're right, Nomi. What was I thinking? I'm sorry. Can you forgive me? How are you, dear? You need anything? Why don't you come home? You can stay with me. It'll be fun. We'll have pyjama parties."

"Ma, I'm too old for pyjama parties and so are you."

"You're never too old for a little fun. Remember that, mamelah. It's very important."

"I'm staying here."

"What's to stay for? Why don't you come home?"

"This is my home, Ma. I live here now."

"Okay. You can't blame me for trying. So? Tell me. Are you okay for money? I'll send a little something to help out."

My mother the millionaire. We weren't exactly the Rockefellers when my father was alive. Now, she gets by on a small pension from an insurance policy my father left her, and part-time work in the synagogue gift shop. "Since when are you so flush? What? Did somebody die?"

"Nobody died. It's Murray."

"What? He gives you money?" Murray Feinstein is the man my mother has been dating. They met a year ago at the cemetery, after my father's unveiling. In Jewish tradition, a head stone is placed over a grave after someone is buried. One year after the funeral, the family gathers at the cemetery to unveil the stone, and remember the deceased. Murray was at the cemetery that day, paying respects to his wife.

"Watch your mouth, young lady. I'm still your mother."

"What did I say?"

"He takes me out three, four times a week for dinner, Chinese, Italian, steak, you name it. So, my grocery bill is a little lower these days."

"Oh."

I pretend to be asleep when Sapphire leaves for work the next morning. We work completely different hours. I tend bar Thursday to Sunday evenings at Patty's Place, a small neighbourhood pub in Bernal Heights. Sapphire's on day shift, Monday to Friday, at Good Vibrations, the sex toy shop in the Mission, which is hilarious. If her customers knew how uptight and repressed she really is, she'd never sell a single dildo. At the kitchen table, I sit with a cold cup of coffee for hours, in a state of shock. Sapphire lived in this apartment with her last lover too. This is Sapphire's apartment. Apart from that one picture of us, all the photos are of Sapphire's family. Her grandparents, Nanna and Poppa, her parents, her two blond brothers and her thin sister. All smiling. No one touches. The furniture, dishes, stereo, TV, the books, towels, knick-knacks are Sapphire's. I have my clothes, a couple of books, comb, toothbrush, gel, my helmet. Once we bought a garlic press together, hers was rusty. And the bed. We both chipped in for a new bed. The rest is all Sapphire's.

When I finally check the clock the whole day has gone. It's time to get ready for work. Sapphire will be asleep when I come home later. I feel like the earth has tilted and I'm slowly sliding into a big empty pit. I don't know what to do.

Tonight Sapphire wants to have dinner with me. I haven't seen her all weekend. She was out when I was home. Or sleeping. I was at work while she was here. She saunters in the door glowing, like someone newly in love.

"Hi, Nomi," she says, all casual, and slips past me into the bedroom. She's an hour late. I fume at the kitchen table. I bet she squeezed in a visit with Rambo. A silent rage bubbles up from the pit of my belly.

"I'm going to grab a quick shower," she chirps from the bedroom, "then we can go out."

I march into our room, fists clenched at my sides. "No, Sapphire. We can't." I say to the back of her head.

She swivels around. "What?"

"You're an hour late."

"Am I?" She glances at the non-existent watch on her naked arm.

"Look, I'm not a fool," I say, although it's not exactly true.

"Nomi . . ." She takes a step toward me.

"You were with *him*, weren't you?"

She sighs.

"That's what I thought." I go to the closet, yank open the door, search through a pile of laundry for my black canvas knapsack. Angrily I heave dirty clothes behind me into the room.

"Nomi, what are you doing?"

"Shit." Frustrated, I grab a tennis racket and toss it clattering onto the hardwood floor. An old bottle of sunscreen, a baseball, broken sunglasses, a running shoe, white extension cord, I hurl them all. "There." I haul out my canvas bag, cram in a few pairs of underwear, jeans, a couple of T-shirts, socks, push past Sapphire into the bathroom. My toothbrush, our toothpaste, my comb, cologne and face soap I stuff into the front pouch.

"Nomi, what are you doing?"

"Sapphire, I think the question is, what are *you* doing?" I fling the knapsack onto my back, wrench the front door open so violently it bangs against the wall and race down the stairs to the street. Fog obliterates the sun, casting a pall over the earth.

I roar down States Street on my red Honda Rebel. On Castro I pull over to the curb. Where will I go? The whole week has been nothing but pain. Every moment in that apartment with Sapphire is salt on an open wound. At 18th, I make a sudden U-turn and stop at the pay phone in front of A Different Light Bookstore, where I call Betty, my best friend.

"Get over here, girl," she orders. Betty lives alone in a one-bedroom apartment in Bernal Heights, not far from where I work. "Living room couch is all yours, babe," Betty says, "for as long as you want. You hear?"

"You're a lifesaver, Betty."

"You can flatter me later. Just get your white butt over here."

I jump back on my bike and ride up the Castro Street hill. Cool wind blows against my hot face. I'm so angry my emotional tremors could trigger a small earthquake.

"It's Sapphire again." Betty pokes her freshly-shaved head through the bedroom doorway, holding the phone receiver. "What do you want me to tell her?"

"Tell her to go to hell!"

Betty speaks into the phone. "Did you hear that? Uh-huh. Okay. Yep. I'll tell her." She passes through the living room to the kitchen, returns with two cans of Bud Light and hands me one. I screw up my face, but accept the beer and swallow a big swig. "How can you drink this stuff? It's terrible."

"You don't seem to mind." Betty sits beside me on the couch. Out of habit, she brushes the air behind her ear where her dreadlocks used to be, then leans back against oversized, multi-coloured pillows. Betty'd had dreads since 1985. Yesterday, she cut them off, shaved her head right down to the scalp. She says she's been cold ever since. "Want to know what she said?" Betty pulls the quilt from the end of the couch up over her legs. With the remote control, she switches on her thirty-inch TV screen. Stereo sound emanates from the speakers. She flips through the channels, stops at "The Simpsons."

"I hate this show," I announce, bitchily.

She looks at me like I've lost my mind. "You love this show."

I shrug. "I hate it. So? What did she say?"

She hesitates, examines my face.

"What?" I say, unnerved by her stare.

"You're not going to like it."

"So? What else is new? Tell me what she said."

"She says she never meant to hurt you. She never meant to . . . you sure you want to hear it?"

I beat my fist on the armrest. "I said I did. Just tell me."

"Okay. She says she never meant tofallinlovewithRichard. It

just happened." Betty spits the words like she can't wait to get them out of her mouth.

This is too much for me. I leap up off the couch. A stream of beer shoots from the top of my can onto Betty. "Richard? Richard! Just happened? Oh great! That's just great. It just happened," I repeat, as sarcastically as humanly possible. "How fucking original. Isn't that fucking original, Betty?"

"Not particularly." She dumps the beer-soaked quilt to the floor, raises her butt, reaches into her back pocket, extracts a blue bandanna and mops beer from her face and chest. Her black sweatshirt soaks up the rest of it.

"I can't believe this." I sink onto the couch, slam my beer can down on the end table, drop my face into my hands and begin to cry. Betty leans over, rubs my back and drinks her beer.

"Oh god," I let the tears flow.

"Poor Nomi."

"Oh shit. I can't do this. I can't cry."

"It's okay, Nomi. I won't tell anyone."

"No. It's not that. I have to work tonight."

"Oh."

I lift my head. "My eyes are all red and puffy already. Aren't they?"

She leans back to take a real good look at me. "Well . . . not so bad."

"You're lying."

She shrugs.

"Shit. I gotta stop crying," I say, which unleashes a new torrent. Betty makes sympathetic noises, strokes my back.

"Why don't you call in sick?"

"Patty'll kill me."

"No she won't. She'll understand. In fact, I think you should take the whole week off. You can't work in this condition." Betty reaches for the phone, hands me the receiver. "Go ahead. Call her."

"You think?" I sniff.

Betty nods.

I dial the number. The dog in the next apartment begins to bark.

On Betty's living room sofa, I toss and turn all night. It's an ancient love seat that does not pull out into a bed. Even at five-two, I am too long. If I lie on my back and stretch my legs out, I have to perch them on the opposite armrest. On my side in the fetal position, my knees bang against the back. Before sun-up, the woman in the next apartment is awake, clattering dishes into cupboards. A pillow over my head does not muffle the clanging of pots. Later, Betty bounds in, wearing longjohns under her jeans and a sweatshirt, even though bright sun streams through the living room window. "I'm going to Café Blue for a cappuccino," she says. "Wanna come?"

I drag the covers over my head. The quilt smells like stale beer. "No! I'm never going there again. Me and Sapphire used to go every Sunday morning."

"Well, it's Saturday."

Betty saves us a table on the patio. I go inside for drinks. Balancing two cappuccinos in one hand, a gigantic piece of chocolate cake in the other and a recent copy of the *Bay Times* under my arm, I squeeze my way through the narrow, crowded café. Almost at our table, I try to push past an unusually tall man. When I look up I'm face to face with Sapphire. The tall guy is *him*. Rambo. For a brief second I consider throwing hot coffee in Sapphire's face. She sees what I'm thinking. Her eyes widen, she looks at the cups, then back at me.

"Don't you just wish I was that immature?" I spit.

She extends her hands out in front of her. "Nomi. Please. Can't we just talk?"

"About what?" I thrust everything into her open arms. I don't look back when something crashes to the floor. Betty follows me outside.

"Okay. So coffee was a bad idea. But you know what I would do?" Betty sits on the living room floor, trying to decipher the instructions for her new CD player. She's nagging me to go out. All I do is mope around her apartment. I can tell I'm getting on her nerves.

"What?" I push a pile of silver paper clips to one side of the coffee table and a pile of brass ones to the other side. I've taken to sorting through Betty's junk drawers. It settles my nerves to put something in order, even if it isn't my life.

"Go out. Get laid. Have fun. Believe me, there's nothing better for heartbreak than sex. Nothing." She waves the CD player instruction booklet at me.

"What's this?" I show her a small metal object that might have once been a plastic keychain, covered in bubble gum so old it's melted. Underneath is a faint illustration of the Golden Gate Bridge.

Betty lunges forward, grabs the chain and hurls it into the garbage can. I decide to go out soon, if only to make Betty happy.

Later that night, Betty has a date. I rent *Moonstruck*, the only movie I can stand to watch. I open a can of Bud Light, pull Betty's quilt over my legs and settle in for the evening. During my second beer, my favourite scene begins. Late night in New York City, Loretta Casterini and Ronnie Cammerari stand outside Ronnie's apartment building. A cold winter evening, light snow falls as the new lovers argue.

"Love isn't perfeck," Ronnie declares. "Love breaks your heart. Love ruins everything."

I know the scene word for word. I speak the lines with Ronnie, imitating a thick New York accent, and just like him, I pronounce "perfect," "perfeck."

"We're not here to make things perfeck. The snowflakes are perfeck. The stars are perfeck. Not us. Not us. We are here to ruin ourselves and to break our hearts and love the wrong people, and—and die."

A single tear rolls down my cheek. I never thought our

relationship was perfeck, but I thought we had a good thing. I miss Sapphire, even though I hate her. As I drift off to sleep the titles roll and Dean Martin sings,

"When the moon hits your eye like a big pizza pie, that's amore.
When you dance down the street, with a cloud at your feet,
   you're in love.
When you walk in a dream
But you know you're not dreaming, Signora,
'Scuza me, but you see
Back in old Napoli, that's amore."

I dream I'm in an old four-poster bed. Around me are scantily dressed women whose sole purpose in life is to make me happy. One is kissing me. Another rubs my feet. Someone fixes me a drink. Someone else pays my rent. It's a lovely dream with a multi-million dollar budget and a cast of thousands, all of them beautiful. Sapphire roams in, wearing a black negligee, slips into bed beside me, pours tiny kisses all over my body. It's just like old times. We kiss. She touches me everywhere with silk fingers. I feel a peace I'd almost forgotten about.

I wake to keys jingling in the lock. Giggling. Betty and some woman I don't recognize creep into the apartment, trying unsuccessfully, in their intoxicated state, to be quiet.

"It's okay," I announce, "I'm not sleeping."

Silence, then, "Hi, Nomi. Sorry to wake you."

"I wasn't sleeping." I drag the covers over my head as they make their way to Betty's room, one paper-thin wall over. I try not to listen while they have sex. With my head under the covers I'm in a cave. It's pitch black. My heart hurts, beating cruelly against the inside of my chest. Quietly, with resignation, I cry. How did my life fall apart so quickly? Sleep creeps over the muffled sounds of Betty and her friend.

The next morning I decide to take Betty's advice. I ask for her help getting back into circulation. Betty knows everyone. She fixes me up with Alison, the younger sister of a woman Betty dated last year.

"Oh. Did I mention she just came out recently?" Betty asks as I'm about to leave.

"What?"

"She's a little shy," says Betty.

Alison and I go to the Castro Theater. They're showing *Forrest Gump*. I missed it when it first came out. Halfway through the film I casually slip my hand into Alison's. It's nice to touch someone again, but I'm acutely aware that the hand is not Sapphire's. It's thinner, the grip is weaker. Tears roll down my cheeks as the movie ends. I pretend they're for Forrest, but really, they're for me. And Sapphire. I fake a smile and suggest a drink at The Café, a second-storey bar overlooking Market.

At the door, Alison is asked for ID. Suddenly, I feel old. My whole life seems ridiculous. Why did I listen to Betty? I don't want to date. I want Sapphire.

"Alison, maybe we should just . . ."

The bouncer gives back her ID and nods okay. She smiles.

"What were you saying?"

"Nothing." We wander over to stools at an empty table by the window. The radio towers of Twin Peaks loom over the Castro.

Alison and I don't have much to say to each other. I'm new at dating and she's new, period. I scramble for small talk. The movie, the weather, our jobs, the community. After two drinks I'm enjoying myself. Maybe Betty's right. Maybe an affair would lift my spirits. I look at Alison. She *is* attractive. I smile. She smiles. The DJ slides on "Mighty Good Man" by Salt 'n' Pepa and En Vogue.

"Wanna dance?" I ask.

She smiles again. I lead her to the dance floor. I watch her hips sway from side to side as we dance. Her breasts are round and full in low-cut spandex. She looks more inviting by the moment. I wrap an arm around her waist. We dance tightly together, her body against mine. She feels different than Sapphire. Smaller around, a little taller and she moves slower. She looks deep into my eyes, licks her lips. I think she wants me to kiss her. I lean forward, slowly bring my lips to hers. She presses her mouth against mine, hard. Her tongue searches inside my mouth, soft breasts against mine, fingers in my hair. Rum and Coke on her tongue. We kiss until the song ends. She grins.

"Maybe we should go somewhere ... more comfortable," I whisper in her ear.

"Mmmm," she says in response.

We ride up Divisidero on my Honda and park on the sidewalk outside Alison's small ground-floor studio apartment on Haight. Her barred windows are covered in grime. Cars rush by, people yell, buses roar, music blares, panhandlers beg, dogs bark. The apartment reeks of cat piss. Footsteps pound overhead. The floor is sticky. Four hundred dishes crowd the sink.

"Oh damn," Alison curses, rushes over to the bed and feels the sheets. "Not again."

"What?"

"My cat's neurotic. Whenever I'm out, she pees on the bed."

"Oh." I laugh, even though it isn't particularly funny. "Come here."

She doesn't.

"What?" I ask gently.

"Uh," she puts her head down, "it's just that ... uh ..."

"What?"

She looks into my eyes, hers dreamy with lust. "Kiss me."

I do. We kiss for a long time. We grope each other through our clothes. My nipples are hard. I'm getting wet. Desire pounds against the stone fortress that surrounded my heart and seized my body the day I saw Sapphire kissing that guy on Castro. I ease Alison's corduroy jacket off her shoulders, toss it away. I undo the first small button on her sweater, the second button and the third. Her body stiffens slightly. Her hand grasps my wrist.

"What? What's wrong?"

She looks down again.

"Alison?"

"Look. Maybe you'd better go."

"Go? But I thought you said ..."

"I did, but I'm . . . just not ready."

"Not ready?"

"You know."

"Oh." I drop my hands to my sides. "Oh." I say again. "Are you okay?" I try to see her eyes, but they're hidden behind her long, straight hair. Maybe she's crying. "Well, okay. I'll go then. Uh, if that's what you want. That *is* what you want, right? For me to go?" I want to part her hair so I can see her eyes, but I'm afraid to touch her. She nods. "Well . . . ah . . . I'll . . . I'll call you. Okay?" I open the door quietly and let myself out.

"Don't be ridiculous, Ma. Of course I know about safe sex." I sip steaming coffee, reclining against the large pillow on Betty's couch.

"All right. I was only asking. Just in case, I picked up a few pamphlets at my doctor's office."

"Don't send pamphlets. I know what they say." Betty meanders into the room, naked from the waist up. She's growing more used to having no hair, and has stopped dressing for the North Pole. She passes the couch, heads for the kitchen, rubbing her eyes, stretching. Her baggy, navy blue Joe Boxers go all the way down to her knees. Sunlight floods the living room.

"It's no trouble, Nomi. A fifty-two-cent stamp I can afford."

"Please, Ma. Keep the pamphlets. Okay?" I hear Betty pour herself a cup of coffee.

"What can I say? A mother worries."

"Don't worry, I know all about it. Anyway, lesbians are a low-risk group." Betty trudges in with her coffee and sinks down beside me on the couch.

"Mamelah, what are you talking about—'low-risk'?"

"Ma. It's hard to explain." Betty raises her eyebrows and smiles broadly.

"I'm listening."

"The AIDS virus is . . ." I grope for words. "More present in sperm and blood than . . . anywhere else."

Silence. Betty puts her ear up to the receiver to listen in.

"Ma?"

"I'm listening. Go on."

I feel like I've entered a Woody Allen movie. This is too absurd for life. I scan Betty's living room for hidden cameras. How did I end up on my best friend's couch explaining HIV transmission to my mother? If I stall long enough, maybe Woody will save me by shouting "Cut!" I look to Betty for help.

Chapter *Two*

A week later B. J., Betty's girlfriend-of-the-week, introduces me to her friend Mimi, a librarian, a few years older than me, also recently divorced. She still lives with her ex. I don't know how she does it. I can barely stand the thought of Sapphire, never mind the sight of her. I ask Mimi out.

A steep flight of wooden stairs leads to a pale green Victorian with large bay windows, a fake front and ornamental trim circling white stone pillars. No one answers the bell. A TV blares the theme song from "Ellen" out an open window on the second floor. I ring again. I knock. I ring until I hear footsteps, nervously run a hand through my short hair to smooth it down. The door opens. Mimi is wearing a silk burgundy dressing gown, bare legs. Long brown hair tied back in a braid. Soft brown eyes.

I smile. "Hi."

"Oh, I guess you didn't get my message."

"Message?"

"I called to cancel. I'm tired. Had a rough day."

"Oh."

"Well . . ."

"Uh, well, would you like to take a rain cheque? We could go out some other time."

"Sure. Ah . . . what the heck. As long as you're here, we could go down the street for a coffee."

"Okay."

"But wait. I've got to get dressed." She shuts the door, leaving me on the front stoop. I lean back against the wall and watch people walk by.

Twenty minutes later the door opens. Mimi is wearing tight

black jeans, a red V-neck sweater, black leather jacket. Her hair hangs halfway down her back. I hold out my arm for her as we stroll down the street.

We talk over double lattes. Her life sounds even crazier than mine. She's spent four years with a big old butch called Nat, formerly Teresa Maria. They haven't had sex in over three years.

"But the first six months were great," Mimi stresses.

She still calls Nat her "partner" even though they broke up nine months ago, when Nat announced she was a "female to male transsexual" and entered the sex-change program at the University of California, San Francisco.

For the last six months, Mimi has been dating a bisexual woman named Wanda, who also isn't having sex with her.

"I go to her place and we watch videos. I come on to her and she says she's tired," says Mimi. "Every single time. I don't know what to do."

I haven't a stitch of advice to give. "More coffee?"

We're having a good time, so we go for steak-and-whole-bean burritos at the Taqueria on 18th and then she wants to go home.

"I'll walk you," I offer.

On the porch at her place, I wait while she opens the door. She smiles, reaches over and brushes hair out of my eyes. "Would you like to come in for a bit?"

"What about Nat?"

"Gone to visit her mother in Sacramento. She's going to tell her tonight."

"Tell her what?"

"About her sex-change operation." She takes my hand. Hers is soft and warm. I squeeze gently. She leads me up a steep flight of stairs and into a large two-bedroom flat with ten-foot ceilings. In the living room an ornate crystal chandelier hangs from a ceiling trimmed in swirls of plaster. A large fireplace with a hand-carved baroque mantel dominates one whole wall. The polished hardwood is covered with a red-flowered throw rug. Built-in glass cabinets are crammed full of video cassettes, CDs and books. We sip bottles of Corona on a beige couch, its wide seat built for long-legged people. I sit forward to compensate.

"So?" Mimi says.

"So."

She sips her beer.

I sip mine. The glass bottle cools my sweaty palms.

"How long did you say you and Sapphire were together?"

"I didn't." I stare into her eyes. She smiles. I move closer.

"Oh." Again she lifts her beer bottle to her mouth, tips it back.

"Three years. Well, it would have been three years next month. Hah. I was going to take her to the Russian River for our anniversary. Anyway, who cares? You have really beautiful eyes." The last person I feel like talking about right now is Sapphire.

She bats them. "I do?"

"Yeah." I grin.

"Thanks."

"I'd like to kiss you," I risk.

Mimi looks nervous, but shrugs and says, "Okay."

I shift sideways, position my lips against hers. I kiss her, but she just sits there, not kissing back. I retreat.

"Don't you want me to?"

"I thought I did," she sighs. Bites her lower lip with her front teeth. "You're very attractive." She plays with my hair. "It's just that I realize I'm still in love with Nat. It feels wrong to kiss someone else."

"I thought you said you broke up?"

"We did."

"And she's a transsexual now, or whatever you call it."

"FTM."

"So how can you be in love with her?"

"I don't know. I just am."

"Well, Mimi." I grope for something to say. "Well. As a friend—that is, if I was your friend—I'd say you're selling yourself short. I mean, you said you haven't had sex with her for three years, and the bisexual isn't having sex with you either."

"Yeah? So? What's your point?"

"Uh . . ." I laugh, unnerved by her building anger. "Well, nothing, I guess. I guess I have no point."

"Cause you don't know anything about it."

"No," I agree.

"It's complicated."

"Yeah?"

"Yeah." She crosses her arms over her breasts.

"Yeah. I mean, yeah, I see what you mean." I stall, trying desperately to coax her back to her former pleasant mood.

She yawns. Suddenly and dramatically. Deposits her beer bottle on the coffee table.

I wait.

She yawns again. I take the hint.

"Well. I guess I should be going." I place my bottle on the table beside hers, and stand, hoping she'll grab my arm, say she's sorry, beg me to stay. She remains silent as I slip on my jacket. "Well," I stick out my hand.

She shakes it lamely.

"Goodbye." I let myself out.

It's a chilly November evening in San Francisco. Most of the year the weather is mild, even warm, but the nights are almost always cool, leather jacket weather. A Sunday night, the Castro is filled with people trying to prolong the weekend. On the corner in front of Walgreens, a young blond boy hands out flyers for a new dance club. Beside him, a thin man with dirty hair asks me for spare change. I take a flyer, shrug at the panhandler, feel instantly guilty, check my pocket, find a quarter and drop it into his plastic cup. I stroll farther up the hill. I'm not ready to go back to Betty's place yet. A light rain begins to fall. I slip into The Café for a nightcap. There are quite a few people inside. Men and women. White, red and blue spotlights reflect off black walls. The music is loud. People are smoking strong cigarettes and yelling in each other's ears. The patio doors are open. Traffic noise from Market Street drifts in. Car engines, a bus, a man yelling for a taxi.

Some serious dykes are playing pool, concentrating on their shots, while others write their names on the green blackboard in white chalk and wait for their turn. A few people are dancing to Gloria Gaynor's "I Will Survive." Nostalgia for disco is big this season.

I order a vodka martini and sit on a high stool at the bar, not really paying attention to anyone else, just concentrating on my own thoughts. I try to make sense of my life.

I fell in love with Sapphire three years ago. I didn't mean to. We met while I was in San Francisco on a trip. I was staying with Betty then, too, representing the Toronto Gay and Lesbian Film Festival Committee. I was supposed to attend the San Francisco Queer Film Fest and meet with people on their committee. Bring back ideas to our group. Betty was my official host.

Betty introduced me to Sapphire, a fact I never let her forget now. Sapphire was on the San Francisco committee with Betty. She had a lover when we met—Marlene—who also worked on the committee. I noticed Sapphire, but knew she had a lover, so I figured she was off limits. Saturday night, the Film Fest dance was in the Women's Building on 18th, in the Mission. The committee had decorated the room with vintage movie posters, *The Wizard of Oz*, *The Sound of Music*, *Singin' in the Rain*—that classic shot of Debbie Reynolds, Gene Kelly and Donald O'Connor, in yellow rain slickers and floppy rain hats. There was a bar in a corner of the room and a rented theatre-style popcorn machine, continuously popping. The popcorn and imitation butter smelled like the movies. I was hanging out against the back wall, with Betty, drinking beer and girl-watching.

Sapphire sauntered over to me, took my hand without a word and led me to the dance floor. She was a little drunk. She rubbed her body up against mine. I could see Marlene watching us from the other side of the room. I told Sapphire. She just laughed and carried on. Moments later, Marlene disappeared. That's when Sapphire really got into seducing me. Guess I should have known right then what kind of woman she is. Insecure. Goes from one relationship to the next, without even bothering to break up with her last lover first. But who pays attention to reality when true love beckons?

"Marlene is all wrong for me," Sapphire explained. "We were about to break up anyway. I just had the guts to do something about it."

Four months later, on one of our late-night phone calls, Sapphire talked me into moving to San Francisco. Actually, it wasn't that hard. I'd often fantasized about moving to the Gay Mecca by the Bay.

"Just give it a try, honey," she begged. "You can always move back. And this way, we'll be together. Isn't that what you want?"

What the heck, I thought. I quit my job—it wasn't a great job anyway, delivering packages downtown as a bicycle courier—gave up my apartment, packed a bag and hopped a plane three weeks later. California, here I come. Figured I'd just go and see what happened.

"Can I get you another martini?" It's the bartender.

I look down at my drink. Empty. Check my watch. "No. No thanks. I'm fine." I slide off my stool, fix my hair in the bar mirror and head out the door into the damp night.

"Who says I'm depressed?" I'm sitting cross-legged on Betty's couch with the quilt over my head, like a tent. Talking to my mother.

"Believe me, Nomi. A mother knows."

"Ma, that is so cliché." I raise the quilt up at the bottom to let in some air.

"Are you eating?"

"Yeah, Ma. Last night I ate a whole box of Oreos."

"You didn't."

"Okay. Half a box."

Betty struggles to sew a button onto a black denim shirt. I've never seen a worse attempt. Jabbing her finger, losing the needle, sewing the shirt closed by accident.

"Give me that." I snatch it and start stitching properly.

"Why don't you come too? We're going dancing at The Wet Spot. It'll be fun. Maybe you'll meet someone."

"No thanks. I'm through with dating. I'm no good at it." I twist the end of the thread into a knot and break it with my teeth.

Betty laughs. "Girl, you'll be fine. You just need more practice. Come on. I'll wait while you get ready."

I check the rest of the buttons on her shirt. "No. I'm going to stay in and watch *Moonstruck*."

"Again?"

I fling the shirt at Betty. She catches it in mid-air.

Betty showers, tries on several outfits, shines her shoes, reorganizes her wallet, clips the chain to her belt loop, re-shaves her head, exchanges the silver stud in her pierced lip for a gold ring. When she finally leaves, I slip *Moonstruck* into the VCR and settle down on the couch with a bowl of popcorn, a bottle of Dr Pepper and Betty's quilt. Dean Martin begins to croon. The telephone rings.

"Hello?"

Silence.

"Hello? Hello? Who's there?"

"It's me," Sapphire says quietly.

Silence.

"Hello? Nomi?"

"Yeah. I'm still here. What do you want?"

Silence.

"I want to see you. Can I come over?"

"No."

"Nomi, please? I want to talk to you."

"Why?" My heart pounds. Sapphire's voice moves me more than I want it to. I put a hand on my rib cage.

"Can't I come over to Betty's? I want to talk in person."

"What happened? Did he dump you?"

Silence.

I laugh cruelly. "He did, didn't he?"

"Yes." Quietly.

Silence.

"What do you want me to do about it?"

"I want to talk. I'm coming over."

"No! Don't bother." I hang up. Loudly.

Ten minutes later the doorbell rings. I open the door. Sapphire's been crying. I want to tell her to go to hell, but I can't. She looks crushed. I hold the door open wide. She slips out of her shoes and plods past me. I follow. In the middle of the living room, hands at her sides, she gazes at me, her eyes soft, full of emotion. It might be love. It could also be regret, or guilt.

"I made a mistake. Nomi. I don't know what else to say. It's over now. Please. I want you back."

I slump down on the couch, snatch up my bowl of popcorn and balance it in my lap. "Are you crazy?"

Sapphire sits beside me. "Maybe I am. I don't know. I miss you."

I shove a handful of popcorn in my mouth and chew loudly. On the TV, Loretta Casterini is fixing Ronnie Cammerari a steak.

"Nomi . . ." Sapphire lays a hand on my arm. Her familiar touch soothes and infuriates me at the same time. I turn to look at her. She's crying. "I'm sorry, Nomi. I love you."

My head feels like a helium balloon straining to float away. I don't know what to do. This has never happened to me before. I leap up, plunk the popcorn onto the end table and pace back and forth on the living room carpet.

"Let me get this straight, Sapphire. You met some guy, fell in love, got dumped and now you want me back?"

She nods her head and sighs.

I laugh bitterly, shake my head. "That's great, Sapphire. That is truly twisted. How do you think I've felt these last three weeks? What do you think this has been like for me? You think I can just forget that you dumped our three-year relationship on account of some *guy*? Some *straight* guy?"

"He's bi."

"Oh great. Even better. I hope you used condoms."

"I know you're mad . . ."

"Mad? Mad? Are you kidding? I'm furious. And hurt. And humiliated . . . and lonely."

"Me too," she says. "I miss you."

I turn my back to her and face the television. With one drastic swing of his good arm, Ronnie Cammerari sweeps the dinner dishes, table and all, onto the kitchen floor. He crosses the room, embraces Loretta and they kiss. The music swells to a crescendo. I face Sapphire. I know her so well. Everything about her.

"You didn't miss me so much last week. Did you?"

"Nomi. Please, don't do this." Sapphire's head follows me like a spectator at a tennis match. I pace again.

"So? Was the sex good?"

"Nomi . . ."

I step closer, so I tower over her. "Was it?"

She bounds up and stands at the window, her back to me. Sounds drift up from the street. Two men laughing and talking.

"Was it?" I scream at Sapphire.

She pivots around and glares at me. Sighs. "What do you want, Nomi?"

"Answer my question. Was it good?"

"It was . . ." she frowns, looks off to the side.

"What?"

"Different. It was different. Okay? That's all. Just different."

I stare at Sapphire. Different. Is that what she was looking for? Something different? She stares back. Frowns. Like she's trying to guess what I'm thinking. And then my body betrays me. I want her. I want to touch her. I hate her and want her at the same time. I imagine what it would be like to just reach over and take her in my arms. It would feel so regular. Like something I do every day. Not weird at all. Outside, there is a terrible screech of car brakes, the unmistakable crunch of metal on metal, a cacophony of horns. A woman screams. I stare at Sapphire, my eyes set, determined. Wordless, I cross the room. She gasps. Her hand flies to her forehead as if she were a Southern belle, dazed from the heat and too much gin.

Outside, a man is yelling. A car alarm sounds.

I seize Sapphire by the shoulders, crush my lips on hers, frantic. She moans, kisses me back, flings her arms around my neck. Like Ronnie Cammerari, I bend down and sweep her up. Carry her to the couch.

"Nomi?"

"Shhh."

I am lost in the sweet familiarity of her body against mine. My desire is reckless, rash. Hands on her face, I devour her lips. Her tongue in my mouth carries me back to our home together, our life. Our first time and all the other times in one climactic moment. I lunge for her breasts. She tears at my shirt. Naked, wild, desperate, flying on angel-hair wings, to the skies, to the sea, to the beautiful sea,

"You and me, you and me, oh how happy we'd be.

When the moon hits your eye, like a big pizza pie, that's amore.

When the world sees a shine, like you've had too much wine,

you're in love."

My fingers are inside her. I know her so well. Know just how she likes it. She moves circles on me, pushing and sliding. Soft and wet. My face in her breasts. Warm, slippery, red fire. Tight waves crash and break. We kiss. She moans. I feel her inside me. Searching, hungry, reaching for my centre, my heart. Oh honey, oh baby, I miss you. I want you.

"Yes, baby, yes!"

Her hair in my face, sweet scent of her, on my tongue, my fingers, my mouth. She bites my nipples. Raw, sweet pleasure. Sliding in and out of her, of me, of my life. We bob on the sea, on the sea, on the beautiful sea, you and me, *you and me, oh how happy we'd be.*

She comes fiercely, head arched back, eyes closed. Her fingernails scratch a trail down to my ass, sharp, razor thin strokes of passion. Longing. Desire. Home. *You and me, you and me, oh how happy we'd be.* Sirens wail in the distance. We lie still. I hold her. The siren stops outside the window. A flashing red light circles around the living room walls. We sweat. And we breathe.

Ronnie Cammerari says, "Love isn't perfeck. Love ruins everything. Love breaks your heart." And I understand how true those words are. I love Sapphire. And everything is ruined. Our home, my trust, our love. I stroke her sweaty forehead, my other arm wound intimately around her. I have no idea what I want to do. I want our old life, but the past is past. And everything is different now. I want to kick her out, make her suffer the way I did. I want to kiss her, make love with her, lose myself in her sweet salty kisses, her familiar embrace.

A key turns in the lock. Betty walks in. Practically drops her iced mochaccino when she spots me and Sapphire naked on the couch. I smile meekly, embarrassed. She flashes a look that says she can't wait to hear about this, smiles and heads for her bedroom. I squeeze Sapphire tighter. We watch the end of the movie in silence. And I decide not to decide anything, tonight.

Chapter *Three*

I wake with the sun, lying on my back on Betty's couch. Sapphire is asleep on top of me, cutting off the circulation in my right arm. Slowly, I slide my dead limb from beneath her. It tingles. I rub it. The hair on the back of my head is damp with sweat. Sapphire nestles closer into my clammy neck. It feels almost like old times, snoozing on my back with my girl-friend snuggled in my arms. Peaceful, dreamy, safe.

But these are new days. Sapphire and I are not at home, in our love nest, happily enjoying a morning together on our comfy queen-sized Sealy Posturepedic bought together on our second anniversary. We are crammed tight on my best friend's narrow, threadbare couch, where I sleep, hurt, betrayed and humiliated.

Last night was a crazy thing. I must have had a complete mental breakdown. One minute I wanted to hurl my treacherous ex-girlfriend out the front window to burst on the street like a bag of rotting trash. The next, I threw my pathetic wounded self into her arms. The sex was more exciting than it had been for a long time. I was an animal, a great lover, I was raging lust, hurtling downstream on untamed passion.

Am I still in love with Sapphire? I study her, try to determine what I feel. Anger. Regret. Indifference. I realize what last night was all about. The final fuck. One last plunge for old time's sake. A long-standing lesbian tradition, like moving in together on the second date, or becoming best friends after breaking up. A lesbo ritual, time honoured and strictly adhered to. Lesbian instinct, like salmon swimming upstream to spawn.

I stare at Sapphire's face. She looks older. Like she's aged five years in the last two weeks. I wonder how I look. Probably like a lunatic. I have toppled over the edge of the falls in a barrel. Who, in their right mind, would sleep with a girlfriend who dumped her for a guy, and then grovelled her way back the second the guy dumped her? Only a complete sucker. A thoroughly miserable, hopeless bottom-feeder, slithering slimily through the muck of a vile swamp. Every angry bone in my body begins to tremble. I disgust myself. Sapphire disgusts me. I want her off me. Out of here. I pull away and sit up. The movement wakes her.

She opens her eyes and smiles. I scowl. Her eyes widen. She sits up.

"Uh-oh," she says. "What's wrong?"

I fold my arms across my chest. "What's wrong? What's wrong? That's a good one, Sapphire."

"What?"

"What do you think?" I fling the covers off us.

"You're angry."

"Good guess."

"So? What's going on? I mean last night . . ."

"Last night was a big mistake. I should have my head examined." I lean forward and drop my unexamined head into my hands.

Sapphire sighs deeply. "So. What are you saying? Are you saying you don't want me back?"

I lift my head and look into her eyes. The rage I feel at Sapphire's betrayal churns in my belly, circles like a tornado. I leap up, shake my fists in the air. I can't speak. I can only breathe, quickly, in and out, through clenched teeth. Sapphire's hair is matted on one side of her head. She looks like the Wicked Witch of the West. I reel away from her, stumble through the kitchen, into the bathroom, and slam the door. Grief rips through me, sobs into my open hands. I turn on the shower to hide the sound of my crying, and step in. Hot water pounds down on me. I'm the biggest fool alive. I can never leave this bathroom again. It's too embarrassing. I don't want to face Sapphire, Betty or anyone else. I take an obnoxiously long shower, until the hot water runs out. When I emerge, Sapphire has gone.

In the kitchen I grind coffee beans. Betty's antiquated grinder roars like the beginning of the next war. The racket pleases me. I empty the dish drainer, bang pots into cupboards, loudly. Betty stumbles in. Her bald head is covered with a backward baseball cap. She is dressed for work in her Super Shuttle uniform, black pants, white shirt, black tie, blue company windbreaker slung over one shoulder. She stands in the doorway. Watches me.

"So, aren't you going to say anything?"

She shrugs. "Any more coffee?" She slips her jacket onto the kitchen doorknob.

"There's lots." I yank open the cupboard, seize a mug, slam it onto the counter, slosh coffee into it, spilling some, and thrust it toward Betty. She tentatively reaches out her hand, gingerly places the cup on the counter. Crosses past me to the cupboard for a bowl and grabs a spoon from the drawer. Betty fills her bowl with Shreddies from the ever-present box on top of the fridge. Betty loves Shreddies, eats them morning, noon and night.

"Interesting times, huh?" Coffee and cereal in hand, Betty strolls into the living room and sits on the couch.

"I know what you're thinking," I say, following her.

"No you don't." She shovels a huge spoonful of cereal into her mouth.

"You think I'm crazy."

She shrugs, chewing.

"You're right. I am. That was a crazy thing to do. I couldn't help it. I love her. No. I hate her. I don't know. It just happened." The second the words are out of my mouth, Betty and I turn simultaneously to stare at each other. Neither one of us mentions the obvious. I sound just like Sapphire.

"Murray asked me to marry him," my mother says later, over the phone. I figured this might happen eventually. They've been dating for nearly a year. Murray seems like a nice man, but I don't really know him. I only met him the once, at my father's unveiling. It's good news, I guess. Ma seems happy when she talks about Murray. It's just that right now, I can't deal with one more thing.

"Nomi, are you listening to what I'm saying?"

"Course, Ma. That's wonderful. So, what did you say?"

"I told him I had to think about it. What else? I'm not a young woman, Nomi. At my age a person doesn't just jump into something like marriage. After all, I've only been seeing him for a little while. What would people think?"

"Ma, who cares what people think? What do *you* think?" My head hurts. I need an aspirin. I stand and tug on the phone cord. It reaches only halfway across the kitchen. The bathroom is another three feet away. I hover in the middle of the room rubbing my temples with my free hand.

"Me? I don't know. I never thought this would happen, Nomi. I thought your father, may he rest in peace, would still be here. How's the weather out there?"

How's the weather? How can she go from my father to the weather? "The weather?" I peer out the window for the first time that day. "It's fine. The sun is out."

"Good. There's a hurricane in Florida. Your Great Aunt Bessie is there. I called earlier. She's a nervous wreck. There's storm warnings out all over Miami Beach. People are supposed to stay inside. Can you imagine Aunt Bessie staying in? She's probably sitting at her usual spot by the pool, playing solitaire. I can't get it out of my mind. I see her being swept away by a fierce wind. Like in that old Judy Garland movie."

"Judy Garland? You mean *The Wizard Of Oz*?" I have to laugh. My great Aunt Bessie is seventy-five. She has one of those old-fashioned women's one-piece bathing suits, with the little flap over the crotch. She wears bright red lipstick, a little dollop of rouge on each cheek, and a huge straw hat, held in place by a bright green kerchief tied under her chin. Her sunglasses are vintage 1955, horn-rimmed, with green and white rhinestones in the corners. Her husband, my Great Uncle Sam, died twenty years ago, and now every winter Aunt Bessie goes to Florida for a month, stays in a low-budget hotel for seniors several miles inland from the beach. Every day she sits in the same folding lawn chair by the pool, plays cards and listens in on other people's conversations. I picture a twister, whirling around the pool deck, swooping down and carrying off Aunt Bessie, chair and all, to the Land of Oz.

"What do you think, Nomi? Should I call her?"

"Ma, I'm sure she has the sense to stay inside if there's a hurricane. You worry too much."

"You don't know Aunt Bessie."

I have to go back to work. Either that or kill myself. It's been almost two weeks since I've made it in to Patty's Place. I'm running out of money and there's only so much Betty is willing to do for me. My job tending bar isn't exactly kosher, if you know what I mean. I'm a Canadian living in America without a Green Card. I want to get one. I don't want to break the law. But in America it's illegal for homosexuals to fall in love with foreigners. Straight people do it all the time. They get married and get Green Cards. Just like that. I found out shortly after I arrived that I couldn't get a Green Card, and without one, I couldn't get a job. I didn't know how long I'd be able to stay. One evening, I was hanging out at the pub with Betty. She was urging me to talk to Patty.

"Just tell her where you're from," Betty whispered in my ear as she shoved me toward the bar, "then tell her your predicament."

"Why?" I dug my heels into the wood floor, so she would stop pushing me.

"Just do it." She nudged me forward.

Patty is Canadian too, born and raised in Sudbury, Ontario. She's been living in San Francisco since 1967, when she moved out here to be a hippie. In those days it was easier to go through immigration. Especially if you were white, or looked white. Patty's one-quarter Ojibwa, actually, but she didn't bother telling the INS that. It's not like she's status or anything. Now, Patty is a legal alien. She showed me her Green Card. It was kind of disappointing. It isn't even green. It's pink. She took pity on me when I told her I couldn't get a job and wouldn't be able to stay in San Francisco much longer. She hired me on the spot. I get paid in cash, under the table. I have to be really careful about who I tell. You know how people are. Mostly, when they ask about my accent, I just say I'm from back east.

"From north of Buffalo," I say. A lot of Americans haven't heard of Toronto anyway, or if they have, they think it's in Ohio. It's nerve-wracking to have to lie like this, but I have no choice.

I pick up the phone and punch in the number, hold the receiver up to my ear and wait. Patty never answers until the fifth ring. She thinks it makes the pub appear busier than it actually is.

"Patty's Place."

"Hi, Patty."

"Nomi? Is that you?"

"Yeah. I've risen from the dead."

"Well, it's about time." Patty is not a tactful woman.

"So I was wondering . . ."

"Course you can have your damn job back. Robert's been filling in for you on Fridays and Saturdays and I've been picking up your other shifts. We're both beat. I tell you, this working for a living is for the birds."

"You saved my shifts for me?" I am truly touched. It's the first nice thing anyone has done for me all month. Well, except Betty, who has earned the Lifetime Achievement Award in friendship by now.

"Course, Nomi." Patty lowers her voice to a low grumble. "We got to stick together. You know what I mean?" She means *us Canadians*.

"You bet we do." I've never been the patriotic type, but for Patty, I'll make an exception.

"So get your buns down here ASAP. I'm tired and I want to go home."

"But it's only Wednesday. I usually work on Thursdays."

"Hurry up, Nomi. Before I change my mind."

"Okay, Boss."

I hang up the phone and haul myself up off the couch. At least I still have a job. It's definitely time to get back into the world. If I continue moping around at Betty's, I'll become a sour old dyke, a butch version of Miss Havisham, the old spinster in Dickens' *Great Expectations*. Years from now, I'll be sitting on Betty's couch, my muscles atrophied, cobwebs draped from my head, my face wizened and lined with sorrow. My grief, frozen in time. I'll be mentioned in gay travel books. Dykes visiting San Francisco will drive by in tour buses, peer through my window to catch a glimpse of the living dead. Once every five years, my story will make it into the *Bay Times*. Younger dykes will shake their heads, warn themselves against ever becoming like me. k.d. lang will write a song and Ellen Degeneres will base a whole comedy routine on my life story. My mother will appear on Phil Donahue, the brave parent of a mentally deranged lesbian spinster. Each time she tells my story on national TV, Sapphire will appear more and more evil, until eventually she'll no longer be able to walk the streets free from harassment and ridicule. Well, that part I could live with.

Getting ready for work I come to the conclusion that life is crazy. After weeks of torture, Sapphire shows up begging me to take her back, and I don't want her.

"I don't want her," I say out loud. "I don't want Sapphire!" I scream at the top of my lungs, testing the words. "I don't want her. Don't want her. Don't want her. Don't want her!" As incredible as it sounds, it's true. She can go straight to hell and never come back for all I care. Shalom, shweetheart. See you in hell. I dress quickly, then tromp into the bathroom to brush my teeth and comb my hair.

Outside, I fire up my bright red, 1985 Honda Rebel 250, wait for it to warm up. When I was buying a bike, I really wanted a black one, but Sapphire thought the red was flashier. I swing my leg over and straddle the seat. I never liked this bike. I wish I had a black bike. I only got this one to please Sapphire. How many other things did I do just for her?

At the bar, I dread going inside. I'm thankful to have my job back, but I know Patty's going to make a big fuss the second I waltz in the door. I stall for a moment and look in the window of Bernal Books. There's an author's reading next week, contributors to an anthology about breaking up. Great. Think I'll skip that one. I love Bernal Heights. Perched high above the Mission, it's cute and cozy. Quiet. A real neighbourhood. The streets of houses and shops twist and turn, up the hill and down again. More and more dykes are moving up here. The houses, though Victorian, are smaller and of simpler design than houses in the Castro. Patty's Place is at the top of the steep hill on Cortland Avenue, surrounded by bookshops, grocery stores, cafés and delicatessens. Two doors down is an Irish pub, called Flannigan's. Its street sign is covered in four-leaf clovers. Patty has a small pink neon sign that reads "Patty's Place." Beside the name is a blue neon martini glass, with the word "Cocktails" written in pink neon script above the glass. Patty's front door is heavy oak. I take a deep breath, jerk it open and step inside.

"Well, look who finally graced us with her mighty presence," Patty booms across the room.

I cringe. "Yeah, you know, I was in the neighbourhood and decided to drop by. Just for a minute or two."

"A minute or two like hell." Patty swoops out from behind the wood counter to give me a bear hug. "Come 'ere, you."

She squeezes me so hard I think she is going to break me in two. For a second I wonder if she is mad at me, she's hugging me so tight. Then, she releases her hold just as suddenly as she had grabbed me.

"Let me look at you." She stands back and surveys the damage. "You look terrible, Nomi. Good thing you're back. We'll have you looking like your old self in no time. Won't we?" she asks a drunk woman sitting on a stool, her hand tight around a glass of Scotch.

The woman nods, scowls and laughs. In that order.

I don't want to be my old self, I want to find a new self. Maybe I already am new. I don't say anything to Patty. It seems like it would upset her.

It is unusually busy for a Wednesday night. I work like a dog, with no breaks, no time even for a cigarette. Though I quit smoking years ago, I still think I should get a smoke break. What I do on it is my business. Maybe it isn't any busier than usual. Maybe I'm just not used to it. Maybe in two weeks off I forgot what it's like to work in a bar. People seem meaner. Drunks seem drunker. Lousy tippers lousier. Maybe I should have just killed myself instead of coming back to work. Easier, less painful and better for my feet. Patty returns at closing time, like always, to count the money and help me clean up.

"Good to have you back, kid," she says. There's a bottle of gold tequila in front of her, and two shot glasses. "Join me in a drink."

"Sure." I can't think of a better idea at this point.

"Sit down a minute, kid. Forget about cleaning up." She pats the stool beside her. I put down my bar rag, walk around the counter to the customer side and hop onto the stool. She pours me a shot of tequila, passes the salt. I shake some out into the hollow between my thumb and index finger, lick it, throw the shot to the back of my throat and suck on a lemon wedge. The fiery liquid burns down to my stomach. Patty downs her tequila, without lemon or salt, just straight as she goes. She rests her glass on the counter, looks over, studies me. Uh-oh. I know this look. She's about to grill me.

"So, what the hell happened to you, huh?"

I sigh, grip the bottle, refill both glasses, lick salt, knock back another shot and suck on a lemon wedge. Patty belts her shot, and watches me, a solemn look on her face. She can wait forever for me to answer her question, and she will. I contemplate another drink. I sigh. "I don't know, Patty. Everything fell apart. It all unravelled."

"How?" She pulls a pack of Marlboros from her shirt pocket, taps the pack against her left hand, slips a cigarette between her lips, lights the end and inhales deeply.

"I don't know, Patty. It happened so fast. For a long time everything was great, then one day it fell apart. I don't know where I went wrong. I guess I wasn't paying attention." I reach for the tequila bottle. This conversation is depressing me. I pour another.

Patty nods knowingly. "That's it, kid. That's it in a goddamned nutshell." She snatches the bottle and refills her glass. "You gotta pay closer attention, Nomi. That's your problem. You're not paying attention."

I stare at Patty skeptically. It's kind of hard to take advice from her where relationships are concerned. In the two and a half years I've known her, she hasn't had a single girlfriend.

"Believe me, I know what I'm talking about. Well." She slaps her thigh, as if something important had just been settled. "Time to get back to work."

Clear this is my cue, I slip off my stool and commence clean-up.

When I open the apartment door noises drift toward me from Betty's bedroom. Sex noises. Loud sex noises. Betty has yet another new girlfriend. She doesn't stick with any woman for long. Betty believes she will never have her heart broken this way. If she never feels much, no one can hurt her much. A few times I've tried to convince her that she'll also miss out on a lot of joy, but Betty has her mind made up.

Betty hasn't always been like this. She used to fall in love at the drop of a hat. Your typical U-Haul dyke, head-over-heels after the first date. That was pre-Donna, back-up singer in the Marlettes, an all-woman reggae band. Betty fell deep for Donna. Bought her an engagement ring and everything. Eighteen-carat gold, with a diamond. Donna left town suddenly one day with the band's new drummer, without even leaving a Dear John letter for Betty. Kept Betty's ring and flew the coop.

That was two years ago. Betty swore she'd never fall in love again. Now she refuses to date anyone for more than two weeks, three at the absolute, and then only if she doesn't like the woman much. If she really likes someone, she won't even go out with her twice. Betty figures that way she'll stay safe.

The new girlfriend is a computer programmer named Nita. Betty met her at the bank. Betty is the only lesbian I know who meets women at regular places like the bank or on the bus. The rest of us meet our girlfriends at dyke bars, softball games or demos. But my friend Betty can find women anywhere. How she does it is beyond me.

I close the door, flop down on the couch, find the remote wedged between the sofa cushions, and flick the television on loudly. I'm not in the mood for TV, but I can't stand to hear the sounds of Betty having sex with whoever she met at some regular place today. I don't feel like having sex with anyone, but I'm jealous all the same. I'm jealous because Betty is happy and I'm miserable. Betty has found a way to protect her heart and I haven't. Betty has a bedroom and all I have is a sofa. She is laughing and kissing someone, and I'm sitting on the couch with nothing to suck but my own thumb.

I turn up the volume outrageously high, so loud the walls are vibrating. For a brief second I worry it will disturb Betty. Then I don't care. I'm half-hoping Betty will storm out of her bedroom and have a knock-down, drag-out fight with me. At least I'd be engaging with someone. Better than sitting here alone, feeling sorry for myself.

I channel surf until I find an "I Love Lucy" rerun, where Ricky and Fred change places with Lucy and Ethel. The guys stay home and attempt to do the housework—burn the ironing, boil so much rice it pours all over the kitchen floor—while Lucy and Ethel get jobs in a candy factory. They sit in front of a conveyor belt, grab pieces of chocolate, wrap them and set them back down. A matronly supervisor instructs them not to let a single piece of chocolate go by unwrapped. Otherwise, they will be fired.

All of a sudden the conveyor belt speeds up. To keep the chocolates from escaping, Lucy and Ethel snatch pieces and eat them, stuff others down their shirts and in their hats. The conveyor belt accelerates. Frantically they seize pieces of candy.

There is chocolate everywhere. On their faces, in their hair, on their shirts. Everything is wildly out of control.

It's exactly how I feel. The conveyor belt is moving faster and faster and no matter how hard I try, I can't wrap the chocolates before they run out the other side. If I don't get my life together soon, the supervisor will show up and I'll be fired.

Chapter *Four*

Ringing jars me from a deep sleep.

"Hello!" I bark into the phone, hoping to scare whoever it is into hanging up.

"Nomi! Is that how you talk to your mother?"

Oh shit. "Ma. How was I supposed to know it was you?"

"Who else would it be?"

The logic of mothers. "Ma, it could be lots of people." I flop down on my pillow, rub my eyes, stretch my free arm. My mother often phones first thing in the morning, oblivious to the three-hour time difference.

"So? How's my favourite daughter this morning?"

"Ma, I'm your only daughter."

"So? You're still my favourite."

I desperately need a coffee, but there isn't any made yet. The phone cord doesn't reach to the kitchen counter and grinding coffee beans on Betty's jackhammer grinder is out of the question. Betty and her newest are still asleep. The last thing I want to do is wake them up. They'd probably start having sex, and I'm already depressed enough. "So, what's up, Ma?"

"Does something have to be up, Nomi? I just wanted to see how you were doing."

I can tell she's lying. Something is definitely up. I also know she won't tell me directly. She wants me to guess. To figure it out for myself, as if I know every little thing that could possibly be going on with her. I try the sneaky approach.

"How's Josh?"

"Who knows? You think your brother ever remembers to pick up a phone and call his old mother?"

"I thought he calls you every Friday night."

"He does. Would it hurt him to call a little more often? He lives right here in Toronto. It's not long distance. Your other brother I don't need to hear from. Let me tell you. A mouth like that on a young man, I never heard in all my life."

Bingo.

"What are you talking about, Ma? What did Izzy do?"

"Tell me, Nomi. Do you think it's right? Should a boy talk to his mother that way?"

My mother has this habit of beginning a conversation right in the middle, as if I've been there all along and know exactly what she's talking about. "What way, Ma?"

"What way? I'll tell you what way. With a big mouth. He's still a pisher in my books. Doesn't even have a regular job. He's cooking hamburgers at McDonald's. Can you believe that? A boy with a college degree. Who ever heard of such a thing?"

"Ma, it's the nineties. It's hard to get any job these days. What did he say?"

"Answer my question."

Oh boy. This is going to be a long one. "What question?"

"Should a son talk that way to his mother? If your father, may he rest in peace, was still here today, he'd raise a hand to that boy. And your father was never the violent type."

I'm about to explode. "Ma! What did Izzy say?"

"What did he say? I'll tell you what he said."

Finally.

"It's about Murray."

"What? What about Murray?"

"Your brother thinks I shouldn't marry him."

"He said that?"

"I mentioned that Murray asked me to marry him and your brother had a fit."

"He had a fit?"

It doesn't sound like Izzy. My brother Izzy is mild mannered, quiet, the brainy type. Self-conscious about his thick glasses, shy with girls, has one or two friends he hangs out with. They play computer games and invent things. I don't remember ever hearing Izzy raise his voice. My brother Joshua is more passionate. He's gorgeous. Curly dark hair, deep-brown eyes, a Greek-god body. He always has girlfriends. Especially since he started playing guitar in the JD's, a local rock band. Josh I can picture raising his voice. But Izzy getting excited about anything besides his experiments seems a little unbelievable.

"Ma, are you sure it wasn't Josh?"

"Nomi, I still have all my marbles. I know which of your brothers opened a big mouth to me. It was Izzy."

"What did he say?"

"He thinks I should wait."

"Wait?"

"To marry Murray. He thinks it's too soon. That I don't know him well enough yet."

"That's what he said?"

"He said he won't come to the wedding."

"The wedding? There's going to be a wedding? You mean you've decided?"

"I'm not getting any younger, Nomi. Murray wants to marry me. What if I say no? He wants a wife. He'll find someone else. Believe me, Nomi, there's no shortage of Jewish widows in this town. Already Sonia Greenblatt is breathing down my neck."

"She is?"

"You better believe it, kiddo. Every time I see her she asks how it's going with me and Murray."

"So?"

"It's the tone in her voice, Nomi. I know what she's really asking."

"You do?"

"Sure. She wants to hear that things aren't going so well, so she can pick up where I left off. She'd steal him right out from under me if she could."

I picture my mother on top of Murray Feinstein, an image I don't want to see. "So? You've decided then? You're going to marry him?"

"What choice do I have, Nomi? I don't want to grow old alone. Believe me, it's not like there's lots of other men where he came from. What if this is my last chance?"

"But, Ma—do you love him?"

"Love? Who knows from love? I loved your father, may he rest in peace."

"You're not in love with Murray?"

"I'm fond of him."

"Well, Ma. What if you're wrong? What if there are other men out there? Maybe there's someone you'd like better." The plumbing pipes squeal as the woman in the next apartment turns her kitchen taps on.

"Nomi! Don't you start with me too. I've made up my mind. It's set. We're getting married week after next."

"Week after next? Ma! Why so soon?"

"It's Murray's birthday. We thought it would be fun to get married on his birthday."

"Ma, that's so soon. I don't even know if I can get a cheap plane ticket on such short notice. You have to book three weeks in advance to get a deal."

"Nomi, you have to. I can't get married again unless my only daughter's here."

"Tell him to set a later date. This is ridiculous, Ma. It's so sudden. Are you sure? Let's talk about it a little." I feel frantic. Like my mother is about to make a huge mistake and there's nothing I can do to change her mind.

"What's to say?"

"Ma. What are you talking about? This is a big decision. This isn't like you. Are you depressed? Is something wrong?"

"Of course there is. Everything's wrong. Everything's been wrong since your father died. Tell me, Nomi, why did he leave me? It was too soon."

There is nothing, really, that I can say. There is no answer. I know it. My mother knows it. She just needs to speak the words out loud. I let her. The conversation goes on like this for a while before Betty wakes, stumbles into the kitchen, turns on the grinder, and, thank god, fills the coffee pot with water.

"Nomi. What's that terrible noise?" My mother is suddenly aware of things other than her depression. "Is there construction next door?"

"No, Ma, it's the coffee grinder," I shout above the roar.

"So loud?"

"It's old." I cup a hand over my free ear to block out the din.

"So? Nomi, you'll come, then? To my wedding?"

"Ma. Of course I want to come to your wedding, but so soon? It's such short notice. A ticket'll cost me a fortune. And I don't know if I can get time off work again right now. I just went back. Can't you wait just a little longer? How about next month?"

"Try, Nomi. Please? Call a travel agent and see. We're not having anything fancy. Just you, the boys, Murray's daughter, the immediate family. A small reception at your Aunt Rhoda's house. After all, a blushing bride I'm not. We don't need to spend a fortune. Am I right, Nomi?"

"Yeah, Ma, you're right. Listen, I'll see what I can do. Okay? But can't you just talk to Murray about next month?"

"Okay, mamelah, I'll talk to Murray."

We hang up.

Betty turns off the grinder, switches on the automatic drip machine, pads past me to her room. I sit, listening to the water gurgle. My mother is getting married. It seems like my father just died. How did two years go by so fast? And who the hell is Murray Feinstein anyway? I don't even know the guy. Am I supposed to call him Daddy? Pop? Murray?

It's hard to feel good about my mother's pending nuptials. Since I left Sapphire, I have become a cynic in the worst way. I haven't a shred of romanticism in my heart. I see only the bad in every relationship. When things will begin to fall apart, and how. When two people should just stay the hell away from each other. There is no forever. Forever is only as long as things last. I will never fall in love again. Love ruins everything. And things are bad enough as it is.

I'll become one of those lonely old dykes with thirty-seven cats. I'll never go out. Not to the bar, not out for dinner, not to parties. I'll go to work and come home. I'll feed my cats (that alone could take all evening), I'll watch the late show or Jay Leno, and I'll fall asleep on my couch, a cat on each side, several by my feet and a couple on my lap. I'll be in control of my life. The conveyer belt will slow and I will wrap every single chocolate that passes in front of me, before it reaches the other side.

As I sit planning my tranquil future, Betty walks by. She bends, peers at me, scowls, sighs and continues into the kitchen. On her way back through the living room, she balances three mugs of coffee. She deposits one in front of me and leaves with the other two. I mean to thank her, but I have no words. I am lost in a lingering depression. I suppose something will have to change soon. Perhaps the answer is simple. I should just go on Prozac like everybody else.

On my way to work the next day, I stop at a red light on the steep hill where Dolores meets 20th. A grassy boulevard in the middle of the wide street separates northbound traffic from south. A long row of palm trees runs down the avenue. Before I moved to San Francisco I didn't know there were so many different types of palms. Some are tall, with huge leaves that shower down like green umbrellas. Some are short and stubby, with trunks like giant pineapples. They remind me of a tropical paradise. A large house on the other side of the street is surrounded in scaffolding. Two men stand on a second-storey plank, scraping paint from a window frame. A warm breeze passes, sweet like blossoms. I breathe deeply. In my peripheral vision pedestrians step off the curb at the intersection. The first two pass by. The third person stops right in the path of my front tire. It is none other than my cheating, lying, ex-lover, What's-Her-Name. I snarl and look right through her.

"Nomi!" she says, all excited, like she's thrilled to see me.

Her voice penetrates to the core of my heart. I grit my teeth, sneer through the face mask of my helmet and say nothing.

She doesn't budge. "Nomi." She reaches out and places a hand on my forearm. I can feel it through my leather jacket. I jerk my arm away.

"Nomi. I . . . I really want to talk. I mean, I'd like to get together."

I laugh sarcastically.

"No, really. I was going to call you."

I snort.

"To see if you'd be into getting together. For coffee or something."

"What for?" I say coldly.

"Nomi. Please. Believe it or not, I still care about you," she whines.

"Yeah. Sure." I twist the throttle with my right hand, to gun the engine. Just for effect.

"Nomi."

The light changes. I pop my bike into first gear, release the hand brake, so the front tire rolls slowly forward. Sapphire does not move out of my way. She grips the handle bars to stop me.

"Please, Nomi. Just for coffee."

The car beside moves ahead. A truck behind honks his horn. I know I should tell Sapphire to go to hell. But the sound of her voice tears me apart. I'm so miserable. How could meeting her for coffee make things any worse? Anyway, I've been meaning to stop by her apartment and pick up the rest of my stuff. "When?" I ask.

The truck driver leans harder on his horn.

"Really, you mean it?"

"Come on, buddy! Move it!" The guy in the truck hollers out the window.

"When?" I repeat impatiently, gesturing with my head at the angry guy to the rear.

"How about tomorrow?" she says quickly. "Oh shit. I can't tomorrow. Uh, how about Sunday?"

"Sunday?" I say blankly, as if it was a day I'd never heard of.

"Yeah. Day after tomorrow." She studies my face.

I hear a screech of tires. The truck squeals out from behind and squeezes into the other lane, passing awfully close to me. "Fuck you!" he screams.

"Okay? Sunday?" Sapphire tries again.

I stare at her, skeptically. Should I just go and check into the nearest loony bin for even talking to her?

"Nomi?" She cocks her head to the side.

"Fine. Okay. Sure."

"Great."

"Where?"

"Uh, how about Café Blue?"

"Fine." I grunt.

"What time?"

"Time?"

"Yeah."

"I don't know. Seven," I decide.

"Good." She leans forward like she's about to kiss my cheek. I lurch my head back abruptly.

"Now get out of my way. I'm late."

"O . . . kay," she says.

She moves a couple of inches toward the curb. I shift my bike into gear, open the throttle full, roar up the hill and away from her.

"Uh-oh," says Patty as I storm into the pub. "Looks like someone's in a bad mood."

"I am not." I march around behind the bar, snatch the rag out of her hand and savagely wipe the counter.

"Whatever you say, Sunshine." Patty shakes her head, raises her thick dark eyebrows. "We're out of Guinness. The Bud Light tap is acting up, so don't even bother serving it. I just got a case of Wells tequila cheap, don't ask me how, it's none of your business, so we're having a special on tequila drinks—a buck-fifty each, even Sunrises. And don't give away all my garnish like Robert does. I'm trying to make a damn living. I'm out of here." She whips off the short, white apron that makes her look more like a short-order cook than a bartender, slips it on the second shelf under the cash register, where she keeps her extra pair of glasses, lucky dice, smokes and comb. "I've got a date."

"What?"

I reel around and stare at her. Patty hasn't had a date in all the time I've known her.

"Which part didn't you get, Einstein? The part about the Guinness or the tequila specials or, god help us, everything I just said?"

"The date. You're going on a date?"

"Close your mouth, kid. You'll catch flies that way. Yeah, a date. I have a date. And you can keep your damn wisecrack comments to yourself, okay?"

"Sure."

I try not to smirk as I remove my leather jacket and hang it on a hook behind the door that leads to the basement. Patty strolls toward the rest room, where presumably she's going to get changed.

It's a regular Friday evening at Patty's. There are a couple of dykes and a couple of straight men lined up on high stools at the bar, drinking pints of beer, or Scotch-on-the-rocks. The small bar television is switched to the news. The two guys are intently watching, making the occasional comment to each other. The anchorman is reporting on the upcoming civil suit against O. J. Simpson. The men watching disagree with each other about the case, and loudly expound their personal theories. The two women are reminiscing about some game they just played. I can't quite tell if it's basketball or volleyball, but it definitely has to do with a gym and a ball and a team. At the pool table are two straight guys who look like they wish they were dykes. They wear plaid flannel shirts, Birkenstocks and jeans. They have a dog who lies curled up in the corner napping. Patty has a loose policy about pets. Regular customers can bring well-behaved dogs into the bar, as long as Patty's cat appears to like them. Marge, an old brown and black Siamese, is usually found on top of the juke box, her tail getting in the way of the selection guide. Sometimes on busier nights, annoyed, Marge will move to the back and perch right on top of the Guess Your Own Weight game which gathers dust in the corner, the least-used piece of machinery in the pub.

I go to the small bar sink to wash glasses. Patty hates doing dishes and always leaves me with a big stack when she's been tending the bar.

"So? How do I look?" Patty emerges from the rest room. Her straight black hair is slicked back more than usual. She's wearing a crisp white button-down shirt, black jeans and a blue flowered tie.

"Wow." I can't hide my surprise. "Patty. A tie and everything. This *is* special."

She gives me a look. "No comments, Rabinovitch. Remember our agreement."

"Hey. You got me all wrong, Patty. I'm just admiring your appearance. You look great. Knock 'em dead. Go on, I'm fine here."

She blushes, then looks around for a moment. "Listen, if it gets too busy in here, call up Robert and see if he can come in. I don't like leaving you alone on a Friday night."

"I'll be fine, Patty. Go. Enjoy yourself."

"I'm serious, kid."

"I know you are. I'll see you tomorrow."

With a huge smile on her face, Patty swaggers to the front of the bar and shoves open the massive door.

The thing I like about my job is that every shift is different. You never know what's going to happen, who's going to walk in, what kind of mood they'll be in, how they'll get along with the others. Patty's Place is a neighbourhood pub. The building is nearly a hundred years old, probably built just after the big earthquake in 1906. Patty's been running the place for fifteen years. It's not a fancy dance club. No DJ or dance floor. Just an old juke box in the corner, that sometimes skips. It's small, barely bigger than the average coffee shop. The floors are real hardwood, unpolished like in an old Wild West saloon. A long oak bar takes up much of the space. There is a small pool table near the door, a couple of tables with chairs and many of Patty's special touches. Patty loves picking up vintage items at yard sales and auctions. The pub is packed with junk.

In a back corner, there's a red leather barber's chair, circa 1930, in which people can sit and put their feet up. There are several clocks, only one of which works, and it's on bar time—twenty minutes fast, so that we make sure to have all the alcohol cleared away by cut-off time. The cops tend to be harsher on gay bars, especially known lesbian bars, and Patty doesn't want to take a chance of losing her licence. Everyone knows the clock is fast, but no one complains. They all know the reason. Anyway, the regulars know that staff can be convinced to pour a drink after last call, when begged to, as long as the customer downs the whole damn thing by two on the bar clock.

The walls are covered with memorabilia, an old "Enjoy Coca Cola" poster, neon beer signs, a toilet seat, a fake Mona Lisa, a yellow-on-red sign from the 1920s which reads "Tables for Ladies," a football helmet, several brown fedoras, a red feather boa, chrome handcuffs and a black-and-white photograph of Craig Russell as Judy Garland. On the ceiling are a five-foot-long poster of Marilyn Monroe, another of Janet Jackson, a limited-edition poster of the Beatles and an original placard from Harvey Milk's election campaign of 1978.

There is an odd mix of customers at Patty's. Although Patty doesn't call her place a dyke bar, word has spread in the community that it's run by "that old bulldagger," as Patty jokingly calls herself, so there's always an assortment of lesbians. Old-time feminists in flannel shirts and Gore-Tex jackets, young bald girls, tattooed and pierced, urban gay professional women, briefcases parked by their feet. Mostly, though, we attract the softball, darts and bowling team type of dykes, the kind with scruffy dogs named Butch and Rover, who work at the post office or for the electric company. Strangely, we also get a steady clientele of straight boys—hippies or dyke wannabes depending on how you look at it—with long hair, flannel shirts and baggy blue jeans, who also have scruffy-looking dogs named Butch and Rover.

It's not a bad job. Could be worse, and it's not the kind of job you take home with you at the end of the night. Occasionally a particular customer stays in my mind, or a tricky situation that I could have handled better, cutting off a drunk customer, or keeping the peace between the dykes and straight boys. But most of the time, the second I step out of Patty's, work leaves my mind. These days I'd be only too happy to be deeply distracted by my job. When your love life is in the toilet, it must be nice to throw yourself into your work. It could be the time you discover the cure for cancer or finish that novel you've always meant to write. At least you have something to show for your misery. What could I possibly do? Invent a new cocktail? Figure out why the juke box gets stuck when you punch selection A3?

"Hey, bartender!"

I look up. A drunk dyke at the far end of the bar is motioning at me, angry. How many times has she called me? I flash her my most conciliatory smile.

"What can I do for you?"

"What do I have to do around here to get a little service?" she bellows.

"Another Jameson? And a pint?"

"Wait until Patty hears about this," she tells her friend, while I fix their drinks.

I sweep my way down the bar, to see who else needs refills.

As I'm mixing a Long Island Iced Tea—four different kinds of booze plus Coke—the phone rings. I pick up the receiver.

"Patty's."

"Your mother called."

"Betty, my mother calls me all the time. What's the big deal?"

"The phone's been ringing off the hook. I haven't been answering. I've been . . . busy. But I just checked the messages. She called four times. Sounds really upset. I just thought you'd like to know."

"Shit."

"Whassa matter?" the drunk at the end of the bar asks.

"Anyhow, Nom, see you later, tomorrow probably."

"Okay. Thanks, Betty. Hey, Betty, what did she say? Did she say what was wrong?"

"Uh . . . something about an argument with your brother."

"Oh, Izzy again."

"No, I think she said your other brother, Josh. Yeah, she said Josh."

"Oh. Now she's mad at Josh, too?"

"What?"

"It's a long story, Betty. Anyway, thanks. But I can't really call her right now, the place is packed. It's nuts in here. Sorry about this. Really. I'll tell her to stop calling so often."

"Don't sweat it, Nomi. You should hear *my* mother go on. It's not your fault. Chill out. You sound stressed."

I put the phone down and go back to my Long Island Iced Tea, which by now is double the usual strength. The woman getting this drink is going to pass out from the fumes alone.

At 1:30 by the bar clock, I yell last call. The heavily intoxicated woman at the end of the counter raises her hand like she's in school. She's so tanked I should refuse her another, but try and fight with a drunk. I jam as many ice cubes as possible into her glass and pour a small amount of whiskey on top.

"Drink up folks!" I yell above Diana Ross and the Supremes singing "Stop in the Name of Love." "Bar's closing. All drinks off the table in fifteen minutes."

It's 1:45, bar time. I want everyone finished and out of here by 2:00. Patty's date must be going well. If not, she'd have come back by now to check on me.

"Come on, bar's closing," I say to the two drunk dykes. They lift their drinks, knock them back and attempt to stand. It's hard to say which one is shakier, but somehow they manage to hold each other up and stagger out of the bar. I pray they're not driving. When they're gone, I close the heavy wooden front door, drop the thick steel bolt in place. I crank the music way up. The Beatles, the Stones and the artist formerly known as Prince fill the empty bar with music. I cash out, rinse glasses, put bottles away and sweep. The key rattling in the lock and the thump of someone pounding on the door startles me.

"Hey! Rabinovitch! Lemme in!" Patty bellows, banging her fists on the door.

"All right. All right." I scoot around the bar to let her in.

"Jesus." She covers her ears with both hands. "Would you turn that down? Whattsa matter? You deaf or something?"

I lower the volume. "Didn't think I'd see you again tonight. How was your date?"

I continue sweeping. Patty shakes her head, sighs, walks around to the other side of the bar and pours herself a glass of Scotch.

"Women," she grunts as she brings the glass to her lips and takes a large swallow.

I stop sweeping. "What happened, Patty? Didn't it go well?"

She glares at me. "What's the matter with women, Rabinovitch? Are they all crazy or what?"

I shrug.

"Get this, okay? She says she likes me, she really likes me, but she doesn't want to see me again, because she likes me too much. She's not ready for a relationship and she thinks she might fall in love with me, so just in case, she doesn't want to see me again. Can you figure that?"

"Sounds like Betty."

"Yeah, you're right. It does. Hmmm."

"What's her name? Maybe she's one of Betty's ex's."

"Aw, what's the difference?" Patty downs the rest of her drink and pours herself another. "So, how'd we do tonight?"

Chapter *Five*

Sunday evening, I'm getting ready for coffee with Sapphire. Betty walks in smoking a big, fat, smelly cigar.

"Come on, girl. Grab your jacket. It's Boys' Night Out."

I wave at the smoke in the air. It smells awful. "What?"

"A new tradition. I just invented it. Boys' Night Out. Like it?" From her shirt pocket she produces a second cigar, peels off the plastic, stuffs it between my lips and holds a burning match up to the end. I tilt back a few inches to avoid the flame, remove the cigar from my mouth. It leaves a sweet taste on my tongue.

"What's Boys' Night Out?"

Betty looks at me like I'm stupid. "I call my butch friends and we do something real guy-like. You know, like smoke cigars and play poker, or go to a strip joint, or meet at Patty's and drink pints of Guinness, eat peanuts, throw the shells on the floor."

"Everyone does that at Patty's."

"Come on, girl. Get ready. Wear a football shirt and a baseball cap. Going to be great." She snaps her fingers high in the air. "I'm going, you, A. J., Guido, Chester, even Patty might hang with us."

"I have other plans." I tramp into the bathroom. She follows.

"Plans?"

"I'm meeting with Sapphire." I smear green toothpaste onto my toothbrush.

"What? You crazy, Nom? What for?"

I turn on the tap, and brush my teeth. Vigorously.

"Nomi, why?"

"Because she asked me to." White foam drips down my chin. I slurp it back into my mouth.

"Because she asked you?" Betty puffs robustly on her cigar.

"You're not going back to her?" She leans one hand against the bathroom door frame, eyes wide with horror.

I spit toothpaste into the basin. Watch it dissipate slowly into the water. Betty's bathroom sink is blocked and drains sluggishly. I reach for my tube of gel. "I don't know, Betty. I honestly don't. She wants to meet, so I'm going. Anyway, I want to get my stuff."

"You think it's a good idea?" Cigar smoke fills the room. It makes me cough.

"I don't know." Absently, I stick one hand into the half-filled sink, press my palm over the drain. Sometimes suction helps it empty quicker.

"Promise me, Nomi . . ." Her cigar sticks out from between her lips at the side of her mouth.

I wipe my hand on a towel, dab some Polo for Men on the back of my neck, squeeze past Betty. On the couch, I pull on my Doc Martens. "What?"

"That you speak to me first. 'Fore you make any decisions."

"I can't promise that, Betty." I reach for my leather jacket from a hook on the wall.

"Fine." She folds her arms across her chest. Thick curls of grey cigar smoke billow up in front of her face. "Then you leave me no choice. I forbid you to go." She stands in front of me, to block my way. I cough, wave at the smoke and walk around her.

"I'll let you know what happens." I open the front door. "Don't wait up."

She puffs on her cigar, removes it, exhales. "Sure you wouldn't rather come to Boys' Night Out?"

The stench of Betty's cigar follows me into the hall.

At Café Blue I order a cappuccino and carry it to a small wooden table in the corner. I leaf through a copy of the *Bay Times*, not really concentrating. The heavenly aroma of fresh coffee surrounds me, along with the muted mutterings of other people's conversations, covered periodically by the hiss and gurgle of the espresso machine. Sapphire is twenty minutes late. I order a second cappuccino. Another twenty minutes ticks by. I can't believe it. This was Sapphire's idea. Why is she not here? Maybe something happened. I want to call her, but there's no pay phone in the café, and if I leave, maybe she'll show up and think I didn't come. I finish my coffee, then decide to risk it. I find a phone booth half a block down on Market. Sapphire answers on the third ring.

"Uh, why aren't you here?" I try to keep the anger out of my voice, give her the benefit of the doubt.

"I'm not coming, Nomi."

"What?" I stare at the graffiti covering the telephone and glass. Symbols and teenage code words.

"I can't."

"But I don't understand. This was your idea. I can't believe you didn't show up. You just left me sitting in Café Blue waiting, like an idiot."

"I'm sorry, Nomi."

"You're sorry?" I pull the receiver away from my ear, shake my head at it, put it back. "You're sorry? That's the best you can do?"

"I was wrong."

"This was your idea, Sapphire. You asked me." Wind blows exhaust fumes under the bottom opening in the phone booth.

"I know. It was a mistake."

"So that's it? You're not coming? You don't want to talk?"

"No." It sounds like she's been crying.

"I don't understand, Sapphire. What's going on?"

"I'm sorry, Nomi."

"Sorry about what?"

A guy in a soiled ski jacket with wild hair knocks on the door to my phone booth. I ignore him.

"Sapphire, what's going on? You said you wanted to talk!"

"I know. It was a mistake. Listen, I can't talk right now. I gotta go . . ."

"Wait a second. Don't you think you at least owe me an apology or something? For leaving me sitting here like a schmuck?"

"I said I was sorry."

The guy continues knocking. I scowl at him.

"Sorry? Shit. What's all this about, Sapphire?"

Silence.

"Huh?"

More silence.

"Oh. I get it. He's come back to you again. Hasn't he?"

"Well . . . no." She sounds defensive.

"Oh, yes he has. I can tell by the tone in your voice. Dammit, Sapphire! Don't lie to me. You at least owe me the truth!" The homeless guy raises his eyebrows at me, shakes his head and walks off. Others pay me no mind. This is the Castro. People have seen behaviour far wackier than mine.

"All right," she admits.

"I knew it!"

"I'm sorry, Nomi . . ." she whines.

"Sorry? Right. Well you know what, Sapphire? I'm sorry, too. I'm sorry I ever met you. You know that?"

A fire engine roars by, siren blaring.

"You don't mean that, Nomi."

"The hell I don't!" I yell over the siren, then bang the receiver down so hard it hurts my hand.

Humiliated again, I want nothing more than to bury my head in the sand. But I really need to be with my friends. Embarrassed or not, I ride over to Patty's to see if Betty and the others are still there.

Betty and the gang are sitting at the big round table near the back. They all have unlit cigars in their mouths. Patty must have forbidden lit ones. They are drinking beer, talking and laughing loudly. I thump over, fling myself into the chair beside Betty, plunk my helmet onto the table in front of me. Everything stops. Betty looks at me.

"Don't say it, Betty. Don't even think it," I warn.

There is dead silence for a moment. Betty's chair scrapes loudly against the floor. She stands and ambles over to the bar.

"Bartender!" she shouts at Robert, a fifty-something gay man. In his younger days he was a celebrity drag queen at Perry's on Folsom. An old friend of Patty's, he's worked on and off at the pub for years.

"Yes ma'am." He curtsies, as if the Queen herself had signalled.

"A large glass of your best Scotch," Betty orders.

"Is this for you, or our unhappy friend?" Robert enquires.

"It's for her."

"Then I think Patty would want this one to be on the house." Robert places a fancy pink umbrella on the edge of the glass before he hands it to Betty.

Betty deposits the drink in front of me. I extract the umbrella, look at it as if it was poison and let it fall to the table. I sip on the Scotch sullenly, as the gang slowly re-enters their festive mood.

"So, this girl asked me out," brags Guido, exhaling a stream of cigarette smoke upward through the corner of her mouth. In her other hand, she plays with her unlit cigar.

"Who?" asks Betty, skeptically.

"I met her in the grocery store," says Guido, grinning.

"No way," I snarl. I thought only Betty met girls in regular places. Now Guido is having that kind of luck too?

"Yeah. At Cala." Cala is a big supermarket right in the Castro. It's 110 percent gay, so it doesn't really count as a regular place.

"Oh," I say, disappointed.

"Yeah. So what happened?" asks A. J.

"She's a check-out girl. I see her in there all the time. She's always checking me out, if you know what I mean." Guido laughs uproariously at her own joke.

"Ha, ha," says Betty, flicking the end of her unlit cigar over the ashtray, as if it really had an ash.

"So what happened?" says A. J., peeling at the label on her beer bottle. A. J.'s been married to her girlfriend Martha for about five million years. We all think they stopped having sex a long time ago but A. J.'s embarrassed to say so.

I sip my drink, listen and sulk.

"Well," Guido leans in close. "I'm at her counter, right, and there's a huge line-up after me, but she goes real slow, picking up all my groceries one at a time, giving me these long meaningful looks as she passes my things over the scanner. Then, when everything's done, she looks right at me and says, 'Is there anything else you'd like to check out?' Can you believe it?" Guido slaps her knee.

"No way," says Betty. "You're making this up."

"Humph," I say.

"Only to you, Guido. These kinds of things only happen to you," Chester says, setting her cigar on the table, running a hand through her wavy salt-and-pepper hair.

"Shut up. Let her finish," says A. J., leaning forward.

I drain my drink, stare at the table, fume silently.

Guido takes a big drag from her cigarette, leans back in her chair, smirking like a really big butch, proud and fierce, even though she's about four-foot-eleven in her boots. "Well, I move in to her real close-like," Guido continues, "and I say, 'Yeah, baby, I'd like to check you out.' "

"You did not," Betty says.

"What'd she say?" asks A. J.

"She said, 'Meet me in the parking lot in half an hour.' " Guido takes a final puff, grinds out her cigarette in the ashtray, pops her cigar between her lips, folds her arms across her chest, and tips her chair backward onto its two back legs. The glint in her eye is positively arrogant.

"So, did you go?" A. J. prods.

"Course she went," says Chester, patting Guido on the back exuberantly. "This is Guido we're talking about here, right Guido?"

I can't stand to hear the rest of Guido's story. With the lousy luck I've been having, I don't want to hear about someone else getting the girl of their dreams. "Aargh!" I scream. "Can't you guys talk about anything else besides girls?"

"What else is there?" Guido asks.

I lunge for my helmet, stand up and storm out of Patty's like the six-year-old I am.

That night, I sleep fitfully. All I can think about is Sapphire and revenge. She doesn't deserve to live. After all she's put me through she must die. I will kill her. It'll be a crime of passion. People will understand. Even the judge will be lenient when he hears my tale. After I've killed her, I'll turn myself in. I'll be sentenced for manslaughter. In jail, I'll find a new lover. She'll be a young femme, someone who really needs me. We'll have a lovely jailhouse romance. I'll write to all my friends about her. We'll be happy together for ten to twenty. Our love will be legendary. If one of us gets out of jail, she'll wait for the other. And meanwhile, Sapphire will be dead. Deceased. Finished. Out of my life. Once and for all. Satisfied with my plan, I try to go back to sleep. I toss and turn. It's useless. I know I'll never kill Sapphire. I don't have it in me. I can barely kill a worm, never mind an ex.

At four in the morning, I sit up in bed and realize what I must do. I've been humiliated beyond reason. The solution to my sorry excuse for a life is obvious. My only hope, now, is suicide. I must buy a gun and shoot myself. I'll go to the Tenderloin district and buy a revolver on the street. This is America, after all. Then I'll go to Sapphire's apartment, knock on her door, wave the gun around in the air when she answers and blow my head off right in front of her. She'll have to live with the gory sight for the rest of her life. With any luck, she'll be completely traumatized, never able to be in a relationship again. Who knows? Maybe I'll be doing society a service. I'll be saving the next five schmucks who would have gone out with Sapphire, only to have their hearts crushed. Maybe I'll wind up in the Lesbian Hall of Fame.

In the morning, I dress casually, black jeans, T-shirt, Doc Martens, black leather jacket. I slide on a pair of dark sunglasses, and slip out the door before Betty is awake. I don't want her to know about my plan until it's too late. I've left a note for her on the top shelf of the refrigerator, explaining the whole thing. It's well written, poignant and heart-wrenching. Perhaps she'll have it published in the *Bay Times* as a lesson to all lesbians, or as my obituary. Maybe she'll copy it and hand it out to all of my friends, so everyone will understand why I had to do it.

I park my bike at Market and Powell, lock my helmet to the front wheel and walk deep into the Tenderloin. I pass a bar, a warehouse, a smashed phone booth that smells like a urinal, and a late-1970s brown Chevrolet with four flat tires and shattered windows. A guy sleeps in the back seat, a dirty red blanket covering everything but his hair, and his feet, which poke out the bottom. He wears brown leather shoes with no laces. In a doorway, another man is sprawled, also under a filthy blanket. His is blue. Under his head is a black nylon bag. He smells like piss and vomit. The stench makes me gag. Two teenage boys head my way, swearing loudly. Both wear baseball caps turned backward, huge baggy pants, oversized sweatshirts and white high-top runners, unlaced. My heart thuds loudly in my chest. I shove my hands in my pockets and try to look mean or crazy or both, hoping they'll leave me alone, although it occurs to me they might know where to buy a gun. I rush past them, close to the wall, as if I have somewhere to go and it's important, so don't fuck with me, okay? After they pass, I let out my breath. A fine bead of sweat has formed on my forehead. This might be harder than I thought. What does a nice Jewish lesbian from Canada know about buying guns on the streets of America?

On the other side of the road is a woman who looks like she might be a hooker. She's extremely tall, long legs in a short, black skirt, stockings, high heels, and enough make-up to stock an entire drugstore. I take a deep breath and cross the street.

"Hi," I say, trying to act nonchalant.

"I don't do girls," she says, one hand on her hip. "Not for less than a hundred."

"Oh, no. That's not what I want." I wave one hand back and forth, palm facing her.

She cracks her gum, looks me up and down.

"I'm not a drug dealer, honey. You're on the wrong block."

"No. Um, actually, I want to buy a gun." Oh my god! Did I just say that?

"Oh." She stares right through me. "Okay. Maybe I can help you."

Oh shit. What have I done? My knees begin to shake. My heart speeds. I can't go through with this. I've never even seen a real gun, much less fired one. I have to get out of here. I feel nauseous, like I'm either going to throw up or faint.

"Look, uh, never mind. Uh, this is a mistake." Oh god. I sound like Sapphire again. "I'm sorry." I back away, trembling.

"Whattsa matter with you?" she yells.

I turn and hurry away.

"You crazy or something? What do you want? A free look? Fucking dyke!" She screams at the top of her lungs.

The guy sleeping in the doorway wakes up and looks directly at me. I race down the sidewalk. Adrenaline courses through me. I suck air greedily into my dry throat. The woman is still yelling. I can hear her faintly, as I round the next corner.

"Fucking dykes! Why don't you stay in the Castro, where you belong?"

As I run toward my parked bike, I debate whether I'll tell Betty about this.

"How'd the suicide go?" she asks when I enter her place later that afternoon with a vegetarian pizza and a six-pack of Dr Pepper.

"Just fine," I answer, dropping down beside her on the couch. She's watching a re-run of "Roseanne," the episode featuring Sandra Bernhardt and Morgan Fairchild as lesbians. We've both seen it twice before. I flip open the box. "Care for a slice?"

"Why, yes. Thank you." She reaches for a piece. "So, what'd you do today?" She glances at me from the corner of her eye.

"Nothing much. Tried to buy a gun in the Tenderloin, but I'm not very good at it."

She turns to look full at me. "You're kidding, right?"

I shake my head and take a large bite of pizza.

"Wow." She turns back to the television. "You have more guts than I thought. So what next, Nomi? What's with the suicide thing?"

I shrug. "It's like I said in the note. I have no choice. She's driven me to this. I have my honour to protect."

I fully expect Betty to go into counselling mode at this point—after all, before she started driving a van for Super Shuttle she was a counsellor at the 18th Street Rape Crisis Center. She's skilled at crisis intervention. She's my friend and she wants me to live.

She just nods and keeps watching TV. "That's cool."

A piece of pizza falls from my mouth, onto my lap. "It is?"

"Uh-huh."

"You're not going to try and stop me?"

"What good would it do? I can see your mind is made up. Anyway, you're right. You have your honour to protect. Anything I can do to help?"

Betty is making fun of me. Doesn't think I'm serious. Well, I'll show her. "Shut up," I say.

On TV, Rosanne's mother is shrieking, "I'm a lesbian, you're a lesbian, we're all lesbians."

"By the way," Betty reaches for a Dr Pepper and flips it open, "your mother called again."

"Oh shit." My mother. I can't deal with her right now. I have a suicide to plan.

So, maybe a gun was a bad idea. I should slash my wrists instead. Razor blades you can buy anywhere. In the corner store. Drugstore. Grocery store. Anywhere. I formulate a plan. I'll buy the razor blades at Walgreens and go to Sapphire's apartment. I'll tell her I want to speak to her. She'll let me in. I'll be dressed all in white. I'll yell at her, maybe cry a bit, then, at just the right moment, I'll pull out a blade and slit my wrists. Blood will splatter onto my white clothes, onto Sapphire's floor, her walls, her couch. She will scream hysterically. The loss of blood will be so swift, I'll collapse onto the floor in seconds. Sapphire will kneel down and hold my head in her lap as I slowly fade away. The last thing I'll see will be her beautiful eyes, full of concern, even love, as the world fades to black and I finally know peace.

Satisfied with my scheme, I go to dress. I realize I don't have my white pants. They're still at Sapphire's. I'll have to settle for blue jeans and a white shirt. I take my time getting dressed, carefully gel my hair, even polish my Docs. After all, you only kill yourself once. I want to look good. When I'm finally ready, I leave Betty's apartment, swing one leg over the seat of my bike, rev my motor, and speed, darting in and out of lanes, all the way to the Castro. At Walgreens, I stroll past the shampoo rack, the cold remedy shelf, the toothpaste and the bath soap section. I stop in the razor blade aisle. It's a bit overwhelming. There are so many different kinds to choose from. I settle on Gillette Ultra double-edged. The expensive kind. Why not? It's not like I'm going to need money after today. Might as well go for the best.

Outside the drugstore, I open the package of blades and shove them into my pants pocket, loose. Then I head up the street toward my parked bike. As I pass the doughnut shop, the smell of freshly baked chocolate doughnuts tempts me inside. Why not? I order two. It's not like I have to worry about my weight now. Or my cholesterol. In an hour, I'll be dead. Who cares if I'm fat? I eat both doughnuts as I continue up the hill. I can't resist a slice of pizza from the Castro Pizzeria, nor a hunk of smoked salmon from Abe's Bagel Shop. At the top of the hill I duck into the ice cream parlour for a butterscotch double dip.

Outside Sapphire's apartment, I feel the icy cold razor blades in my pocket. Then I knock on the door. Nothing. I knock again. Still nothing. I knock louder. Silence. I reach for the key ring on my belt, inspect it. I still have the key. With any luck she hasn't changed the lock. My key slides in. Turns. The door opens.

"Hello," I call out.

No answer. I go into the bedroom to look for my clothes. Inside the closet are several boxes with my name scrawled on top in magic marker. My things. Didn't think I had so much stuff. All packed up for nothing. After today I won't be needing any of my earthly possessions. My stomach is bloated from all the food. I go back to the living room and collapse on the couch. Jody, Sapphire's old grey cat, saunters over and plants herself in my lap. The kittens scamper back and forth in the living room, excited by my company. I close my eyes. I'll just rest for a few minutes.

I wake to the feel of a hand on my arm. I flinch, open my eyes. I'm staring into Sapphire's.

I glare at her. Say nothing. She waits for an explanation. I stand slowly, without taking my eyes from hers. Jody prances to the other side of the couch. I thrust my hands deep in my pockets. Stare at Sapphire, determined.

"Nomi? What's going on?"

Inside my pocket, I run my finger lightly down the length of a blade, to check for sharpness. It feels plenty sharp. I grasp the edge of it with my thumb and forefinger, slowly pull my hand with the blade from my pocket, raise my other arm out in front of me ceremoniously, with my eyes locked on Sapphire's. I hold the blade high above my head.

"Nomi!"

I shake it at Sapphire, like a weapon.

"No!" she yells, but does nothing, just stands where she is.

I lower the Gillette Ultra toward my arm. The earth stops turning. I imagine that everyone else on the planet knows what I'm about to do and has frozen in their tracks. The world holds its collective breath while Nomi Rabinovitch ends it all. Sapphire's eyes are huge. Jody jumps down from the sofa and rubs her body against my leg. I feel the warmth right through my pants. I freeze in my position, right arm halfway in the air. My left arm remains extended. I check out Sapphire's face. She looks frightened. And depressed, a little tired even. Like she's going through a bad time too. Jody sits down, right on my foot, purring. I have the urge to reach down and pet her. I breathe in deeply. I like breathing. I like the feel of a cat on my foot. I don't want to kill myself. I want to live. My greatest revenge would be to get on with my life. To be happy again. I smile. Like a madwoman.

"Nomi?"

I laugh. Loudly. Hysterically. Drop my arm and the razor blade falls to the carpet. It doesn't even make a sound when it hits. I keep laughing as I turn, open the apartment door and leave.

Back at Betty's place, the phone is ringing. Like an idiot, I answer it.

"Nomi? Is that you? Oy, mamelah. I've been calling for days. I was so worried. Where have you been? I left messages. Did you get them? How are you? Oy, you wouldn't believe what's been going on around here. It's been mishugenah. Are you listening?"

I slip off my jacket, toss it onto the chair. Take a deep breath. "I'm here, Ma. What's up?"

"Why didn't you return my calls? I must have called five times."

Six.

"I've gone back to work, Ma. I worked the last three nights. What's up?"

"You'll never guess."

I walk Betty's brand-new cordless phone into the kitchen. Thank god for small mercies.

"So? Tell me."

"Guess."

I open the fridge and peer in. Nothing much. A can of Dr Pepper. I reach for it. "You just said I'll never guess, so what's the point?"

"It's about Murray." She sounds excited.

"He just won a million dollars and he's sending me a cheque to cover a year's rent." I take my drink to the small patio off the kitchen. A warm sun beams down.

"No. But close."

"Close?"

"He's buying your plane ticket out here for the wedding. As a gift. You leave day after tomorrow. I told Murray to send it special delivery. You should get it in the morning. Isn't that great?"

I open the can and take a long swallow, plucking dead blooms from Betty's potted nasturtiums.

"Great," I say glumly.

"Nomi, aren't you happy?"

"Ma, why didn't you check with me first? How do you even know I can get away the day after tomorrow?"

"You'll get away. You'll get away. How many times does your mother get married? Only twice. This is it. My last time. Believe me. I need you here. I want you to be my bridesmaid."

"What? No way, Ma. No bridesmaid. That's where I draw the line. You can just forget about that. I'll come, okay? I'll come. I'll be there, I'll help you, but I can't be a bridesmaid. And I can't wear a dress."

Dead silence.

"You hear me, Ma?"

"I hear you, Nomi, but I don't understand. What is it? Why do you have to be so difficult?"

How do I begin to explain? "Ma," I say, "trust me. I'm a bad choice. Why don't you ask Aunt Rhoda? I'm sure she'd be honoured."

"Fine. I'll ask my sister. I only thought . . ."

"What? What did you think, Ma?"

"Never mind. I'm just happy you'll be here."

"I'll be there. I'll be there."

"Your brothers will pick you up at the airport. Oh, and it's snowing. Bring something warm."

It's 2:00 a.m. the following night, and I'm throwing clothes into my black canvas knapsack. Betty's loaned me a black blazer, a white dress shirt and a suit bag. My plane leaves at 7:00 a.m. A key turns in the lock. Betty walks in. Alone.

"Where's your girlfriend?" I toss a couple of T-shirts into the knapsack.

"My what?" She seems depressed.

"What's-her-name, who's been here every night for the past three days." I grab four pairs of black socks and shove them into a side pocket.

"Oh, Daria. We broke up. It was time."

"That's what I like about you, Betty. I barely have a chance to memorize your girlfriend's name before she's history."

"What's eating you?" She perches on the armrest of the black leather chair she inherited from her friend Reggie, who died last year.

"Sorry. I'm just nervous. I always get this way when I have to go to Toronto. Plus, I hate weddings. They're depressing. Especially my mother's wedding. It makes me sad. I keep thinking about my father. I keep wondering what he would think."

"How long you gonna stay there?"

"Twelve days."

"Where?"

"My mother's."

"Nomi! Have you lost your mind?"

"I know what you're thinking."

"You'll fight."

"I know. But it'll be the last time she'll be alone. I want to spend time with her. Once she marries Murray she'll be a wife. It won't be the same, ever. He'll come first. He'll always be there. I just want one last week with her before that changes."

"You'll regret it."

"That's the other thing I like about you, Betty."

"What?"

"You're such a goddamned optimist. Does my heart good."

She tosses a cushion at me. It bounces off my chest, onto the couch.

"If you want to make yourself useful, you could go into the bathroom for my toothbrush and comb."

"Sure. What about your cologne?"

"Betty. It's a family visit. It's not like I'm going on a date or anything."

"Don't be too sure."

"I am sure."

"Uh-huh." Betty shakes her head from side to side, all the way to the bathroom.

Chapter Six

*O*n the airplane, I have a window seat. Beside me is a middle-aged het couple. I plug myself into my portable tape player to let them know I am utterly unsociable. Don't even bother trying to converse with me.

A hazy day, the vague outline of the sun is barely visible. As we fly out, the top quarter of the Golden Gate Bridge rises out of thick white fog. I shiver at the thought of Toronto weather. I don't have winter clothes anymore, nothing warm enough for December in Ontario, just my leather jacket and one big wool sweater. I phoned Josh and asked him to lend me a ski jacket and gloves. He and Izzy are going to pick me up at the airport. I haven't endured a real winter since I left Toronto three years ago. I could never stand the cold. Even as a child. While the other kids made snowmen and snow angels, and had snowball fights, I'd stand in a corner of the schoolyard shivering, praying for the end of recess so I could go back inside the warm classroom. Growing up in Toronto, I lived for July and August, the only two months I was ever truly warm. Now I'm a spoiled West Coast brat. I adore the mild Northern California climate. No snow, no ice, no frost. Warm all year round. Green bushes, palm trees, flowers blooming twelve months of the year. San Francisco's "winter" rainy season feels like spring to me.

When I told Patty I was going to be out of town for a couple of weeks, she wasn't too thrilled. I just started back at work, now I'm off again. Still, she understood.

"You've only got one mother." She sounded older than I'd ever heard her sound before. "When she goes, that's it." She snapped her thumb and middle finger in the air. "Do me a favour? Bring me back a six-pack of Export."

Molson Export. A classic Canadian beer that's hard to find in San Francisco. "Sure, Patty. Anything."

It feels good to be travelling. So much has happened in the last three weeks. Maybe by leaving town, I'll get some perspective on my life. The flight takes a million years. The pilot informs us we'll be circling the Toronto airport for approximately twenty-seven minutes. A blizzard has covered the entire city. Only two runways are cleared for landing. There's a line-up. We are number twenty-three. After circling for close to an hour, the plane finally lands. I'm exhausted and sweaty.

Josh and Izzy are laden with clothes.

"Nomi!" Josh rushes over to me, huge strides with his long legs through the airport crowds.

"Hey, Nomi," Izzy trails behind.

"Here," Josh holds out his arm.

"What did you guys do? Rob a clothing store?"

"You said you'd be cold," Izzy reminds me, tilting his head back to see. His glasses have slipped, as usual, to the end of his nose.

"Yeah," Josh agrees. "Hold out your arms." He hands me things. "Here's a wool sweater, here's another, a scarf, down-filled gloves, longjohns, a parka."

Izzy passes me his bundles. "A ski vest, a hat, earmuffs, wool socks, and this, this is great." He reaches down into a shopping bag. "This is a thermal sub-arctic outdoor camping quilt, guaranteed to keep you warm and dry even in a snowstorm. And," Izzy searches in his pocket, "warm packs." He holds up a clear plastic bag with small square objects. "A special combination of chemicals. You put them in your pocket and squish them. The friction creates heat. I made them myself. I use them all the time. I tried to patent them, but somebody beat me to it. Anyway, here." He tries to give them to me, but I gesture that my arms are completely full.

"Oh yeah." He laughs. "I'll hang on to these for you." He shoves them into his pocket, then finally pushes his glasses back into position on his nose.

"Great. Now you guys have to help me with the rest." I put on the parka, scarf, gloves and a hat, let them carry everything else. "Okay. This ought to do. Is it really cold?" I sling my canvas bag over my shoulder, suit bag over my arm.

"Nah, not too bad," Josh promises, steering us toward an exit. The automatic door slides open. A blast of freezing air attacks my face, almost knocking me over.

"Shit," I say, "as bad as I remembered."

"Worse yesterday," Izzy offers, pointing to a large parking lot and his old green Pontiac.

As we walk up the front steps, the door to my mother's house flings open. "Get inside." She waves us in with a long-handled wooden spoon. "It's cold out there. Nomi! You're here." Ma bends to kiss my cheek, then wraps her arms around me, drawing my whole body in for a soft, full hug. My mother is five inches taller than I am. I feel like a ten-year-old in her embrace. "Let me see you." She pulls back and looks me up and down. She frowns, touches the nylon of my jacket, Josh's jacket really. "Whose coat is this? It's too big. It looks ridiculous."

"Hi, Ma. You look nice, too."

"Come inside, kids. Izzy, is there snow on the driveway? Do me a favour?"

"Okay, Ma," he zips his jacket back up, pushes his glasses up with one finger and tromps out the door. "I've got it."

I follow my mother into the kitchen. She's wearing green polyester slacks, a flowered blouse, yellow fuzzy slippers and a pink-and-black apron which reads, "I'm bored with housework." The smell of chicken, onions and soup fills the air. The kitchen window is fogged up. It is blessedly warm. My mother's kitchen looks the same as always. On the family-sized table is a white plastic cloth covered with little gold Stars of David, and the words Happy Chanukah. In the middle of the table is a sugar bowl, a plate with individual pink packets of Sweet'n Low, pink flamingo salt and pepper shakers my father bought in Miami Beach twenty years ago, a matching pink flamingo napkin holder with a small stack of napkins and a plastic container of low-sodium imitation salt.

The counters are covered in mixing bowls and cooking utensils. My mother's small desk in the corner is stacked with phone books, a pile of bills, ledger books for the synagogue gift shop, a large "things to do" pad, and several romance novels from the public library. Her old black telephone perches precariously on the phone books. The radio sits on the corner of the counter by the sink, playing the oldies station. Paul Anka sings "Put Your Head on My Shoulder." My mother hums along.

"How was your flight? Nomi dear, you'll help me make matzah balls."

"Fine. You're making matzah balls? Ma, you're really going all out. Who's coming?"

"Everyone. La, la, la, la, la, Baby," she croons with Paul, opens a cupboard above the stove, rummages for the orange-and-green box of Manischewitz matzah meal. "Here." She hands it to me. "Recipe's on the back."

"You want me to do it myself?"

She puts her hands on her hips. "Nomi, it's easy. You have to learn sometime. You never know, maybe one day . . ." She stops mid-sentence.

"Maybe what, Ma?" I ask coldly. I know she means maybe one day I'll get married and have to cook for my husband. She secretly hopes my whole life is a phase. Any day now, I'll go straight, meet a nice Jewish man and have nice Jewish babies. Then she could be proud of me, instead of ashamed.

"Never mind." She opens the oven door and pulls the rack out a few inches. The aroma of roasted chicken makes my mouth water.

"I'm not going to change, Ma. Don't you know that by now?" I hold the box of matzah meal in front of me. On the back, in small white print, is a recipe for matzah balls.

"Okay, I only thought . . ."

I open the avocado-green fridge for a carton of eggs. "You only thought what, Ma?"

"You *know* . . ." She ladles the cooking juices over the chicken.

"No, Ma. I don't know." I find a large stainless steel bowl, which I place on the table.

"Well, now that you and your friend aren't living together . . ." She slides the chicken back inside the oven and closes the door.

"Ma. I'm still a lesbian."

"Shah." She makes a brisk downward motion in the air with her hand. "I don't want to hear that word today. People are coming over." She lifts the lid from a pot of boiling egg noodles and stirs.

"So what? You think they don't know?"

"Murray doesn't."

"You haven't told Murray?"

She shrugs. "It never came up." From a cupboard, she removes a red plastic colander, places it in the sink.

"Ma, you have to tell him. Otherwise I will." I tear open the box of matzah meal with my teeth.

"Nomi, I'm getting married in a week and a half. Please don't start. Why do you have to flaunt it?" Ma lifts the pot from the stove, pours its contents into the strainer in the sink. Steam blasts up. "Oy," she says, blinking from the heat.

"Flaunt it? Ma, give me a little credit, okay? It's not like I'm going to walk up to Murray and say, 'Hi Murray, I'm a lesbian, how 'bout you?' But, if he asks how come I'm not married or something, I won't lie. I'm not ashamed and neither should you be." I pour a heap of unmeasured white crumbs into my mixing bowl.

"Who said I was ashamed?" She turns to me, a hand on her hip. "It just never came up."

"Oh boy." I slump down at the table and re-read the recipe.

Chapter *Seven*

Two hours later, the dining room table is set, food is warming in the oven, and Josh's huge green salad dominates the middle rack of the fridge. My mother is in her bedroom getting ready. I still haven't changed. I've just finished reloading the dishwasher for the hundred-and-fiftieth time. Izzy is back outside, shovelling snow, which has been falling relentlessly since I arrived. Josh is somewhere in the back of the house. The doorbell rings.

"Josh! Get the door!" I don't want to answer it. I'm not dressed and I'm a mess from helping my mother cook. If it's Murray I don't want to deal with him yet. I'll have to talk to him. He'll probably ask why I'm not married, first thing out of his mouth.

"Josh!"

"What!"

"Get the door!"

"I can't. I'm in the bathroom."

"Josh!"

"You get it."

Damn.

In the front hall, I smooth down my short-cropped hair with the palm of my right hand, tuck in my shirt, swing open the door. It's Murray. He wears a thick grey overcoat, brown felt derby with a small feather in the brim, black scarf, thick black leather gloves—the kind with a seam up the side of each finger—and black rubbers over brown dress shoes. A light layer of snow powders his shoulders and hat. In one hand he holds a white cake box and in the other, flowers. He smiles. His eyes pass over my whole body, stopping for a long moment on my hair, an inch at its longest and shaved above the ears and in the back.

"Nomi. Good to see you again."

"Come on in, Murray." He notices my jeans and rumpled T-shirt. Frowns. "Uh, we've been cooking," I explain. "I haven't had a chance to get changed yet."

"Course not." He enters the small vestibule, stamps the thick wet snow from his rubbers on the grey Rubbermaid mat in the entranceway. He stands awkwardly, arms full, unsure of how or where to proceed.

"Oh. Let me take those," I say, snatching the cake box by its string and the flowers by their stems. He bends to remove his rubbers. They remind me of my father. Especially here, in my mother's house. Unexpected grief lodges in my throat. I cough, smile bravely and go into the kitchen to deposit the cake box and flowers. A minute later Murray enters, free of his coat and hat.

"My mother's getting changed," I say. "I'm sure she'll be out in a minute. Can I get you a drink?"

He waves one hand. "No. Don't bother. Actually, I'm glad you answered the door. Gives me a chance to talk to you for a minute before everyone else arrives."

Uh-oh.

He stands in the middle of the room facing me. He's not really tall—for a man. Same height as my mother. About five-seven. He's wearing a brown suit, white shirt, brown tie with a black diamond design, gold tie clip and matching cuff links. His shoes are brown leather Florsheims, the expensive kind.

"I know you don't exactly trust me, Nomi."

"You do?"

Murray nods, raises a hand, shakes a finger at me. "I can see it in your eyes."

I frown.

"I'll do right by your mother. I care about her. A lot," he assures me.

I say nothing. Merely stare.

"So," he says, rubbing his hands together, the matter now settled. "How was your flight?"

"Uh, fine," I answer. "But Murray, I should get changed. Before the others arrive. Help yourself to a drink. My mother will be out any second, I'm sure."

I retreat to my childhood room, where I'll be staying, and close the door. Nothing much has changed since I left home twelve years ago. Same bed. Same dresser. In the closet some of my mother's clothes hang. Guess she has too many to fit in her room. I used to have posters taped to the walls. Patti Smith, The Rocky Horror Picture Show, David Bowie, Tina Turner. My mother's replaced them with two of my father's paintings—both portraits of her. One is an early painting. My mother looks young, probably in her twenties. Her gaze is intensely on the viewer. Thoroughly in love. The portrait hung for years in my parents' bedroom, above the bed. I wonder why she moved it. The other is the last painting my father ever did. My mother as she looks now.

I should feel something, sitting here on my childhood bed, in my old room. Nostalgia at least. But all I feel is irritation. Murray gives me the creeps. My mother's in a total panic. I'm not officially out to most of the relatives, although I figure they all must suspect by now. I'm thirty, unmarried, live in San Francisco. I have a buzz cut, three silver earrings in my left ear, I don't shave my legs or underarms and I never wear make-up. I wear black, ankle-high Doc Martens, baggy jeans, loose T-shirts. And there hasn't been a man in my entire adult life. I open my black travel bag, rummage through it, pull out a fresh pair of black jeans and black socks. Inside Betty's suit bag, I find her white cotton long-sleeved button-down shirt. Over it I add a brightly coloured vest, also borrowed from Betty. I bought it for her last December as a Kwanzaa present. She loaned it to me for the trip.

"Give you a little colour," she joked, "pun intended."

I'm about to put on my leather studded belt, when I realize that the studs might shock my family more than please. I go belt-less. Dressed, I pad down the length of my mother's faded blue shag hall carpet with my plastic case of toiletries.

Josh emerges from the bathroom in black jeans, studded belt, white shirt and a multi-coloured vest. His hair is tied in a ponytail.

"Twins again," he says.

We laugh. Josh and I have an uncanny way of dressing alike without discussing it beforehand.

I look my brother up and down. "I left off my studded belt. Thought it wouldn't go over big."

He looks down at his. "You think?"

I shake my head. "Not on you. Boys are allowed more than girls."

"Really." He eyes his belt again, then removes it. "I won't wear mine either. Not fair."

Good old Josh. Always knows the right thing to do. I stand on my toes, reach up to hug him. He's four years younger and eight inches taller.

In the bathroom, I squeeze a liberal amount of gel into the palm of my hand, mush it around my hair. I'm sure my 'do is not going to be a big hit with the relatives. But it could be worse. Betty keeps urging me to shave right down to the skin.

"It's amazing," she tells me. "Feels like freedom."

It looks good on Betty, but I have a lima bean head. All my lovers have said so. You need a nice round head to look good bald. I check myself in the bathroom mirror and, satisfied, trudge back to the bedroom for my shoes. Josh is talking loudly to Murray. I can't quite make out what they're saying, something to do with basketball. The doorbell rings. Aunt Rhoda comes barrelling down the hall, almost knocks me over as I leave my room.

"Oh," she says. "Nomi. You're here already. Let me see you." She clutches both my hands, stands back, looks me scrupulously up and down. I suck in my breath. "You've lost weight. Congratulations." She clasps her hands together, thrilled, as if I'd just won an important award or graduated from law school, top of my class. Rhoda is obsessed with weight. She attends the Diet Workshop every week, weighs all her food on a tiny scale, chews sugar-free gum, drinks diet cola, eats pounds of lettuce and carrots, and gains and loses the same ten pounds over and over in an endless cycle.

"Aren't you going to put on a dress, Nomi? And your hair," she starts in before I even have a chance to answer the first charge, "what have you done to your hair?"

The last time I saw Rhoda was a year ago at my father's unveiling. I wore my hair longer then; Sapphire liked it that way.

"What do you mean, Aunt Rhoda?" I bat innocent eyes at her.

"What do I mean? What do you think I mean? It's so short." She leans in close and whispers in my ear. A stray curl of over-dyed, over-sprayed auburn hair hits my cheek. It scratches. "You look like a boy."

That hurts. I tried. Borrowing Betty's vest and not wearing my belt. My shirt is freshly dry-cleaned. "You look nice too, Aunt Rhoda. Have you put on weight?" I whisper in her ear.

Aunt Rhoda pulls away and, with horror in her eyes, peers down at her own body, then back at me. "You think?"

Instantly, I feel bad. Probably she's been starving herself all week to squeeze into that tight green cocktail dress.

"I don't know, Aunt Rhoda. Maybe I'm wrong. The light's bad. Come to think of it, I think you lost."

A smile stretches across her face. "You think, Nomi?" She smoothes both hands over her hips.

"Yeah, I think."

"So when did you get in? How was your flight? How long'll you be staying? How's your mother? Is Murray here yet? What do you think about your mother getting married again?"

"Three o'clock," I say. "Fine. Until next week. She's fine. Yes. I don't know."

She frowns. "You don't know. Come on, Nomi. You're twenty-eight years old."

"Thirty."

"Already? Where does the time go?"

I shrug.

"Anyhow, you're not a kid any longer. You should be thinking about getting married yourself one of these days. I know," she holds up one hand, like a crossing guard, "you're too much of a feminist. You don't want to get married. Your mother already told me, but mamelah," again she leans forward, whispers in my ear, "you're not getting any younger. You know what I'm saying? You have to start thinking about your future. Maybe while you're in town I'll take you out for lunch and we'll talk. Meanwhile, your mother's getting married, what do you think? You think she's doing the right thing, or what?"

I shrug. "Or what."

She sighs. "That's what I think, too. Anyway, it's none of my business. Your mother's the older sister. You think she'd listen to a word I have to say? So? Where is she? I want to say hi."

I point in the direction of my mother's room. Rhoda squeezes my arm, a little on the hard side, pushes past me and starts talking again.

"Faygie, I'm here. Let me see how you look. You need help? With your make-up? Don't forget, I took that ten-week course with Maybelline—I know how to put on a good foundation. Your foundation's the most important thing. Did I ever tell you that?"

"A hundred times, Rhoda," my mother says.

I take a deep breath, put one foot in front of the other until I'm in the living room. Seated on the couch are Rhoda's husband, Stanley, and their youngest daughter, Rachel. Her head leans against his shoulder. Their eighteen-year-old son, Mark, stands talking to Josh. Murray is across from Stanley. He looks nervous. Izzy is still outside shovelling snow. The doorbell rings. I answer it. A woman my age stands on the front porch. She looks like a typical Jewish-American Princess, only more athletic. She wears a full-length mink coat and leather gloves, and has enough spray in her Hillary Clinton hairdo to raise Clairol's shares by at least six points. Her make-up is impeccable. Maybe she had help from Aunt Rhoda. She smiles the phoniest of smiles and extends a hand with long, sharp, red nails.

"I'm Cheryl," she says in a sing-song voice.

I drop her hand and hold the door open. "I'm Nomi."

"Sheldon, that's my boyfriend," she clarifies, in case I thought he was her girlfriend, "is parking the car. He'll be here any minute. Is my father here?" Her father is none other than the blushing bridegroom himself, Murray Feinstein.

"He's here," I assure her, lest she worry she might be eaten alive by the Rabinovitches before her father arrives.

She swings off her coat and dumps it into my arms. "It's mink," she explains, in case I was about to mistake it for polyester. "Please put it on a bed. I don't want it touching anyone's wet ski jacket."

She looks disdainfully around and I understand. Murray has money. We are too lower class for Miss Uppity's taste buds. My mother's modest three-bedroom bungalow in a not-so-chic sub-urb of North Toronto does not meet Miss Feinstein's standards.

"Of course," I answer, "I'll call the butler in. He'll know just what to do with it." Then I scream, "Oh Jo-osh," at the top of my lungs. One more second alone with this bitch and I'll rip the lay-ers of Oil of Olay right off her smooth olive skin, undoubtedly darkened to its current shade through countless hours spent at an expensive Yorkville tanning salon.

"What's up?" My trustworthy brother rushes to my side.

I thrust the mink coat into his arms. "Hang this in the cedar closet," I order, "it's priceless."

"The what?" he asks, eyes fixed on Miss Feinstein's heaving bosom, which at this point is quite exposed. Minus her fur coat, Cheryl wears nothing but a slinky, low-cut black dress. Neither Josh nor I will be able to utter a single word to her for the rest of the evening without ogling her expansive cleavage. As long as I don't talk to her, Cheryl Feinstein might prove to be a valuable member of the wedding party after all. Her bare arms reveal the kind of muscle definition and bulk achieved only after hundreds of hours pumping iron. Miss Cheryl, it appears, works out. At the Jewish Community Centre, maybe? Suddenly, in mid-gawk, the front door swings open and a big, hulking, stupid-looking man wearing a designer trench coat enters. He must lift weights, too. Maybe they met at the gym. He nods at me, glares at Josh and possessively takes one of Cheryl's muscular elbows.

"Sheldon!" She turns to him and throws herself into his arms, as if she hasn't seen him in over a year. "Oh. You're all wet. God." She backs away, gives him a look of disgust. He shrugs, then removes his snow-laden coat. Izzy throws open the door, banging into Sheldon's arm.

"Ow," Sheldon complains.

"Oh, sorry," says Izzy, breathing hard. His hair is covered in an inch of snow. Bright red ears poke out from under pale blue ear-muffs. He steps out of his snow-covered boots, rubs his frozen hands together. His glasses fog up.

I reach past Sheldon and seize Izzy by the arm, hauling him further inside the house.

"You're freezing. Come into the kitchen and warm up." The oven has been on all afternoon and the kitchen is the warmest room of the house. Izzy nods, breathes and pushes past Sheldon.

"Everybody get to the table," my mother shouts.

"Ma, Maria's not here yet," Josh whines.

"So? She'll join us when she gets here. She's late," my mother barks back nervously. Maria, Josh's latest girlfriend, is not Jewish and therefore a criminal in my mother's mind. A shiksa, not really welcome. In fact, if my mother had the courage, she'd forbid Josh even to date her. My father would have. Not that it would have stopped Josh—he's twenty-six and lives on his own—but my father would have tried. My mother feels she's being lenient, allowing Josh to invite Maria to this family dinner. If we start without her, so what?

"What about Irma and Joe? They're not here yet either," Rhoda shouts to my mother, from the living room to the kitchen.

"I decided to invite family only."

"She's your best friend."

"Family only," my mother says firmly, entering the dining room with a huge braided challah on a platter.

"Uh-oh," says Aunt Rhoda.

"What?" My mother sets the challah down at the head of the dining room table.

"How did I know? You need some help with the table?"

My mother stops, hands on her hips. "How did you know what, Rhoda?"

"She's your best friend. It was only natural . . ." Rhoda slinks into the kitchen.

"What did you do, Rhoda?" Ma follows.

The doorbell rings. It's Irma Kushner and her husband, Joe. I smile.

"Hello, Nomi dear." Irma reaches out, takes my face in her two hands, squishing my cheeks, planting a big sloppy red kiss right on my mouth.

"Oh my god!" my mother screams suddenly from the kitchen. On the verge of hysteria, she darts into the front hall. "We forgot about Bubbe! Where's Izzy?" Bubbe, my late father's mother, lives in Sholom Aleichem, the Jewish old folks home ten blocks from my mother's house. "She's been waiting in the lobby for over an hour. Where's Izzy? Josh?"

"Ma? How does she feel about all this?" I ask. It must be hard for my grandmother to know that her daughter-in-law is about to remarry.

My brother appears. "Izzy! Oh, there you are. Do me a favour. How does she feel?" She turns to me. "How should she feel? Izzy, go and get Bubbe. She's waiting in the lobby."

"Sure, Ma."

"Hello, Irma!" My mother stretches out her arms, kisses her friend on the cheek, acts like she knew she was coming all along. "Come in. Come in. Josh'll take your coats. I'm just finishing up."

"You want help?" Irma removes a brown, fake-fur coat, flings it into her husband's arms.

"She doesn't mind?" I trail my mother back into the kitchen. Irma follows me.

She sighs. "Mind? Of course she minds. That's all I hear from her. She shakes a finger in my face."

"What does she say?"

"What does she say? What do you think she says?"

I shrug.

" 'It's not right.' "

"Huh?"

"That's what she says. She says, 'It's not right. It's too soon.' "

"How do you handle it, Ma?"

"She's an old woman. She's entitled to her opinion. I don't say a word. What can I say? She's your father's mother. Oh, your Aunt Shel may be coming by later with that husband of hers. She feels a little uncomfortable too."

Aunt Shel is my father's younger sister. Bubbe refers to her as "an accident," because she was born thirteen years after my father, when Bubbe and my grandfather thought they'd have no more children. Aunt Shel has three kids, all a lot younger than me and my brothers. No one calls Shel's husband by name, because every five years or so she accuses him of beating her, leaves him, takes the kids and moves in with one of her friends. Six months later she goes back. The second time she left him, we began to refer to Uncle Jerry as "that husband of hers." My father's older brother, Uncle Solly, we aren't expecting. He and his wife Belle divorced years ago. Uncle Solly lives in Florida, mostly. I haven't seen either of them in years, although I'm close to their son, Henry. My cousin Henry is the only other queer in our family.

The bell rings again. I open the door. Although we've never met, I know it is Maria. She's an attractive woman in her early twenties with striking dark eyes.

"You must be Maria." I hold open the door for her.

She smiles and nods. From out of nowhere, Josh is at my side, taking her two hands in his. "Back off, sister. I saw her first," he jokes.

"Don't worry. She's not my type." They both gape at me, slightly insulted. "She's straight," I explain, leaving them to their greeting.

Back in the kitchen, Aunt Rhoda flounders in the middle of the room with a hot casserole dish of noodle kugel. "Where're your serving spoons, Fay?"

"Where they always are, Rhoda." My mother opens the oven door. A blast of heat permeates the air.

"You didn't pull them out?"

"In the wha-cha-ma-call-it."

"The what?"

"Help me with the chicken. It's heavy."

Exasperated, Aunt Rhoda sets the hot dish on the counter. Irma slices pickles at the table.

"Need some help in here?" I volunteer.

"Yeah," my mother says, as she and Rhoda hoist the heavy roasting pan out of the oven and plunk it on the stove top. "Get some serving spoons."

"Okay. Where are they?"

"In the wha-cha-ma-call-it."

"Huh?"

"The thing," she says, as if that clears it right up.

"Oh." I wander around the room, searching.

"The thing. The thing," my mother repeats, annoyed, as she opens the fridge.

I look to Aunt Rhoda. She shrugs.

"You're both driving me crazy. Over there." Ma points to the dining room. "The thing. The buffet."

"Oh." I laugh. Another Faygie-ism decoded. I carry an armful of large spoons and knives back into the kitchen.

The front door swings open. Bubbe shuffles in, clutching Izzy's arm for support.

"She forgot about me?" Bubbe asks in a loud booming voice, craning her neck to look up at Izzy, who isn't particularly tall. Bubbe is extremely short, maybe four-foot-six.

"That's not what I said, Bubbe." Izzy sounds frustrated.

"See? My son Harry, may he rest in peace, not dead a year even and already she's forgotten about me. Wasn't I her mother-in-law for twenty-eight years? And now, look at her—getting married again already. Not even a year yet."

"Bubbe, it's been almost two years. Let me take your coat."

"You see?" My mother yells to no one in particular. "You see what I put up with?"

"He was a young man, your father. When he died. It's not right. Is it, tatelah? You'll do me a favour? Help me with my boots. Oy, it's so cold out there. What's the temperature?"

"I don't know. Why don't you sit on the chair and I'll help with your boots?"

"Yeah, but be a doll? Help me with my boots." Bubbe is practically deaf. She refuses to wear a hearing aid, it would make her look old. When she wants to, she hears quite well. Bubbe has selective hearing.

"Sure thing, Bubbe. But sit down first," Izzy yells, loud enough to be heard in another country.

"Tell me, tatelah. About your mother. What do you think? You think it's right?"

"Lift your foot," says Izzy.

"I don't know why I bother," my mother says.

Minutes later we all cram around the crowded dining room table to eat. My mother has added a portable card table at one end, covered in a white cloth. Murray sits at the head of the main table. My mother is at the other end, closest to the kitchen, so she can get up and down throughout the meal. Newly engaged and already they act like an old married couple who've been together for years. Murray stands. Everyone quiets down to listen. He pours red Manischewitz wine into a long-stemmed crystal glass, holds it up.

"Ahem." He clears his throat dramatically. "I'd like to propose a toast to my bride-to-be, Faygie Rabinovitch, who I had the pleasure of meeting not so long ago and who, as you all know, has agreed to be my wife. To Faygie." He raises his glass high and grins at my mother. She smiles back.

"To Faygie," others agree, although no one else has any wine. Murray realizes and starts pouring Manischewitz into glasses, passing them around.

"It's not right," my grandmother says to Maria beside her.

Maria looks confused, but she smiles at Bubbe anyway. "Who are you?" Bubbe asks suddenly.

Josh, on Maria's other side, leans over her and shouts. "I told you already, Bubbe. This is Maria, my girlfriend."

"Your girlfriend?" Bubbe looks Maria up and down, then leans across her and asks loudly, "Is she Jewish?"

"And Sunday after next," continues Murray, "I will have the great honour of walking down the aisle with you, Faygie."

"You don't walk down the aisle together, Murray," corrects Rhoda. "The groom waits for the bride under the chupa."

Murray laughs nervously. "Of course. Of course. I forgot. It's been a long time since I got married. In any case, I just wanted to say, thanks all for coming to have dinner with us tonight. L'chaim."

"It's not right," declares Bubbe.

"Shah," says my mother.

"L'chaim," says everybody else.

"So, let's eat," Murray suggests.

Like the king of the castle, he sits and waits to be served. I jump up to help my mother with the first course, chicken soup with the matzah balls I managed to make. The other women, Rhoda, Irma, Maria, even Cheryl, get up to help too. The feminist in me is appalled. I want to stand on my chair and make a speech about how the women are not here to wait hand and foot on the men, but I don't. I go back to the table. "Hey Josh, Izzy. Come here," I say. "Come on. Give us a hand."

"Oh right," says Josh.

"What?" says Izzy.

"Come on." I grasp his sleeve and drag him to his feet.

It feels like days before dinner is over and most of the guests have left. The kitchen is a disaster. Josh helps me load the dishwasher. Murray has cornered Maria, boring her with stories from the old days. After the honeymoon, Murray's going to move in here. My mother's keeping the house. She insisted they live here.

"Since his wife died," my mother explained to me earlier, "he's been eating take-out on paper plates. After their daughter moved out a few years ago, they sold their house and bought a condominium by Steeles. I told him I won't live in an apartment. This is my kitchen. I don't want to move. So? He agreed. Men don't care where they live, Nomi."

"They don't?"

"He agreed right away."

When most of the mess has been cleaned, Josh and Maria leave. Izzy follows with Bubbe in tow.

"I still say it's not right. It's too soon," Bubbe says on her way out.

"Careful, Bubbe," Izzy says, "it's icy."

"What, tatelah?"

Murray lingers in the living room. My mother goes in to talk to him. I have an overwhelming urge to scrape grease out of the bottom of a roasting pan. I'm curious about my mother and this man, but I feel awkward. I'm not ready to be with just the two of them. I'm still not used to my father being dead, or my mother being with another man. She comes back into the kitchen. Murray is leaving. "Goodnight girls," he calls out, closing the door behind him.

"Oy, Nomi. I thought he'd never go."

"Tired, Ma?"

She sighs deeply, then drops into a chair at the kitchen table. I abandon my roasting pan, sit opposite her.

"Ma, what's the matter?"

She bursts into tears. I reach over and take one of her hands. "Ma, what is it?"

"I'm making a big mistake."

"What?"

"The whole thing. The wedding. It's a big mistake. It's not right." Tears stream down her cheeks.

"Ma . . . are you worried about what Bubbe says?"

"If he wants to be with Sonia Greenblatt, she can have him," she scoops a scrunched-up Kleenex from inside her shirt sleeve, blows her nose loudly.

"What?"

"I can't worry about it anymore."

"Ma, what are you talking about?"

"Just what I said. If he leaves me for Sonia, then that's it."

"Ma . . ."

"I'm not ready for this. I only said yes because otherwise he'll run off with Sonia Greenblatt."

"He will?"

"He's a man, Nomi," she says, as if that explains everything. "He has needs. He wants a wife. If it isn't me, it'll be someone else. Sonia's just waiting for something to go wrong, so she can scoop him up."

"Ma? Would she really do that?"

"She's been alone for five years already, Nomi. A good man like Murray Feinstein doesn't come along every day."

"Ma, she's your friend."

"We'll see." She dabs at her eyes with the Kleenex.

"So . . . you only said yes to Murray because you were scared if you didn't, he'd leave you for Sonia?"

"Oy, Nomi. What have I done? I barely know the man. I can't live with him. I can't have him sleep in your father's place. I'm too old to start again, Nomi. I'm scared."

"Oh boy." I rub the back of her hand. We sit for a while, mother and daughter. I wish I knew what to do. I've barely been able to keep my own head above water. Treading against the current. In my weakened state, how will I keep my mother from drowning too?

Chapter *Eight*

At ten-thirty my mother goes to bed. I'm still on West Coast time, so it's only seven-thirty for me. I've had enough of heterosexuals for the evening. I borrow my mother's car and head downtown. After all this talk of weddings and dresses and make-up and family, I need to be around other homos. There's a dyke bar called The Rose I used to go to when I lived in Toronto. As far as I know, it's still open. I drive in that direction.

I find a parking spot right on Parliament. The bar is three blocks north. I take a deep breath and, for the first time today, relax. Three gay men pass, heading in the other direction. Even in the cold, two are wearing black leather jackets. The other sports a lined denim coat. No gloves, no hats. Acclimatized to the weather. I'm bundled up in Josh's parka with a scarf, gloves, earmuffs, wool sweater and long underwear. And still I'm freezing. I hear snippets of conversation as the guys pass me.

"And to think I trusted him. Did you see the child he was with. . . ?"

"I told you about him, Michael. Didn't I?"

A truck rumbles by, drowning out their voices.

I'm thankful for the gust of warm air that greets me inside the doors of The Rose. I hesitate for a moment in the doorway as my eyes adjust to the darkness of the bar. There is music playing. Not too loud. I stroll inside, away from the door, take a seat on a stool at the bar, unzip my jacket, and leave it on. I'll never be warm again. The bartender is a woman in her late twenties. Head shaved on the sides, a bright orange ponytail sticking straight up from the top of her head, she reminds me of Pebbles Flintstone. She smiles, places a round paper coaster in front of me.

"What can I get you?"

"Vodka tonic."

She nods, reaches above for a highball glass. I look around. There are only a few women in the bar, twenty or so. Some dance on a near-empty floor. No DJ tonight, just taped music. Two women sit on high stools at the other end of the bar. Tables here and there are occupied. Smoke from Canadian cigarettes is thick in the air, less raunchy than the American brands I'm used to.

"Three-seventy-five," the bartender says as she sets my drink in front of me.

I reach into my back pocket for my wallet, pay, then pick up my glass, swivel around in my chair to watch the women on the dance floor. After family hour at the Rabinovitches, it's great to be in a dyke bar, an anonymous butch, sipping on a drink. It takes a minute to sink in. At first it's a vague feeling, in the pit of my stomach. Then it's a sureness. I stare at her, dancing with another femme. Swaying their hips, laughing, talking. Julie Sakamoto. I've had a crush on her for years. When was the last time I saw her? Two years ago? Three? She's as lovely as ever. She has a sensuous energy that is infinitely attractive. In the way she moves, how she dresses, so femme. Like a real girl. Radiant, dazzling. Tight blue jeans hug curvaceous hips. A black, low-cut sweater exposes her bare neck. Long black hair bounces on her shoulders. I could sit and watch her all night.

She probably still won't talk to me. Some things never change, no matter how much time has gone by. I wonder if she's still with ... what was her name? Renni? Lenni. That's it. Lenni. I'd love to talk to her, dance with her. Just once. But I don't dare approach. She doesn't like me. The music changes and she strolls off the dance floor with her friend. They join another woman at a table in the far corner. I can see her clearly from across the room. The last time I tried to talk to her was right here at The Rose. She barely gave me the time of day. Answered my questions sharply, then turned back to her own table. Her lover had been there, behind, watching. Later I realized I had been out of line, flirting with her, with her girlfriend right there. But I couldn't help myself. She's so enchanting I lost all sense of boundaries.

Lenni isn't here. What does that mean? Have they broken up? Or is Julie just out with friends, while Lenni waits for her at home? Maybe this is my chance to talk to her. Maybe things have changed. She looks in my direction. My heart speeds up. Quickly I swivel and face the bar, wondering if she noticed me. I am horribly nervous. Julie is a woman I could really fall for, someone who would matter. Who am I kidding? It's like I told Betty. I'm through with dating. I'm no good at it. Alison and Mimi were disasters. It's too soon to try. I'm still grieving. I look and smell like a wounded animal. When you're in this state, people run screaming from you. I might as well be a skunk. Pepe Le Pew. That's me. I need a trenchcoat, a stripe down my back and theme music. I'll just sit here by myself. A lesbian skunk. Anyway, if I approached Julie what would I say? Probably something stupid I'd regret for the rest of my life.

I finish my drink and head downstairs for the bathroom. It's time to leave.

On my way back up I bump right into Julie. Her eyes lock on mine. I stop. The most amazing thing happens. She grins. A huge, friendly smile, as if she really likes me.

"Nomi," she says. "It *is* you. I thought so."

I pick up my hand and wave. Feebly. "Yeah. It's me." Oh boy. Has she been watching me? I feel like the class geek. "Nice to see you."

"Yeah," she says. "Nice to see you too. So . . . are you leaving? I mean, do you have to?"

"Uh, well . . ." Her huge almond eyes sparkle. At me. This is too incredible to be true.

"Do you want to join us?" She points to her table of friends.

I look. The femme she was dancing with waves at me. Oh god. I bet Julie was talking about me. "Well, I don't want to intrude . . ."

"It's okay. Why don't you come and sit down?"

"Well . . ."

She smiles wider. My heart melts. I know I should leave. A siren sounds loudly in my head. Danger, danger. Everybody leave the building. Run for your life.

"Okay," I say, recklessly.

"Good."

I follow her, confused. She's never been friendly to me. I don't know what's going on.

Julie introduces me to her friends. I wish we were alone, so I could really talk to her.

"I haven't seen you in . . . a while," Julie says.

"Yeah. I moved. To San Francisco." Oh god. My tongue feels like sandpaper in my mouth.

"That's what I heard."

"Oh yeah?"

"Yeah." She stares at me. Just stares. I don't know what to do.

Like a heaven-sent gift, her two friends get up to dance.

I'm dying to ask Julie about Lenni, if they're still together, but I can't think of a tactful way to bring it up.

"So. You're still living here," I state the obvious. And the sky is blue. The earth is round. Oh boy. I must sound like a fourteen-year-old. Like someone who's never talked to a beautiful woman before.

"Yeah," she says. "Still here. I never really thought of moving anywhere else. Was it hard moving to San Francisco? I mean, I would find it hard to start all over somewhere new."

I shrug. "Well, I love San Francisco. It's really beautiful. Have you ever been?"

She shakes her head. I try not to stare at her mouth, but it's hard. She has big, full, soft lips, just like Betty Boop. I imagine kissing her.

"Oh, you should come sometime. You can stay with me. I mean . . ."

She raises her eyebrows.

"You know. If you need a place to stay." What am I talking about? I don't even have a place myself right now.

I smile. She smiles.

Something beeps, muffled.

"Oh." Julie fumbles in her purse for a small black pager. "I have to call in—check my message." She excuses herself, rushes past me toward the pay phone. I sit at her table and wait. Red and blue strobe lights flicker. I play with a pack of matches. Cigarette smoke drifts across my face from the next table. I crane my neck, look for a waitress. Wish I had a drink. Julie's friends return.

"I love that song," one says, fanning herself with a paper napkin. I smile.

Julie rushes back. Her mood has changed. She takes in a breath, sighs deeply.

"What's up?" one friend asks.

"That was Roger. Henry's lover. He's at the hospital. Henry's been bashed."

"Oh my god."

"Did you say Henry?" My pulse speeds up. How many gay couples named Henry and Roger could there be in Toronto?

Julie nods.

"Henry Rabinovitch?"

She nods again, her eyes grow wide. "Oh god. I didn't realize . . ."

"He's my cousin."

"I didn't make the connection before."

"Where is he? I want to go."

"Wellesley Hospital."

"That's not far." I know exactly where it is.

"No, it isn't," Julie agrees.

"I gotta go." I stand.

"Wait, Nomi. I'll go with you."

"Okay."

She grabs a long grey coat off the back of her chair.

We rush out together into a wall of ice-cold air. I fumble with the zipper on my ski jacket.

"My car's three blocks south," I tell Julie.

"It's faster to walk. Parking's a nightmare around here. Come on."

She's two steps ahead of me. We race up Wellesley Street toward the hospital.

The last time I saw Henry was at my father's unveiling. He looked good, but he's been HIV positive for years. A bashing could seriously affect his health. "Did Roger say how he was?"

"No."

I picture my cousin on a cold sidewalk, kicked and punched, over and over. Shaken, I focus my eyes on Julie's back. Her long black hair bounces against the back of her coat as she runs. This is almost surreal, this moment. Everything's moving too fast. So much in one day. The conveyor belt has speeded up. Chocolates are falling. This morning I was miserable and warm in San Francisco. Now I'm running down the street in Toronto, freezing, following a woman I've had a crush on forever, on our way to the hospital to find out if my cousin is dead or alive. My chest aches from gulping frozen air. My eyes tear and my nose begins to run.

"Come on," Julie says, opening the emergency ward entrance.

Breathlessly, I follow her inside.

Part 2

Monkey Business

Chapter *Nine*

*E*ither this is the worst hangover of my life or I'm dying. Where the hell is Roger? Green walls, fluorescent lights, Lysol. I'm in a hospital. How convenient. Roger works in a hospital. Hope I'm in his. He's probably on the next floor, tending someone else. Has anyone told him I'm here? I need morphine, heroin, a vodka martini. Roger, come save me.

The drugs are wearing off. There's a dull ache in my back. Pain is distant, but closing. My teeth throb. A fiery pain grips my chest. A steady beep muffled in layers of cotton. Muted voices, footsteps. Am I awake? Someone is standing beside me. Can't open my eyes. A hand on my arm, stroking my skin. Soothing. Is it you, Roger?

Ouch. A needle. Drugs, thank god. Warm spreads through my veins and I'm limp as cooked noodles. Sinking into the bed. Floating to the ceiling. Through the tiles. Oh god. I'm disintegrating. Call 911. I'm dying of an overdose. Someone, tell Roger and touch up my face before the police photographers show up. Wouldn't want to look lousy for my obit. I'm so bagged. Haven't been this tired since New York. A few lines of crystal, stayed up for three days. Crashed the fourth for two days in bed. Washed up, like an old movie star. A has-been. Five more minutes. Just five more minutes of sleep, Roger. Then I'll get up. Why don't you go and make coffee? I'll meet you in the kitchen. Just five more minutes. I'm so tired. So damn tired.

Footsteps click on the pavement behind me. I barely notice. Two men on their way to the bar, no doubt. The whack on my head comes out of nowhere. I'm down, on coarse pavement. Money? Take it. Wallet's in my back pocket. Right side. Cash? It's yours. All of it. Credit cards? Take them. My watch? Take it, too.

Black boots. Thick soles. Motorcycle boots. Cowboy boots. Into my ribs, my stomach. Red hot pain raging. The taste of blood.

"Faggot. Fucking faggot. Teach you a lesson. Fucking cocksucker." Boots slam my side. Relentless. Frenzied. Something cracks. Splits. There's fire in my chest. A scream in my throat. Footsteps. Shouts. Behind? Ahead? Echoing footsteps.

Where was I going? Strolling along Church Street, on my way to . . . Woody's. For a drink. Roger on night shift. Too quiet in the apartment. One beer. That's all. Then I'll go home. Just one beer. Maybe two. One more block. I can see the red awning up ahead. Wonder who's working the bar tonight. Dave? Or that cute guy, Randy, maybe. Harmless flirting. Haven't touched anyone but Roger since we met. No one believes me, but it's true. It is. I can be faithful, you know. For a hunk like Roger, it's a piece of cake. Just one beer. That's all I want. Didn't see it coming.

Head lead-heavy, sinking into the deep dark. I'm a little boy, running across the street, chasing my father. I slip, skin my knee on pavement and clutch my leg. A howl escapes my throat, tears run down my cheeks. My father approaches. I hold my arms out. He will pick me up, like Mommy does. He raises one arm, slaps me across the cheek. I stare at him, terrified.

"I'll give you something to cry about. No son of mine's gonna be a crybaby. You're a big boy now."

I sit on the ground in the middle of the road and watch as he walks back to the house, shaking his head, muttering under his breath. I stop crying. Choke back my tears, stop them in my throat. Look, Daddy. Look. I'm not crying. I'm a big boy. Just like you said. My throat closes tighter. I can't eat, can't swallow. Doctor says tonsillitis. I can barely breathe. They rush me to emergency. Rip my tonsils out. It hurts. It hurts. It hurts. But I don't cry. I'm a big boy now. My throat aches for a long, long time. I tell my mother. She tells the nurse. Nonsense, says the doctor. It's been over a week now. They send me home. I throw up blood. My throat is on fire, like swallowing knives. Fever a hundred and four. My mother takes me back to the hospital. An infection. I am delirious. I sleep, dream, sweat, shiver. My mother sits by my bedside all night long, singing, holding my hand. My father is not there. I ask for him. I'm not crying. I'm a big boy, I tell her. It hurts but I do not cry. She weeps when I ask for my father. She looks away and doesn't answer. Days go by. I sleep. Wake. My fever breaks. Slowly the vice around my throat loosens. I can swallow. I can eat. When they send me home, my father is not there. My mother doesn't answer when I ask. Every night I wait for him. Ask for him. I want my bedtime stories. My dad's stories.

"Scoot over, Pardner," he'd say every night when I'd get into bed. He'd lean against the wall, his legs stretched out, beside me. "There's this guy, see," he'd say. "Hank. Yeah, that's it. His name is Hank. He's a bit like you, Sport, only all grown up."

"Like me?" I'd say, imagining myself an adult.

"That's right, just like you. And Hank has this buddy, see? And they've staked out this bank, see?"

"Solly!" My mother would shout from the kitchen. "Stop with the bank robbery. Can't you tell him a nice story?"

"Never mind, Belle. This is a good story," he'd yell back.

"He's five years old, Solly. He doesn't need to hear about banks."

Solly would wait until we could hear dishes clatter in the sink, then he'd go right back to the story. It was our ritual. I didn't see my father much. He was always out somewhere. Working, he'd say. But he would always be home for dinner, and every night I would hear a bedtime story.

This time when I get home from the hospital, he's not around. Not for dinner. Not for bedtime. Summer comes, school is out. It's just the two of us now. My mother grows fat. Fatter. And fatter still. Big round hard belly. In September my mother goes to the hospital. I stay with Bubbe and Zayde. When they bring me back home a few days later, Mommy is there with two new babies and is no longer so fat. Two new baby boys. Now, we are four.

"You're the man of the family," she tells me.

I am six years old. I try to picture myself a man. I would be like my father. Big and burly, with a loud rolling laugh. A little mustache over my lip, like him. And my face would be scratchy with tiny black hairs. I'd wear suits and big wide ties with colourful pictures painted on them. An ocean and palm trees. Or the one my mother hates, with two girls in bathing suits. And I'd have black suspenders that snap when you tug them. I look down at myself. I don't have suspenders. Or a mustache, a tie. How can I be a man?

The new babies cry and cry. One, then the other. Someone is always crying. When my mother isn't looking, I hit them. "Crying is for babies," I shout, "Act like a man."

Someone is coughing, hacking. Someone close by. I wake, chest ablaze, coughing. My tongue is thick. Coated, dry. Slowly, I open my eyes. Roger's handsome face drifts into focus.

"Henry." Roger's voice penetrates. "Oh, Henry. No. Don't try to sit up." He leans over, kisses my face gently. My eyes fill with tears. I throw my good arm around my lover. Safe. Finally. His beautiful sweet smell, sweat from a night's work, surrounds me, lovingly. I sob quietly in his arms. He holds me, rocks me, kisses me. "That's it, baby. Roger's here. I'm here. I've got you. You're safe now." He brushes at my tears with his big soft hands. Nurse's hands. "Are you hurting? Do you need more painkillers?" He reaches across my body for my chart at the bottom of the bed, looks it over.

"They put me to sleep."

"That's good. You need rest. You're due for some more. You must be in pain now. Do you want me to get you some?"

I nod. As he stands, I grab at his arm, panicked to see him leaving. He caresses my hand gently.

"I'll be right back, Henry. It's okay." I release my grip. He smiles, leaves the room, and returns a minute later with a syringe.

"Ready?"

I nod.

He sticks it into my arm. I feel the drug numb my skin instantly.

"Roger?" I say.

"Yes, Henry. I'm here."

"Don't go away."

"No."

"Please."

"I'm right here." He kisses my cheek. My heavy eyes close. I sink into the mattress. I hear Roger's voice faintly, feel his weight on the bed. His hand on my forehead, lulling me to sleep.

"Hi," Roger says the moment I open my eyes. He sits in the hard orange chair by my bed. His white uniform is rumpled. He looks as if he's been trying to sleep in the chair. My head pounds. My chest aches, my legs are stiff, my mouth is dry, my eyes are sore, my jaw, arm, nose, everything. I feel like Joan of Arc, burning at the stake.

"You look terrible," I tell Roger.

He laughs. "That's kind of funny coming from you, Henry."

"Have you been there all night?"

"Yeah, and all morning too." He shifts in his chair, uncrosses his long legs, leans forward, kisses my cheek. Even that hurts. I smile bravely.

"Are you hungry?" Roger asks. "How's the pain?"

"Will painkillers knock me out again?" My jaw is sore when I talk. My lip is thick.

"How about some Tylenol 3's? They'll ease the pain without putting you under," he suggests, leaving.

It's daylight. The sun is high in the sky. How long have I been sleeping? My right arm is in a sling, in bondage. I'm hooked up to an IV. I'll have to ask Roger what they're pumping into me. Probably glucose and water so I don't dehydrate. There's a rather large bandage across the bridge of my nose, and my chest is taped up. I remember being kicked over and over in the ribs. Are they broken? Cracked? What else is injured? Frantically, I check under the covers with my good arm. Thankfully, everything seems to be intact. Without my favourite body part, life as we know it would not be worth living. Roger returns with a food tray, places it in front of me. Hospital food. Something mushy and grey, a boiled chicken leg, canned green peas, red Jell-O. Why do they serve such abysmal food in hospitals? Reminds me of a high school cafeteria. They should be tortured, at least arrested, for serving this horrifying slop. Julia Child would die at the sight. I scoop up a forkful of the pulverized grey lump, bring it up to my nose. Potatoes. I touch it skeptically with the tip of my tongue. It does not send me instantly into uncontrollable convulsions, so I tentatively taste some. Roger watches me try to eat. He sighs a lot. Something is troubling him. I wait, toy with my food. Peel slivers of chicken from the bone with my teeth, chew them cautiously.

"I knew something like this would happen," Roger says, finally.

"What?"

"I told you, Henry."

"What?"

"You can't go around making waves the way you do without consequences." He scratches the back of his head, hard and fast. It's a habit he has when he's stressed out. Roger hates that I'm in ACTOUT. It's the main thing we don't have in common. He is a conservative guy. Roger grew up in foster homes. He learned early to stay out of trouble, do his job, pay his taxes, keep his nose clean. His mother, a runaway, had him when she was fifteen, tried to keep him for the first couple of years on her own, working the streets to take care of him. She was picked up, charged, convicted. Social Services made him a ward of the state. When he was five, she got him back for a year. Tried to get a straight job, but drifted back to the streets. The Ministry intervened. Roger's mother kept her visitation rights, but he never lived with her again. Roger was shuffled around from home to home. Six different sets of foster parents. After high school, he worked his way through college and nursing school. He could have been a doctor if there'd been anyone to help him through school. Roger just wants to feel secure.

I guess it's true what they say. Opposites attract. We met at a party. Mutual friends. I was smitten with him instantly. His quiet dark looks. Thick, black hair that dipped over his forehead, Christopher Reeve before his terrible accident. Superman-ish— solid, capable and sweet. Roger was in the corner of the room in a deep conversation with the host, Michael, about the latest experimental drugs. I gravitated toward them, joined the conversation. I'd been HIV positive for five years at least. I always try to keep up on the latest drugs and treatments, for my friends and for myself.

I joined ACTOUT as soon as a chapter formed in Toronto. I was still working then, as a staff photographer for an arts and entertainment weekly. I was originally trained on a low-budget, political gay paper in New York. Worked for them for years. Didn't make much money, just enough to get by. When I moved to Toronto, I got a job with full benefits and steady pay. Nine to five. I was Ward Cleaver himself. For the first time in my life, I wasn't short of money. There was always some left at the end of the week. Two years ago I retired. Didn't want to work right up to my deathbed. I've watched too many friends take that route. I figure I'll live longer if I'm not working full-time. I'm one of the lucky guys. I had long-term medical disability coverage. My doctor signed all the appropriate forms so I could go on permanent disability. I get sixty percent of my former wages, which is not that much, but it's enough to live on, sort of. Well, I have a few sidelines too, but Roger doesn't know about them. We don't discuss money. Never have. Miss Vanderbilt herself would agree, I'm sure. Never discuss money, religion or personal hygiene with your beau. I continue to pay half the rent and half the groceries. Roger pays the cable, phone and electric bills, because he makes a lot more money than I do. If he knew some of the stuff I did to bring in extra cash, he'd kill me. He's so conservative, sometimes I can't believe we're still together. Almost four years now. I'm crazy about him. And he treats me so fine. So I stay with him, even though we disagree on absolutely everything.

"Roger," I say calmly, scooping a bouncing spoonful of red Jell-O. I can't remember the last time I had Jell-O. My mother's house, a million years ago. "It's not that simple." Slowly I raise the Jell-O to my lips. What the hell is in Jell-O anyway? What kind of a thing is this to serve sick people? Enough preservatives in this shit to choke a goddamned horse.

"That's where you're wrong, Henry. It is simple. I don't know what you guys are trying to prove." He frowns while I poke the Jell-O with my tongue. "That looks disgusting."

"You mean the Jell-O or what I'm doing to it?"

"The Jell-O."

"Why do they serve Jell-O in hospitals, Roger?"

He gives me a condescending look.

"Anyway, we're not trying to *prove* anything. We just want to expose the truth."

"You can't fight city hall, Henry." He throws his hands up in the air.

That's one of Roger's favourite lines. We've had this exact argument billions of times. He hates ACTOUT. Thinks we're a bunch of drug-crazed ex-hippies, ripping up our draft cards, burning our bras, and giving all homos a bad rep. That line about city hall is his trademark. He uses it every time we have this fight.

"Roger." I drop the spoonful of Jell-O back into the dish from a foot above. With my left hand I'm a klutz. Red gel splatters my arms and my lovely green hospital frock. "I have to do something. I don't know why you don't understand that. I can't just sit around, waiting to get sick. This is my way. You knew this about me when we first got together." It's true. He did. I told him that first night we met.

"What do you do?" he'd asked. I've always hated that question. People really mean "what do you do for a living?" But most of us do a lot more than just what we do for a living. So I said, "I play poker Wednesday nights with some old buddies, I'm a balcony gardener, I love to cook, I'm an unofficial 'big brother' to the son of some lesbians I know, I fuck as many men as possible each week, I'm a member of ACTOUT. Oh, and I'm a photographer."

It made him laugh.

"Dammit, Henry. Look what's happened to you! You could have died on fucking Church Street. Don't you get it?"

"Roger. I was gay-bashed. What are you talking about?" I stir my Jell-O until it turns liquid.

"Yeah, Henry. But why do you think they picked you?"

I stare at him. "I don't know. My cute tush?"

He sighs. "Henry, what were you wearing when it happened?"

I shrug. "Jeans. Sweater. Leather jacket."

He nods his head quickly, repeatedly. Goes to the grey metal locker at the other end of the room, pulls out my black leather jacket, turns it so its back is facing me.

"This, Henry, is what I'm talking about."

"Oh." I have stickers all over my jacket. Silence Equals Death. Heterosexism Kills. Queer Nation. Dykes Rule. Boycott Shell. We are all innocent victims. Hug me, I have AIDS.

"Who do you think they're gonna pick, walking down the street? Me? Or you?"

"Roger, I won't closet myself."

"I'm not asking you to. But do you have to antagonize people?"

I've never seen Roger so angry. But this is my life. Activism is what I do. I'm fucking retired at thirty-eight. Put out to pasture in my prime. Like an old milk cow. Does he want me to roll over and just wait to die?

"Huh? Henry? What's going to be next?"

"Roger! You know damn well I'm not going to stop. I can't. I have to fight back and you know it. If I stop, that's giving up. You don't want me to give up, do you?"

The cough rises in me all at once, an explosion, bursting from my lungs. I buckle forward. My ribs are so sore, I can only take in short, shallow breaths. Roger rushes over, sits beside me, rubs my back. His warm hands radiate love. His touch heals. Slowly the coughing subsides.

"Oh Henry," Roger says. "That doesn't sound good. You should lie back now. You need rest. I think I should give you more Demerol. You need to sleep. I'm sorry I shouted. I just get scared.

I'm so scared for you sometimes. That's all. I'm scared, Henry."

I lie back against the pillow. Reach for his hand, squeeze it tightly. There is a vice grip around my chest. I try to calm my breathing. Roger leaves and returns with a syringe. Shoots me up again. I hold his hand and wait for the drugs to take effect.

Chapter Ten

This is it, folks. The moment we've all been waiting for. My very first opportunistic infection. How convenient. I was already in the hospital when it hit. Dr. Green noticed a tiny lesion just below my shoulder blade. He says it'll take two days for the biopsy results to come back, but we all know what it is. Dr. Green's entire practice is PWAs. The man knows a KS lesion when he sees one. Apparently, the beating weakened my already devastated immune system. My T-cell count is under 200 for the first time. I probably lost a lot of CD4 cells out there on the pavement, while my head was being kicked in by those creeps. Yes folks, hundreds of my precious T cells catapulted into the atmosphere from a cold city sidewalk.

I guess in a way I've been lucky. I've been asymptomatic for years. Longer than most of my friends. I figure it's because I didn't work myself to death. I haven't had the daily stress of a full-time job in over two years. I get lots of sleep, plenty of exercise and I take Geritol twice a day. Well, I guess I still have my sense of humour. And my self-esteem. And you know what Louise Hay says, if you love yourself, really, really love yourself, you won't die. I love myself plenty. It's AIDS I don't love.

Roger finally went home this morning. I made him. He was exhausted. He's been sitting vigil in that fucking vinyl chair for two days. He's had to keep going to work in between. He needed a good night's sleep in our bed. He protested. Said he wouldn't sleep anyway with me here and him there, but I forced him to go. Frankly, he's been getting on my nerves. And I know it isn't true. He probably fell asleep the second his head hit the goddamned pillow. Now I wish I hadn't sent him away. I'm getting plenty bored. They have me on painkillers again, Demerol and Valium, to which I owe my current pleasant demeanour. Now that every tiny movement is not a new adventure in pain, I am bored, bored, bored. I've already read the one *People* magazine that Roger brought and it certainly isn't good enough to read twice. I wish someone would bring me an *Advocate*. Or a *Poz* magazine. A *Diseased Pariah News* would cheer me right up. Maybe I'll pay to have the TV connected.

Someone is in the doorway, kind of hovering. I can't see around the corner. I wait, as patiently as possible. Finally, they come in. My cousin Nomi and her brother Josh. I have a vague memory of Nomi visiting before, my first day in the hospital. With Julie Sakamoto. Do they know each other? Or was it a dream?

Nomi looks worried. She stands by the edge of my bed. "Henry. God. What happened? You look worse."

So she *was* here on Wednesday. "Just depressed. Doctor found a lesion. Probably KS."

"Oh, Henry."

She reaches down, rubs my arm. Her hand accidentally brushes over the IV needle taped to my forearm. Her eyes follow the cord up to the plastic bottle. Sulpha drugs against PCP. Just in case. With such a low T-cell count I'm now a walking target for PCP, CMV, MAI. I'm a grown man terrified of three-letter words.

"Oh, Henry," she says again.

Josh frowns.

I smile weakly.

Josh looks scared. Maybe he's not used to being around sick people. He has a look in his eye I barely remember. The fear that healthy people have. People who think this will never happen to them. Straight people who don't even know anybody with AIDS. I had that look in my eye once, a million years ago. A million and one.

The nurse bustles in with a lunch tray. She says I should sit up for a while and eat. Nomi perches on the edge of the bed. Josh sits in the chair. I pick up my fork, remove the pale green plastic cover from my plate. Fish sticks, canned peas again, were they on sale?

Fruit cocktail from a can. Don't these people know how to cook? Would it hurt them to serve real vegetables? How am I supposed to recover on over-cooked Swanson TV dinners? If I had a little more strength, I'd storm into the kitchen, tie up the cook and throw together some edible meals. I'd be the most popular patient on the ward. Nomi and Joshua stare at my lunch. Joshua has that look again. I sigh. Stick out my tongue.

"Blah."

He laughs, finally. I cut into a piece of fish, put it in my mouth, slowly chew. It tastes like cardboard. Roger's going to have to bring me some real food soon or I'll never get out of here.

"Tell the story again. Of why you moved to New York," Nomi says. We have a ritual we never tire of. We tell each other our coming out stories every time we get together. It started many years ago, when Nomi was first coming out. She phoned me in New York. She was so scared, just a kid. It took her over an hour to spit the news out.

"What was it like?" Nomi asks. "You moved there all by your-self. You were so brave. God. You were so young."

"Seventeen." I picture myself then, a mere child.

"You were seventeen?" Josh is impressed.

"I had to go. My mother caught me sucking Morris Silverberg's cock. Right in our apartment."

"She kicked you out?" Josh doesn't flinch when I mention the part about Morris Silverberg's cock. Good sign. Nomi's trained him, I guess.

"Kind of ran away. She didn't stop me. The twins were only twelve. Sherry was nine. She had her hands full. Anyway, she couldn't control me."

"What was it like?" Nomi absent-mindedly picks up a piece of soggy fish from my discarded plate and tosses it into her mouth.

"It was great. At first. Morris came to New York with me. We ran away together. We were young and gay. Living in Greenwich Village. A dream come true. We were in love. We had everything. Except for money. We had no money. But we didn't care, or at least I didn't. Guess Morris did. When his father tracked us down, he went back home. Never saw him again."

"Never?"

"Uh-uh. Don't know what happened to him. Don't even know if he's still alive. I've asked around. No one knows him. Maybe he went straight, married some poor woman, had a brood of kids."

"Does Bubbe know about you?" Nomi devours another fish stick.

I sigh. "I visit her sometimes. It's hard. 'When are you gonna get married?' That's all she says."

"I know. I have the same problem," Nomi complains.

"Not out either, huh?"

She shakes her head. "Well, I've never said. I mean, what can I say? She's an old woman. I've wanted to, but I don't think she'd understand."

"She understands," Josh says, quietly, looking down at his shoes.

"What?" says Nomi. "What do you mean?"

"Well . . ."

"What? What did she say?"

"You won't like it."

"What?"

"Oh god. I can't say it." Josh leans forward in his chair, elbows on his knees, head in his hands.

"Josh! Come on. Say it!" Nomi demands.

"It's awful."

"What did she say, Josh?" Nomi speaks through a small crack between gritted teeth.

He sighs deeply. Opens his mouth. We wait. "She said, she said, oh god . . ."

"Josh!"

"I can't."

"What is it?"

He shakes his head.

"Come on Josh. You've already said this much."

"Oh boy."

"Josh."

"Okay. She . . . thinks . . . she said . . . she said you're cursed by God."

Nomi and I look at each other. Eyes wide. Josh sighs deeply.

Nomi leaves to drive Josh to the subway, says she wants to come back later for more of a visit. I miss Roger. I hope he's getting sleep. He has to work tonight. He promised to come see me before his shift. I told him to bring some food from home, or at least get some take-out. I don't know how much more of this horrifying hospital food I can handle.

High heels click on the polished hospital floor. Julie Sakamoto strolls into my room. Julie is one of those feminine lesbians you'd never pick out on the street. Long black hair, dark sultry eyes, cheekbones like a model. She wears dresses, high heels and make-up. She doesn't need to be a bull dyke to be tough. Julie is in my ACTOUT group. We're on the Direct Action committee together.

A few months ago, a man named Albert Maxwell, a gay doctor from New York, walked into one of our Monday night ACTOUT meetings and changed our lives. Albert has been trying to expose a government experiment that began in the late seventies and was responsible for unleashing AIDS into the gay community. He's spent the last seven years doing extensive research. He's written two books explaining the experiment. He's been banned from presenting his findings at the International AIDS Conference, which is suspicious all on its own, if you ask me. He's sent copies of his books to every magazine and newspaper in the United States and to the governor of every state. Not one politician responded. Not one member of the press. He approached our Toronto ACTOUT group for help six months ago. He figures the American media is too afraid to speak out against their own government. Albert is hoping the Canadian press will have just enough distance to take the risk. Albert's theory sounds unbelievable at first, but when you read through his research, it all adds up.

Albert says HIV is not a "new" virus that originated in Central

Africa in monkeys, as the scientists would like us to believe. He says HIV is a man-made disease, created intentionally by the U.S. military. As a weapon of germ warfare. The virus was tested on gay men, secretly hidden inside the Hepatitis B Experimental Vaccine. Trials for the vaccine were conducted in Manhattan in 1978 and in San Francisco in 1980. In Africa, tens of thousands of people were exposed to HIV through the smallpox vaccine programs of the late 1970s.

When Albert first approached our ACTOUT group I thought he was a few sandwiches short of a picnic basket, if you know what I mean. Biological warfare? Hidden in vaccines? Administered right in Manhattan? By doctors? I'd heard rumours about government conspiracy before, but I'd dismissed the idea as hysterical. People with AIDS were dying from government neglect. This I could fathom. But Albert was flat-out accusing the government of *creating* HIV and purposely testing it on an unsuspecting gay community. Impossible.

At that first ACTOUT meeting, I argued against working with him. But some of our members wanted to hear more. So Albert returned the following week with Xeroxed copies of his seven years of research. I spent two weeks reading Albert's evidence. I was chilled right to the bone. Albert traced it all the way back to the sixties. The Cold War was still in full swing. The U.S. government was intent on developing systems of germ warfare. Millions of dollars were granted to scientists working in the field.

As I read through Albert's documents, I became more and more convinced. His theory that HIV was created in laboratories and tested on humans is no more bizarre than the theory the medical establishment has been tossing at us for years. About green monkeys and how the virus "jumped species" into the African population, made its way to Haiti to end up some time later in gay men in Manhattan. I mean, come on, green monkeys? How does a virus "jump species" anyway? And land up in three completely separate areas of the world at the same time? I mean, get serious. Sounds like a bad Stephen King novel.

Albert says it all started in 1969, the Summer of Love. He says it's all in the library, you just have to know where to look. He obtained copies of official government documents through the Freedom of Information Act which revealed that the United States Department of Defense received funding from Congress in 1969 to "perform studies on immune-system-destroying agents for germ warfare." Well, if that doesn't sound like AIDS, I don't know what does. In 1977, the World Health Organization launched a major campaign against smallpox in cities of Central Africa, which just happens to be exactly where the incidence of AIDS is the highest. If the virus originated in green monkeys in the wilds, don't you think rural Africans who lived in the bush would be the first to get it? Instead of people in the cities? Makes sense to me, and I didn't even finish high school. Albert says it was the intention of the government not only to test the virus on innocent people in Central Africa, but to "reduce" the population. In other words, kill people.

I remember the Hepatitis B Vaccine Trial. Some of my friends signed up for it. Morris had gone back home, but I was living in the Village in '78. According to the health department, there was a hepatitis B epidemic among gay men. The New York Blood Center needed volunteers to test a brand-new experimental hepatitis B vaccine. It would end the epidemic, they said. Gay men could help our community. They said hep B was rampant among sexually active gay men. Well, who wasn't sexually active? I mean, come on. This was 1978, in the Village. The height of The Party.

The doctors said we could be of service to our community. Plus, the vaccine was free, and in America, honey, nothing, especially to do with health care, is free. There was a huge questionnaire. My friend Joe filled one out. It asked scores of questions about the most personal things. Name, rank and serial number, of course, but also what you did in bed, with whom, how, how much, with how many and how often. There were full-page ads in the *Advocate*, in all the bar rags and on bulletin boards in the VD clinics. There were bloodmobiles that would drive up and down the streets of the Village, horns blaring—Free hep B testing, protect your health. Be of service to your community, they said. Volunteer for a free vaccine. And you know what? They touched a nerve. Thousands of healthy young gay men signed up for the trial vaccines. Government doctors were coming round to our neighbourhood saying they cared about fags. Enough to start a whole program to address our special health needs. For the first time in our lives, someone in authority was saying we mattered. Most of us had fathers who wouldn't speak to us. This kind of validation from doctors and officials from the health department, hey, it was the approval we'd have died for from our families. No pun intended.

All the cute guys signed up. It was a trend. I'm telling you, the line-up to get into the study was longer than the one at Studio 54. Fags signed up by the thousands. Ten thousand, originally. They took a thousand for the first experiment. Only young, healthy, mostly white, mostly middle-class, educated gay men who would return for three injections, who had a permanent address and phone number, who were willing to show up for regular follow-up blood tests and who were particularly promiscuous. Like laboratory rats. They needed a very specific control group in order to do their research. They needed promiscuous guys who were previously healthy and considerate enough to show up for the follow-up research. The experiment would have been useless without the follow-up contact. Albert is convinced that the AIDS virus was "introduced" into the gay men who served as guinea pigs in the hep B experiment. Once they injected the virus into someone, they needed to keep track of what happened to them. Later, the scientists used these blood samples to prove how HIV was spread sexually in the gay community.

Joe signed up. He was the first man I knew who got sick. He died from pneumonia in 1980—before we'd heard of PCP or AIDS. Al says it's no accident they picked gay men. They needed a group of people that everyone else despised. That way they could get away with dragging their heels on finding a cure. They don't want to find a cure. They're scientists. This is an experiment. They want to study the progression, the effects of the virus and take notes, write papers, win Nobel prizes.

Albert says there was not a single case of HIV before the hepatitis experiments. According to his research, in January 1979, two months after the beginning of the New York City Hepatitis Vaccine Trials, the first case of AIDS was discovered in a young gay man living in the Village. The western vaccine trials began in March 1980, in L.A. and San Francisco. Seven months later, the first cases of AIDS were discovered in those cities. Al says it's all right there in the reports. You just have to read them. Of the first twenty-six cases of AIDS, all were gay men, twenty were from New York City and six were from L.A. or San Francisco. That's too much of a fucking coincidence, if you ask me.

Anyhow, I wouldn't put it past the U.S. government. Look at all the other creepy stuff they've done. And then covered up. Agent Orange in Vietnam. LSD experiments with unknowing victims in the 1950s. Albert told me about the Tuskegee experiment: Four hundred poor, black men with syphilis were examined yearly by Public Health Service doctors in Tuskegee, Alabama, to watch the destructive effects of untreated syphilis. The men were never informed they had syphilis. They were told they were receiving treatment for "bad blood." When penicillin became available in the forties, they weren't allowed to receive it. Other doctors in the county were forbidden to treat them. Scientists were convinced that the effects of syphilis in black people were different than in white people. The Tuskegee experiment was set up to prove that hypothesis. I mean, can you fucking believe that? Some racist scientists in lab coats sit around one day and decide that black men get syphilis differently than white men, and to prove their little theory, they use real people, and no one blinks.

The experiment continued until nineteen fucking seventy-two. And here's the kicker—Al says the Tuskegee experiment was supervised by the Centers for Disease Control and Prevention, the very same folks who now oversee the AIDS epidemic. The simple truth is that the U.S. government's been doing this kind of stuff for decades.

Of course, no one wants to believe Albert's theory, it's just too horrible. We're all in collective denial, a huge dysfunctional family. Like no one wants to believe that mommie dearest is beating us, or daddy is raping us nightly. Albert wants the story out to the public. If enough people know, something will be done. Julie and I have been working together trying to hook Albert up with gay journalists, or people involved in the media. So far, we haven't found anyone.

Julie shifts in the vinyl chair beside my bed.

"Henry, you don't look so good."

"That's what everyone says these days. Don't you like my hair or what?"

She smiles. "You've still got your sense of humour."

"And my figure. Don't forget about that."

"Albert's coming to town."

"He is? When?"

"Couple of days. He planned the trip without asking anyone. I told him he should wait until you're better. But he insisted. Said he needed to see us. He got really upset when I told him what happened to you. He said, 'Shit, I should have known. Damn. How did they find him too?' I said, 'Who?' He said, 'Never mind.' Then he said he was coming here, soon. That he'd explain more when he got here."

"What do you think he meant?"

"I don't know."

"Who knows if we're ever going to find a reporter to write the article anyway. The few I've talked to so far don't want to hear about it or they think it's impossible. They don't believe me."

"I guess you kind of have to hear the whole thing for it to make sense."

"What whole thing?" Nomi says, sauntering into my room. She waltzes right up to my bed. Julie and Nomi smile at each other.

For a long time. I'm about to introduce them when Nomi says, "Hi, Julie." Julie sticks out one hand in a femme way, like a real girl. I watch as Nomi takes her hand. They look deeply into one another's eyes. Little sparks ignite. I can feel electricity in the air. My cousin's eyes sparkle. She swaggers a little, even though she's standing still. It's a slight shifting of the feet, very butch and charming. Hunky. If she were a man, she'd be a real dish.

"Nomi," Julie says, "I thought I might see you here again."

So that's why Nomi came back. Nomi grins. They continue to hold hands, an extended handshake. I start to wonder if maybe I should leave, or at least pretend to read a magazine.

"Henry and I were talking business." Julie smiles wider, bats her eyes in a way that is probably designed to show off her exquisite cheekbones.

"Oh," my cousin says, disappointed. I hear a slight catch in her throat. I wonder if this effect is spontaneous or cleverly rehearsed. It works wonders on Julie, who smiles and preens.

"You can stay though, Nomi." Julie glances at me for confirmation.

I shrug.

Nomi nods, as if something important has just been decided. Awkwardly, they release hands. I can see neither wants to.

"You two know each other," I state the obvious.

"We ran into each other at The Rose the night you were bashed. But we knew each other before that. You know, from the community," Julie explains.

"So you *were* here the night I was bashed?"

"Yeah. I don't think you were conscious though," Nomi says.

"Kind of."

Nomi sways from foot to foot, then perches at the edge of my bed. "Well," she says, "Don't let me get in the way of your meeting." She grins at Julie in a boyish way. I'm enjoying the show. It's kind of cute, sweet, not that much different than two guys, except more subtle. Two men would be well into sexual innuendoes by now. With these two, it's all in the eyes. Where they look, how they hold their hands, their bodies. The way Julie crosses her legs, one over the other, lets her skirt slip just a bit, exposing more thigh. The way Nomi sits, legs spread wide, head cocked back, like a boy. A handsome young college boy.

"Was there more?" I ask Julie.

She tears her eyes from Nomi, turns to me, flipping her long hair over one shoulder. Thinks for a moment. "Well, not really. Just that Albert said he wanted to come sometime this week. He was vague about it over the phone, said he didn't know exactly when, just soon. His voice sounded different."

"Different?"

"Yeah, I got the feeling there was something he wasn't saying. You know."

"Like what?"

She purses her lips. "I don't know, Henry. He was different. Uh, like he was quiet. You know how Albert usually is . . ."

"Yeah," I laugh.

Albert is wired for sound. Too much coffee maybe. Or because he lives in New York. I don't know. He talks really fast, and a lot, interrupting people, speaking at the same time they do. I don't think he means to be rude. He just has so much to say and he's afraid he's going to run out of time, so he's always saying something. Expounding this theory or that, excited, racing around. "He was quiet?"

"Yeah. Quiet. Slow. He was slowed right down. And he sounded sort of weird. Like maybe he had been to the dentist or something and his mouth was frozen. You know what I mean?"

"Did you ask him?"

"Yeah. I asked if he was okay. Then he got into sounding a bit more like his usual self. Anyway, I guess he'll be here soon."

"Who'll be here soon?" Roger hurries in, dressed in his uniform. He carries a tray with Styrofoam cups and bowls, a couple of juice boxes. "Oh, hi Julie. Hi Nomi." He walks around to the other side of my bed. "Move over." Roger sits beside me, leans back against the headboard, puts his feet up, right alongside mine. Wish I could warn Julie not to say more. Roger hates the work we're doing with Albert. He thinks it's nothing but trouble.

"Doctor Maxwell," Julie blurts out.

I cringe, instinctively creep a little away from Roger.

He looks at me sternly. I shrug, helpless.

Julie checks her watch. "I should go. I have some work to do at home."

She stands. Nomi leaps up, like she's afraid Julie will get away if she doesn't do something fast. I am inside a lesbian soap opera, watching fate unfold before my very eyes.

"Can I give you a ride somewhere?" Nomi offers. Nice technique.

Julie's whole body smiles. "That would be lovely."

I get a kiss on my cheek from each of them. They wave to Roger and stroll toward the door. Nomi hangs back just a little, like she's protecting Julie, ready at any moment to hold open doors, lay her jacket across a puddle, slay dragons, climb mountains. Chivalry seeps from her every pore.

"They make such a cute couple," I tell Roger.

"Are they a couple?" He lifts the plastic lid off a Styrofoam bowl of chicken noodle soup. Steam rises. The noodles are thin and short, like in Lipton instant.

"We'll see," I say. He pushes the bowl toward my side of the tray.

"How are you feeling?" He brushes the hair off my forehead.

I pout. "Depressed."

He attempts a smile. "We'll get through this, Henry."

We. He said we. "Will we?"

His eyes are soft and dreamy. Like a man in love. "Yeah." He gently presses the bandage on my broken nose. It keeps coming up at the edges. I've been sweating. It's so damn hot in here and Roger won't let me have the window open. Says it's better for me to sweat.

"I want you to eat this." He hands me the spoon.

"Okay, Roger," I say and snuggle closer to him, slipping my hand through his arm. Roger is the first boyfriend I've had in a long time. It's still a thrill whenever he does something just for me.

"Go on," he says. With Roger by my side, I can do anything.

Purposefully, I lift a spoonful of the hot steamy liquid to my mouth.

Part 3

Life, Liberty and the Pursuit

Chapter Eleven

Oh god. I'm about to drive Julie Sakamoto, the most beautiful femme dyke in the universe, home. I can't believe this is actually happening. If this is a dream, I hope I never wake up. I open the front passenger door of my mother's car and wait for Julie to step in. I close her door, walk around and glide into the driver's seat.

"You're a real gentleman, Nomi," Julie smiles.

"Oh. Yeah, I guess." Is she flirting? I start the engine. There's a light snow falling. A thin layer covers the windows. I grope for the brush on the floor between Julie's legs.

"Excuse me. Sorry." My hand brushes lightly against her calf. She doesn't move out of the way. "Have to clear the windshield," I explain, as if she couldn't have figured it out. My cheeks are hot. I open my door quickly and slip out. It's freezing, but I'm so flushed, I undo the zipper of Josh's ski jacket a few inches to let cold air in. Julie smiles at me through the windshield. I grin back. By the time I slide back inside, the car is warm.

I ease the stick into drive. "So, where to?"

"Bathurst and Harbord. I'll show you when we get close, okay?"

"Sure."

"So, I didn't get a chance to ask you the other night . . ." Julie says.

"What?" Her legs rest a mere two feet from mine. Her whole lovely body is within reach.

"What brings you to town?"

She crosses one gorgeous leg over the other. I try not to gawk. "Oh. My mother's wedding."

"Oh. Divorced?" With her left hand, she brushes stray hair away from her face.

"Widowed. My father died two years ago." I pump the brakes, slowing the car to stop at a red light.

"Oh. Sorry."

I smile bravely into Julie's soft eyes. My stomach back-flips. I'm dying to ask if she's single. "So, you still live with Lenni?" I try.

"Who told you we lived together?"

"Oh. No one. I thought maybe you did." The light turns green. I touch the accelerator gently and enter the intersection.

"Nope."

They could still be an item, without living together. How am I going to find out? I decide to change the subject and then try again later. "That sure sounds fascinating. The work you're doing with Henry."

She faces me. "It is, Nomi. Gives me chills, actually. I've read a lot of the material Dr. Maxwell sent us. It's frightening. When you see the government documents, it all makes sense. More sense than the usual theory."

"Oh yeah? What's that?"

"That the virus has always been around, dormant in monkeys, in Central Africa. And for some unknown reason was passed on to humans in the late seventies. If you ask me, it's pretty racist. Why Africa? Who says it didn't start in New York? Most of the early cases were there. In white gay men. How come the scientists don't think it started in New York and then moved to Africa or Haiti? Huh?"

I remember Julie from my political days in Toronto, a radical dyke of colour, and take the coward's route. "I don't know."

"Exactly. Because there is no reason. It's racist, that's all."

I nod. Even if she's not still with Lenni, if I asked her out for coffee, she'd probably say no. If she said yes, then what? Like I told Betty, I'm here for Faygie's wedding. And that's it.

"You know, now that I've read Albert's theory about AIDS, I can't believe more people don't question the whole thing. You know what I mean?"

"Huh? Yeah." Whatever you say, beautiful. Sounds weird to me. It's not like I trust the government or anything, but how could they get away with purposely infecting so many people? Someone in charge would put a stop to it.

"It makes me so mad. What do you think, Nomi?"

Oh god. Don't ask me what I think. Should I lie to get on her good side or tell the truth? "Well . . ."

"You don't believe it," she declares. "I can tell by your face."

"Julie, it's just that you and Henry sound like you walked right out of a science fiction movie."

"More like science *fact*, Nomi," she says with an edge.

"Well, I mean . . ." I backpedal vainly. "It's just that, well . . . probably if I read more about it like you have . . ." Why am I even bothering? All femmes are crazy, anyway. You can't win. No matter what you say. Even if Julie liked me a little, she'd only break my heart. And my heart can't take another break right now. Frazzled, I forget to turn onto Harbord Street and end up waiting at Bloor to turn left.

"All right. Why don't you come upstairs and read some, then? I have copies at my place." Ohmygod. Did she just invite me up? The light turns red. I screech past the Jewish Community Centre and head west. There are Christmas decorations, red and green lights, in store windows. Saturday afternoon shoppers rush along Bloor Street. Julie smiles.

"Sure," I mumble, and my stomach drops clear through to the street below. I run right over it. This is dangerous. I should just drop Julie off, forget I ever met her. I should drive directly back to my mother's house and the wedding preparations. Julie is too beautiful. Too charming. Way too sexy. If I go any further, there's no telling what will happen.

"Okay? Nomi?"

I grip the steering wheel tightly. A trickle of perspiration runs down my chest. Who do I sound like? Betty. That's who. The old keep-your-heart-in-deep-freeze approach to love and life. Don't go after someone who might matter. Don't fall in love. Don't look for happiness, because where there's joy, there's pain. "Okay," I say.

"Good. Oh, hang a left after the next light."

"More coffee?" Julie asks. We've been sitting on her living room floor for three hours. She's been handing me report after report to read. She's right. It's chilling. A few times the hair on the back of my neck stands on end. The more I read, the more convinced I am that AIDS was created in laboratories, on purpose. According to the documents, the president knew about it. The secretary of state oversaw the project. The whole thing has been covered up with millions of dollars from the government of the United States. Julie returns from her small kitchenette off the living room with the coffee pot, refills my cup.

"I could really do with something stronger at this point," I say, rubbing the back of my neck.

"Oh, sure." She gets up and opens a cupboard above the stove. "I have brandy. How's that?"

"Great." I put down the page I'm reading, watch her set two small snifters on the counter. Julie is a knockout. Hair to her waist, full red lips. Long red nails.

I glance at my watch. Shit, 5:30. I promised my mother I'd be back at her place by six. We're having a family dinner tonight. Just her, me and my brothers. "Uh, can I use your phone for a minute?"

"Of course. It's beside the couch. See it?" she says, without turning.

"Yeah." I pick up the receiver and dial my mother's number.

"Hello."

"Josh!" I'm always happy to hear his voice.

"Nomi!" He answers, as if he hasn't talked to me in three years. Josh and I genuinely like each other. I've never been that close to Izzy, but Josh and I have always had this great connection.

"Hey, is Ma home?"

"No. Aunt Rhoda came by and picked her up. There was a sale on dresses or something. She said she'd be home soon. Are you coming back up for dinner?"

"Yeah. Except I'm going to be a bit late. Can you tell her?"

"Sure."

"Just say I'm on the way, and I'll be there soon. Iz there yet?"

"Nah. His car wouldn't start. He's waiting for JoJo to come over and give him a boost."

"He still hangs with JoJo?" JoJo Klepfeld and my brother Izzy have been friends since elementary school. JoJo used to be small, like Izzy. When they were really young, the other guys would pick on them both. Then puberty hit. JoJo became a giant. He's six-four, weighs in at two-fifty. He and Izzy make quite the pair walking down the street, because Izzy never did grow much. He takes after my father's side of the family. Short and stocky.

"Yeah, Iz and Jo are still tight. See you soon?"

"Yeah. Thanks Josh."

Julie sits down on the floor beside me, hands me a snifter. She's a foot away. We're separated by a thin stack of government documents. I sip the brandy. The warm liquid slides down my throat. The whole world has shifted. My stomach flutters. I'm not sure if it's the AIDS conspiracy or the close proximity of Julie Sakamoto. I take another drink.

"So, why'd you want to know about Lenni?" she asks.

I practically choke. "Uh, no reason."

"Liar," she challenges. I glance sideways. She smirks.

I take another sip, for courage. "Okay," I say. "You caught me."

"Thought so. You want to know if I'm single?"

I laugh. Nod.

"Do you think I would have asked you up here if I wasn't?"

"Oh. I don't know."

She shakes her head. "Butches," she mutters.

"Huh?"

"You're so slow."

"I am? I mean, we are?"

"Nomi . . ."

I turn my head toward her. Her eyes are so big, I could jump inside and never come out. "Yes, Julie?"

"Kiss me."

A siren wails inside my guts. Sheer panic. I'm afraid I'll screw this up. The last two times I tried to kiss a woman, I ended up outside and alone so fast it made my head spin. But this is Julie Sakamoto, and she wants me. I place my glass on the carpet, lean over, and slowly move toward her, like in a perfume commercial, or a made-for-TV movie. Two lovers have been separated for years, have waited for the day when they can be together. Finally the moment has arrived. A beautiful sandy beach at sunset. They run toward each other, so slow it makes your heart break. The camera pans from one to the other. Back and forth. Running, running. It takes excruciating centuries.

My desperate lips connect with Julie's. Even softer than I imagined. Paradise. Her tongue slips into my mouth. I moan. She caresses my face with soft fingers. A fine mist of desire washes over my skin. We roll, the research papers crinkle underneath us. Her perfume is everywhere. We neck frantically, her hands reach for my nipples. They harden under her touch. I groan, slip my hands inside her lacy bra.

"Ohh," she moans.

The phone rings. We hesitate.

"The machine'll get it," Julie says, and throws her mouth on mine again. I hear Julie on the tape. The machine beeps. Then a loud voice emanates from the speaker.

"Hello. I'm trying to reach my daughter, Nomi."

"Oh my god! It's my mother." I leap for the receiver. "Ma?"

"Nomi! There you are."

"Ma!"

"What?"

"How did you get this number?" I can't keep the irritation out of my voice.

"Call display."

"Oh."

"And you don't have to get snappy with me."

I sigh. "Sorry."

"Well, where are you, Nomi?"

"A friend's. Visiting."

"Nomi, the boys are both here. We're waiting for you."

I check my watch. Shit. It's six o'clock. "What time is it?" I ask.

"Nomi. Doesn't your friend have a clock? It's almost six-thirty already."

"Ma. It's six."

"I thought you didn't have a clock."

"I just noticed one."

"Mamelah, we're waiting. When can we expect you?"

I sigh. "Soon. Okay. I'm leaving right away. Sorry. I didn't realize how late it was." Or what planet I was on.

"Good. So we'll see you in, what? Half an hour?"

"Sure, Ma. I'll be right there."

"Okay. And drive carefully, dear. It's a crazy world out there these days."

"Okay, Ma. See you soon." I hang up. Julie giggles. "Sorry about that," I say.

"Do you have to go?" She pouts.

I nod. " 'Fraid so."

She stands, wraps her arms around my neck and we're kissing again. Fifteen minutes later, I manage to steer us toward her door, necking all the way there, knocking into her bookcase, tripping over shoes in the entranceway. Still entangled, I slip into my boots and coat, fumble for the doorknob.

"Call me." Her lips brush against my ear.

"Love to." I taste her neck, run my tongue along her skin. My feet are in the hall, my upper body is still entwined with Julie. "What's your number?"

"Doesn't your mother have it?"

"Oh yeah." I pull free, reach back and squeeze her hand. "I forgot." She leans forward and kisses me again. It takes ten more minutes to separate, but somehow we do. I bound down the stairs to the street.

Chapter *Twelve*

My father, Harry, used to drive this car, a 1989 four-door station wagon. Harry always had wagons, to haul wood home for frames, transport finished paintings to shows and deliver commissioned works to people's houses. My father was an artist, a painter. That was the thing I liked most about him. His creative, adventurous spirit, uncharacteristic for his generation and upbringing.

"You gotta be happy in this world, Nomi," he'd say to me. "It's the most important thing."

When my parents were engaged, my mother's mother forbade the marriage.

"She was ashamed," my mother told me. "She wanted me to marry an educated man, a professional, a doctor maybe, an accountant, or better yet, the rabbi's son, Marty Fishbein. Between you and me, Nomi, Marty Fishbein is a schlemiel."

My grandmother, who died when I was a teenager, never liked my father. She didn't respect his art, thought he was ruining her daughter's life. Whenever my father tried to talk to her, she'd grunt. Harry wasn't exactly a genius, but he had talent. Perhaps if he'd never married, if he'd had only himself to support, he'd have lived on a pittance, and spent all his time on art. He might have become famous. As it was, after my parents married, his best friend Meyer hired him as a stereo salesman at Sears. Meyer was the department manager. He gave Harry afternoon and evening shifts, so he could paint in the morning.

Harry's studio was a corner of the basement. Some days he let me and my brothers watch as he worked. He painted portraits mostly, though occasionally he'd do buildings from photographs. Harry was convinced that one day he'd make it big, become rich and famous. That kept him going. Faith in himself. He sold paintings periodically, for modest prices. Kept working at Sears. Kept painting in the basement. Never struck paydirt, but Harry was a happy man. He did what he loved. A fire blazed in his eyes when he painted, singing along with jazz on his scratchy portable record player. Benny Goodman, Louis Armstrong, Peggy Lee, Judy Garland, Ella Fitzgerald and Frank Sinatra. He selected his music as carefully as his colours. The music was as much a part of the process as the brushes he used. I envied my father. He knew what his calling was. Me, I'm still trying to figure that out. But, I did learn from him how to follow my heart. I wouldn't have come out at eighteen otherwise. The car still smells like him. His aftershave embedded in the upholstery. The faint scent of paint thinner in the carpeting. It's almost like he's still around, watching over me. Silently.

I head north on Bathurst Street, steering the car in between two lanes to keep the tires from slipping into streetcar tracks in the road. The snow has stopped. City workers have already plowed the main roads, leaving dirty brown piles by the curbsides. Parked cars are trapped behind long lines of snowbanks. Pedestrians trudge over huge white mounds to get to the sidewalk, stepping deeply into tracks left by others. Through my half-open window, exhaust fumes drift in. Before I moved to San Francisco I lived in this neighbourhood. Like most cities, Toronto doesn't have what you'd call a dyke area. Just a lower-income downtown neighbourhood where a lot of us live. Older houses, tall, narrow, red brick, semi-detached, with big porches and long narrow back yards. Immigrant families live here too, with artists, musicians, young het couples. When my parents were young, the immigrants were mostly Jews, Italians, Irish and Chinese. Later on Portuguese, Vietnamese and West Indian families moved in. The earlier immigrants moved uptown, to the suburbs.

Bathurst Street is second-hand clothing stores, roti stands, cheque-cashing businesses, dollar stores, butcher shops. Honest Ed's, a giant bargain centre, is lit up twenty-four hours a day, a splashy carnival of miraculous cut-rate prices, obnoxious signs in every window. Red and brown brick buildings line the way uptown. Barren trees against hydro wires complete the winterscape. Compared with the lush bright foliage of California, Toronto depresses me. Reminds me why I live in San Francisco. Year round, something is in bloom. Deep-red bottle-brush trees, orange birds of paradise, wild nasturtiums, forest-green palms like natural umbrellas over Market Street. I love the large gay community in San Francisco. In the Emerald City there are groups for every kind of lesbian. There, I don't stand out. I can walk down the street and feel like everybody else.

Further north on Bathurst Street are ranch-style bungalows built in the 1950s, with painted garages and eavestroughs. Pink, green, blue and white. Every third house looks the same. Post-war baby-boom suburbs. My parents bought their house in 1964. The storefront shops of downtown are replaced by strip plazas with huge parking lots. When I was a teenager we used to hang around the plaza, smoking cigarettes stolen from our mothers' purses, sharing Cokes and chocolate bars, planning our futures away from home. My old high school, Northview Heights, brings a pang of memories, good and bad. In high school I fell head over heels in love with Brenda Stern. Brenda was everything my parents wished I was. Beautiful, charming, popular with boys and, most importantly, femme. She wore her brown hair long, parted in the middle and blow-dried back in a frizzy version of Farah Fawcett. On someone else it might have looked terrible, but Brenda looked glamorous. She wore real girl-clothes, lots of jewelry and make-up, perfume even, one of those inexpensive eau de toilettes popular with teenage girls. One day, when she was walking toward me in the hall a huge, invisible sledgehammer burst through the ceiling and slammed me over the head. I felt faint. My knees were mush. I leaned against my locker door for support. As she passed me, Brenda waved, in that cute teenage way.

"Hi Nomi," she said. My stomach flipped. I was in love.

After that I puppy-dogged Brenda all the time. She enjoyed the attention. I offered to walk her home from school, even though we lived in opposite directions. She let me. I carried her books, listened faithfully while she told me of her dreams, agreed with everything she said, hung on her every word. It came to a head the weekend Brenda's older brother gave us a joint. Brenda had invited me over to listen to Patti Smith. Her parents were out. In the basement, Brenda lit up the joint and we shared it. Maybe the grass broke my inhibitions, maybe Patti Smith did, singing "Because the Night." Maybe it was the way Brenda looked at me, her eyes penetrating my soul. Maybe it was simply that we were finally alone. I leaned over on Brenda's family's couch and kissed her on the cheek. She smiled and sat back against the cushions, which I took as a sign of encouragement. Though I'd never kissed a girl before, I'd dated several boys and we'd necked a little, so I knew how to kiss. Some invisible force urged me on. Brenda's eyes were shut. I moved closer and planted my lips on hers. I still remember my surprise at the softness of her lips, not like boys' lips at all. At first I think she just ran with her feelings, because she kissed me back. No tongue, but definitely a *kiss*. My passion spilled out. I pulled her tighter to me. For the briefest second we continued necking, then I felt her stiffen. When I opened my eyes, the horror in hers startled me. She threw me off of her.

"Nomi! God!" she fled to the bathroom, turned on the water.

Terrified by her reaction, I leapt from the couch, flew up the stairs and out the door.

On Monday, school was a disaster. It was obvious Brenda had told her friends. She wouldn't look at me. Other kids stared and sneered as I passed. On Tuesday, someone wrote LEZZIE on my locker in black felt pen, and all of my friends kept their distance. Eighteen, my last year of high school. For a while, I was miserable, the only teen homo on earth. I knew of gay adults, but no teenagers. I was still in love with Brenda. And she hated me. There was no hope for happiness. I was a freak. There wasn't anyone I could talk to. I wanted to die.

Then my Uncle Solly visited. We didn't see my father's older brother much. He often travelled out of town on business. Uncle Solly was between jobs. He ended up staying with us for two weeks. My father set up a cot for Solly in a corner of the basement. That's how I found out about my cousin Henry. Henry had moved to New York City when I was ten. No one ever told me why. Late one night I overheard Solly and my father talking.

"He's queer as a three-dollar bill, Harry. How the fuck did I get a fruit for a son?"

"Relax, Solly. Who's to say? Have another beer." My father was never great with words.

Queer. The word ricocheted inside me. Adrenaline pounded through my veins. My cousin was like me. I should have guessed before. I didn't sleep that night. I thought about packing a bag, emptying my bank account of the one hundred and thirty-two dollars I'd managed to save from my part-time job, jumping on a Greyhound to New York and searching for Henry. Except I knew that New York was enormous. There was no way I'd find him without an address. The phone was my only hope.

The next day I asked Uncle Solly for Henry's number. I waited three excruciating days until no one was home. I didn't know you could call long distance from a pay phone. Sunday afternoon, Uncle Solly was out running errands. My family had gone for a drive. We used to do that on Sundays, go for a drive. Out to the farmers' markets for fresh vegetables and fruit. I told my mother I had exams coming up and needed to stay home and study. Ten minutes after they left I sat down at the kitchen table and picked up the phone. I dialed the number. On the fourth ring, a man answered. My cousin. His voice was kind and relaxed.

"Boy, Nomi. Last time I saw you, I think you were about eight."

"I was ten."

"So you must be seventeen now?"

"Eighteen." I fiddled with the teaspoon in the sugar bowl, lifted up sugar, and let it spill back in little hills.

"Great. In your last year of school?"

"Yep."

"Good. So . . . how's it going?"

"Fine." I switched to the pink flamingo salt shaker, tipped it upside down, watched tiny grains bounce on the table.

"Great. So, uh, how's . . . your family?"

"Okay." I didn't want to talk about school, my age or my family. I wanted to talk about me and Brenda. But I was sweating scared, my heart racing.

"So? Uh, Nomi?"

"Yeah?" I laid the salt shaker down in the pile of spilled salt, flicked the flamingo's beak with one finger so that it twirled around like a miniature game of spin the bottle.

"Did you just call to say hi?"

Silence.

"Nomi?"

"No." Barely audible.

"No?"

"No."

"Oh."

"Yeah."

Silence.

"So? Is everything okay, Nomi?"

"Uh . . ." I flipped the flamingo again. Round and round and round she goes. Where she stops nobody knows. Grains of salt dusted the table top.

"Nomi?"

"Uh . . ."

"There's something you want to tell me?" he asked gently.

"Yeah."

"Is it about you?"

"Yeah."

"Okay. Well, good. I'm here, Cuz. Whenever you're ready."

He knew. I could tell that he knew. "Henry?"

"Yeah?"

"How did you know . . . uh . . . you were . . . uh . . . gay?"

"Oh." He laughed. "Because of Morris Silverberg."

"Yeah? Was he a friend?"

"We were in school together. We fell in love."

"Oh." I was relieved and heartbroken simultaneously. "You mean, he was in love with you, too?"

"Well, I was more in love than he was, I think."

"Was Morris gay too?"

"Kind of."

"Brenda's not gay at all," I said glumly.

"Brenda?"

I sobbed out the whole story. Henry told me everything I needed to hear. I was okay. The world was full of gay people. He told me how to look for a gay and lesbian support group in Toronto, that there might even be a youth group. At the end of the call he said I could phone him anytime and even visit him in New York. When he called me Cuz, I felt mature, grown-up, like him. I found a gay and lesbian youth group at the 519 Church Street Community Centre that saved my life and helped me through the rest of high school.

Coming out to my parents took longer. I left home the following fall, but couldn't bring myself to come out to them for another six years. I was at their house for a family dinner. I'd already come out to Josh and Izzy, both of whom shrugged and said, "we knew." My mother had bought a blueberry pie. For me, she said, because blueberry was my favourite. My father had been on my case about living away from home. He didn't understand why I left.

"I'm gay, Pop," I blurted, shoving a huge forkful of pie into my mouth, popping the small sweet blueberries individually with my teeth and tongue. No one said anything for a few moments. The only sound was chewing. "You know, I like girls," I went on, in case my parents hadn't understood the first time.

"Impossible!" my father shouted. "No daughter of mine is going to be queer. I forbid it!" He waved his fork at me. A glob of blueberry filling plunged to the table. We all watched it land.

"Harry . . ." My mother tried to soothe him.

"Pa . . ." Josh shook his head. Izzy frowned, struggling for something to say.

"Pa, you can't forbid it. I just am."

"No," he said, stabbing his pie.

"Pa . . ."

"I don't want to hear another word," he ordered, and began to eat furiously, purple juice collecting in the corners of his mouth.

"The world's changing, Harry." My mother stood and seized the plate in front of him before he finished his last bite. "What have you been saying for twenty-five years, Harry? 'You gotta be happy.' "

My mother snatched the plates from the rest of us, pie finished or not, and piled them on the counter. I didn't expect my mother to stick up for me. When I fantasized coming out to them, I assumed my folks would stick together.

"Isn't that what you said to your parents when you were a young man? Isn't it, Harry? 'You gotta be happy. That's the most important thing.' You've been saying that for twenty-five years. So? Your daughter listens to you. She wants to be happy. Why should you be so surprised? You, of all people." My mother squirted a stream of pink liquid dish soap onto the plates and turned on the hot water tap. The sink filled with little white bubbles.

"It's not the same thing," he hollered, pushed back his chair and departed to his studio.

Izzy drove me home.

Over the next couple of years, my father adjusted more to my life. I don't think he ever really liked that I'm a lesbian, but he accepted it. He was always trying to figure out why. As if there had to be a cause. "I think you get it from your mother's side of the family," he'd say. Or, "Is it because I let you cut the grass when you were little, Nomi? That's a boy's job, you know. I never should have let you."

I told him some people just are gay. But he didn't seem satisfied. He felt guilty. He feared it was caused by some parenting flaw on his part. When he died suddenly of a heart attack, the hardest thing was that we had never really resolved it. I always thought we'd have more time. That we'd keep talking about it, now and then. My father had gone against his own parents to follow his heart and his dreams. My expectations were high. I had fantasies that one day my parents would join PFLAG. I pictured Harry marching on Gay Pride Day with a hand-painted sign. Maybe with a picture of me and him, and a slogan like, "My daughter's gay and that's OK." But he died before any of that happened. He died with the belief that I would never be happy. My father is a lump I carry around in my throat. Sometimes it slides down enough that I don't notice. Sometimes it bubbles up, then every time I swallow, I push against a wall of regret.

Almost at my mother's house, my thoughts swirl back to Julie. I can still smell her perfume, taste her lips, feel the silk of her hair against my cheek. Desire floods through me. My body swoons at the memory. Excitement clears the Sapphire fog. I can see the forest through the trees. I have an unexpected, magical moment of clarity. The words "meant to be" spring into my head. As ridiculous as my life seems, I am on the right track. Everything that has happened was necessary to bring me to this place. Sapphire dumping me. My mother's wedding. Coming to Toronto. A whirlwind gusts inside me, a raging current gathering steam. Just like when I leaned across the couch and kissed Brenda Stern, now I'm at a turning point in my life. At the place where river meets ocean and spreads out, the possibilities are infinite. There is nothing to do but be swept away.

I turn onto my mother's block. Izzy's Pontiac is in the driveway. I pull in behind and park. Josh opens the front door.

As I remove my jacket, he says, "Hey Nom. What have we here?" and pulls down the collar of my shirt.

"What?"

"A hickey! You have a hickey!" He grins widely.

"Shh. Shh. Where's Ma?"

"In her bedroom getting ready."

"Shhh. You have to help me. Quick, I need a scarf or something." I grab his hand and drag him into my bedroom. We rummage in my mother's things, searching for something for me to wear around my neck.

"Here." He holds up one of my mother's scarves. Red sheer, with yellow flowers all over.

I scowl. "Too femme. There must be something else."

"I don't think so."

"Well, keep looking."

There is nothing else. Reluctantly, I allow Josh to tie it around my neck. "Can you see it?"

He stands back. "Well, the hickey's high up. Whatever you do, don't let the scarf slip," he says dramatically.

I check in the mirror. I look ridiculous. I don't remember Julie sucking so hard on my neck, but the mark on my skin reminds me deliciously of her lips and I smile.

"Nomi?" My mother's voice from down the hall. "Josh? Was that Nomi?"

I reach for the doorknob. Josh grabs my arm.

"Hey. Aren't you gonna tell me?"

"Tell you what?" I say innocently.

"Come on . . . who gave you the hickey? Where've you been? Who've you been with? What'd she do to you? Spill, sister." He tickles me mercilessly in the ribs.

I laugh. "Okay. Okay. Stop. I'll tell you." He stops, waits. "Her name is Julie. She's gorgeous. I'm in love."

He punches me playfully in the arm. "You're always in love, Nom."

"I am?"

"Joshua?" We see the knob turn, the door swings open. "Nomi!" My mother shouts. "It *is* you! Good. We're all here. We're going out to eat. I didn't feel like cooking. How about Chinese? Nomi, is that my scarf you're wearing? It looks nice. You should wear scarves more often. It gives you some colour for a change. Softens you right up. You like that one? It's yours. You can have it." My mother is so excited to see me wearing a feminine accessory, she barely pauses for breath.

"Okay, Ma. Thanks."

"Izzy!" She yells over her shoulder. "Ready? Nomi's here. Oy, I'm starving. You kids hungry?"

Josh and I both nod. I hold my breath as I pass by my mother and into the hall, hoping the scarf stays in place.

Spring Gardens Restaurant, in the plaza around the corner from my mother's house, serves what we refer to as Jewish-Chinese food. Chinese owned and operated, the restaurant caters mostly to the many Jewish families who live in the area and who order dishes like sweet-and-sour chicken balls, chicken chow mein, and consommé soup with hard, crunchy noodles. No hot sauce, no pork, no Chinese vegetables. Broccoli, maybe some bean sprouts. And lots of MSG. The walls are painted bright red, covered with rice-paper fans and bamboo blinds. White cotton covers each table. My family has been eating at Spring Gardens for decades. The waiters and the owners know us by name. We order a massive amount of sweet, bland food and pass the plates around among us. It's been a while since I've had dinner with my brothers and my mother. It feels comfortable and easy. When we are well into our second plates, my mother begins to talk.

"When I was young and just about to marry your father," she begins, "I was so sure he was the man for me, I wasn't nervous. My girlfriends who were already married talked about wedding-day jitters, but I didn't have any. All I felt was calm. Even though my parents weren't thrilled with my marriage to your father—my mother didn't smile once the whole day—I was so happy I didn't care. Your father was a good man . . ." Her voice cracks. Josh, who sits on her left, puts down his plastic chopsticks and takes her hand. We all stop eating to listen. "Sorry." My mother reaches into her sweater sleeve for a bunched-up tissue, which she pulls out to wipe the tears that have formed in her eyes. "I thought your father and I would grow old together. What can I say?"

"It's okay, Ma," Josh strokes her hand. "You're worried about what I said, right? And what Izzy said."

She bounces her head from side to side in hesitant agreement.

"Cause Izzy and I want to talk to you about that. Right, Iz?"

"Yeah." Izzy absent-mindedly picks up a crunchy noodle from the bowl in the centre of the table, dips it in sweet-and-sour sauce and plops it into his mouth. Like my father, Izzy doesn't have a way with words, though his heart is usually in the right place.

"We want to apologize for what we said, you know. That you shouldn't marry Murray. We were just . . ." Josh searches for the words, ". . . worried about you."

"He's a good man," my mother says to my brothers. "Believe me. I wouldn't be doing this otherwise."

"We know," Izzy says.

"I'm not trying to replace your father." My mother speaks what we have all been thinking. She blows her nose, then stuffs the Kleenex back up her sweater sleeve. "No one will ever replace my Harry, may he rest in peace. Your father was my childhood sweetheart. He was the love of my life. You kids know that."

"We know, Ma," I say, looking across the table into her sad eyes sympathetically.

It's contagious. My eyes fill with tears. Josh wipes at the corners of his eyes. I hear Izzy clear his throat. We are all about to break down, right here in Spring Gardens. I pick up my glass of Coke and sip through the straw. What's it like to be married to someone for twenty-eight years and see them die? The hole in my mother's heart must be enormous. She and my father were deeply in love, right to the end. I wonder if I will ever be that much in love. My longest relationship to date was with Sapphire. Not even three years. What's it like to lose someone you grew up with? Raised kids with? For the first time, I understand why my mother is getting remarried. Why she made her decision so suddenly. It's simple really. She's just plain lonely.

"Also," my mother picks up her fork and fills it with chow mein, a signal that we, too, can resume eating, "I told you about Sonia Greenblatt?"

"Yeah, Ma," I say, shoving a chicken ball into my mouth. Sweet sauce coats my tongue. "She's breathing down your neck."

"You better believe it." My mother looks around furtively, then lowers her voice, "You should have seen her face when I invited her to the wedding."

"You invited her?"

My mother looks at me like I've lost my mind. "Course. She's my friend. Izzy, you'll do me a favour?"

"I know, Ma." My brother doesn't even look up from the heap of chicken fried rice he is devouring. "Pick up Bubbe for the wedding. She'll be waiting in the lobby."

"Yeah, but something else also . . ."

"What, Ma?" He looks up over the top of his glasses.

"You'll do me a favour and take care of her. All right?"

"Huh?" Izzy prods his glasses back into position.

My mother shrugs. "You know your Bubbe."

I stare at my mother, try to figure out where she's going with this.

"Naturally I want her at the wedding . . . but . . ."

"But?" I ask.

My mother sighs. "Most of the time I ignore Bubbe when she goes on and on. Aren't I a good daughter-in-law? She's not even my mother. Even when your father, may he rest in peace, was alive, I went to visit her twice a week. I understand this is hard for her . . . but . . . it's upsetting. She won't stop with the finger-waving. 'It's too soon. It's too soon,' she says, over and over. I don't want she should blurt it out at the top of her lungs in the middle of the ceremony. I'm worried maybe Murray's gonna get cold feet."

"So . . ." Izzy says, "you want me to keep her quiet during the ceremony?"

"Please, doll."

Izzy scrunches up his forehead. "How, Ma?"

We all know he's got a point. My mother glances at me. Looks me in the eye, like she's trying to come up with an answer. Then I see her gaze shift down to my neck. She leans forward.

"Nomi! What's that mark on your neck?"

The boys start to giggle.

"A bruise?"

Part 4

'Til **Death** Do Us Part

Chapter *Thirteen*

*T*he biopsy results came back. Surprise, surprise. It *is* KS. I officially have AIDS. Roger, bless his heart, is being a doll. When Dr. Green broke the news to us, Roger held me while I cried. I've been waiting for this moment for years. I knew it could happen at any time, didn't think I'd actually cry when it arrived. But I did. Sorry, Pop. You were right. I *am* a cry-baby. Cried my heart out. Roger climbed into bed with me. Held me while I had my little nervous breakdown. Stroked my face. Kissed me. He says it could be worse. In his profession, he ought to know. Could have been PCP or CMV or toxoplasmosis or any number of other delightful opportunistic infections which would have left me blind or demented, or struggling for my every breath. Dr. Green doesn't want to take any chances, cause my T-cell count is alarmingly low. He wants to keep me here a few more days for what they call observation. And he's been bugging me to think about going on anti-virals. The latest rage in HIV care. Anti-AIDS cocktails. An ounce and a half of AZT over crushed ice, two ounces of ddI and a generous shot of a protease inhibitor, topped with a maraschino cherry and a wedge of lime, served three times a day on an empty stomach. Go ahead and call me ungrateful. I'm just having a hard time trusting pharmaceutical companies, after everything I've learned from Albert. Besides, these drugs are still in the experimental stage. No one knows if they work long-term. Not to mention the lovely side effects one can expect. I told Dr. Green he'd have to tie me down and force-feed me if he wanted me to take the drugs. He looked worried.

"Do me a favour, Henry. Will you at least think about it?" he begged, leaving a stack of drug-company-produced glossy brochures for me to read over.

"Sure, Doc." And maybe I'll think about nuclear war, serial killers and global warming while I'm at it.

I let Dr. Green keep me on the IV sulpha drugs, so I'm sentenced to a few more days of mushy fish sticks, canned peas and red Jell-O. I told Roger I'd recover faster at home, in my own bed, with real food, some peace and quiet. He laughed and said I was better off staying put. So here I lie. Bored, bored, bored. Norma Desmond herself couldn't be more bored, all alone in her huge empty mansion with her creepy butler, Max.

People come and go. I've been getting a lot of visitors, but there are long stretches when no one is here. I've taken to watching television but now I remember why I don't. How can people watch this stuff? It's boring. And it's het. Het, het, het. I'm sick of watching hets in angst, hets in love, hets getting rich, hets dying. Hets, hets, hets. I am sick, sick, sick of them.

I switch the fucking TV off and stare out the window. This morning I remembered the dream I had about my father the first day I was here. The recurring dream, that I was never man enough for Solly. My father. Mr. Tough Guy. Mr. Gangster. No one told me why he went away. Six years later, I saw him again, and the truth just tumbled out.

"When I was uh . . . detained, if you know what I mean," Solly puffed on one of his endless cigarettes. Du Maurier's. We were sitting on a park bench. I hadn't seen or heard from him in six years. Then with no explanation, he was back for a visit every Sunday afternoon. Once in a while we'd take the twins too, but they were only six and scared of him. They had lived their whole lives without him. Solly is not my sister's father—my mother won't say who is—so he never offered to take her. Sometimes Solly took me to the movies. One time he got tickets to a baseball game. Mostly though, we'd just go to the park, sit and talk.

"You couldn't get a decent smoke," he continued. "You had to take what you could get. And the food. Dammit, Henry. The food's the worst. Stay out of jail if you can, son. The food in there is shit. I lost a lot of weight in the joint."

I stared at my father. For six years I thought he'd gone away because I was a crybaby. Because I cried when I fell down. No one told me he'd been arrested that very night. Held in custody.

"You know, Sport, I couldn't stop by and see you, cause we didn't have money for bail in those days." He explained matter-of-factly, dropping his cigarette butt on the ground, crushing it with one foot.

I stared at him.

"What? You didn't know?" He slapped the side of his own face, held his hand there. "Oy vey, Henry. Your mother didn't tell you?"

Slowly, I shook my head as this information avalanched over me.

"Oy yoy yoy. I had no idea. I thought she was gonna tell you years ago. How old are you, Sport?"

It was the third time that day he'd asked my age. "Twelve," I managed.

"Twelve years old. Well, looks like I got out just in time for your bar mitzvah. You're having a bar mitzvah, aren't you?"

I nodded. We weren't that observant, but earlier that year I'd started taking lessons from Mr. Bloom, the assistant rabbi of my grandparents' synagogue. My mother had long ago given up on God, but Bubbe and Zayde made her promise to have me bar mitzvahed.

Solly pulled another cigarette from the pack in his shirt pocket, lit it with a shiny silver lighter, took two deep draws. He blew out a thick stream of smoke. It was a warm spring day. The snow had finally melted. Clouds had given way to blue sky and a warm sun. I watched his rugged face with my mouth gaping. He looked me in the eye, squinted. I held his gaze.

"I'm not a bad guy, Henry. Okay? I didn't exactly hurt anyone. You could say I made what you might call a bad business deci-sion. You understand what I mean?"

I didn't.

He began a long story. When Solly was a young boy, he'd been involved with the Mob. Not the Mafia, a local Jewish Mob. Solly'd been a runner for a man known as Shorty.

"He was a fucking giant." My father shook his head. Apparently the Mob had a sense of humour. "When I married your mother, I broke all ties with those guys, you understand. She insisted. But sometimes in life, shit happens, Henry. We make mistakes, you understand?"

I shrugged. Nobody seemed that understanding when I made mistakes.

"I ran into a buddy from my gang days," my father went on. "Whose name I don't like to bring up on account of just the mention of the momzer gives me heartburn in the worst way, but just so you know who to stay the fuck away from, I'll tell you: Sid Walensky. And that's the last time you'll hear me mention his name." He spit on the ground between his feet. "You were five years old. I just found out your mother was knocked up again. We barely had a pot to piss in, Henry. We were living in a three-room flat on Dufferin near College. Sure, I had a job. You gotta understand I didn't have whatcha call advantages. I was the oldest son. Quit high school when I was not much older than you are now, a year after my bar mitzvah. Got a job so I could bring money into the house. Not like your Uncle Harry, my younger brother. The sensitive type. Ma wanted him to finish school, maybe go to college and get an education, become a professional man. My mother, bless her heart, had a crazy dream. Who had money for college? We didn't have what to eat some days. Harry finished high school, but that was it. Anyway, what good did it do him, huh? My brother the artist works as a fucking clerk at Sears, plays with his paint-by-numbers in the basement. A grown man. Anyway," he took one last drag of his cigarette and flicked it into the park, "like I said, I had a job. Used to get up at four every goddamned morning and go down to the Jewish market, Kensington they call it now, and unload stinking fish for your Great Uncle Moe—my father's brother—you probably don't remember him, cause he died pretty soon after. I don't like to talk bad about the dead, Henry, but you're lucky. Uncle Moe wasn't a nice guy like me. He had a fish shop. He was a meiser oisvorf. You know what that means, Sport?"

I shook my head rapidly.

"A cheapskate. My uncle didn't have the heart to pay me half decently and I was his own flesh and blood. I went to him when I found out your mother was expecting. I asked him for a raise. You know what he said?"

"Uh-uh."

My father spit on the ground again. "He told me as soon as I learned how to really work, he'd give me a raise. So naturally I told him to go fuck himself."

"Wow." I didn't know you could get away with talking to grown-ups that way, even if you were one.

"I was so mad I walked the streets for hours. The sun came up and everyone else was just going to work, not like me, the poor schmuck who had to get up at four in the fucking morning to get to the market by five—even in the winter. I ended up at the Italian pool hall on College, and there was the goniff, whose name I won't repeat now that you heard it once." Solly glanced hastily in both directions.

Sid Walensky, I thought.

At this point my father leaned over and looked me right in the eye. "Now, if I could do it all over again, I'd spit on the momzer if he was dying in the street, walk right by as if he was a cockroach, but that particular day I was in a bind. How could I go home and tell your mother I had no job? You know what your mother's like, Sport."

I nodded. My mother is what you might call high-strung. I've seen her lose it over a chipped nail. I could imagine how my father felt at the thought of telling her he'd been fired.

"It sounded so sweet when the yutz explained. We couldn't lose, he said."

I listened to my father, wide eyed, lapped up every word, just as I had when Solly told his bed-time bank robber stories.

He looked around again, as if he was worried someone was listening. Then he reached into his shirt pocket for another cigarette and held it unlit between his first two fingers, real butch, right down at the knuckles. "I won't go into all the details, Henry." He waved his cigarette in an upward motion in the air, shook his head, frowned. "The ins and outs of the whole mess ... not important. Sid ... I mean, the yutz of all time, had this idea, an insurance scheme, you might say. Nobody got hurt. Wasn't families like us or little old ladies or anything. We sold whatcha might call an unauthorized policy to a huge firm. A big hospital supply company. We were sure they'd been Nazis anyway, had a German name, you know. So it seemed kind of like, whatcha call it? Justice. Anyway, the shit on the end of the stick is I never should have listened to the putz. He made a big mistake and we got caught. End of story. Only here's the kicker, Henry. He hired a fancy-shmancy lawyer, got the dough from his wife's side of the family, who everyone knows are filthy rich. Me? I hired a schlemiel, a kid, barely out of diapers, never mind law school. Your mother found him in the phone book. The yutz got off easy. They sentenced him to two years, and he was out on parole in six months. Me? As you know, I wasn't so lucky. Served six years."

I leaned back against the hard wooden bench. My father lit his cigarette and I watched him smoke for a while. Neither one of us said anything for a long time.

"So, you'll promise me, Sport?"

I looked into my father's eyes, feeling much older than twelve.

"Stay outta jail. It ain't worth it, kid. Trust me."

Later that evening, my mother was sitting at her dressing table getting ready for a date with Jacky Shecter, a large man who wanted to be a prize fighter. He was never good enough to make it big, so he ran a sporting goods store on Yonge Street. I watched my mother in the oval mirror as she applied a thick layer of red lipstick to her pale lips.

"Belle." Sometimes I called my mother by her first name just to bug her. Especially when I was angry. "How come you never told me Pop was in jail?"

"I didn't tell anyone, Henry. I was ashamed." She reached for a brush and applied blue eye shadow to her lids. "You'll open a couple cans of cream of mushroom soup for dinner, okay, hon? And make toast. Maybe you can get the twins to eat an apple or a banana. I don't know what it is with those kids. I can't get them to eat a piece of fruit if my life depended on it."

As the oldest child of four, I was my mother's built-in baby-sitter, cook, bottle-washer and all-round hired help. In a way I didn't mind. It's in my nature. I'd make a great housewife. A regular baleboosteh. I was—still am—a better cook than Belle. If she'd tell me to open up a can of Campbell's mushroom soup, I'd search around in the fridge for things to make it more exciting. Toss onions, garlic, parsley, zucchini into the canned soup as it was warming. Grate cheese, pour in a little cooking sherry, place the cheese on top and bake it in the oven at a high heat for five minutes. Mushroom soup à la Henry. My brothers and my sister ate everything I cooked. They would eat fruit when I served it, because I'd make it more exciting. I'd slice a banana down the middle, place it on a saucer, pour chocolate syrup all over it. The kids would gobble it up. I don't know why my mother never thought of stuff like that. Wasn't where her talent lay, I guess. Whereas I am a natural Susie Homemaker.

My mother worked full-time in the make-up department at Eaton's, until six every night. On the bus, she wouldn't get home until seven. It was my job to get dinner ready. I was kind of a loner, so I didn't mind. I felt important, older than the other kids my age. They could just go and play. I had work to do. When my brothers were little and my sister was just a baby, my mother hired a baby-sitter to watch us until she got home from work. Mrs. McGee was a round, older Irish woman who lived down the street. She was clean and cooked well, basically a nice woman. But a devout fundamentalist Christian, who truly believed our whole family was going straight to hell because my mother was divorced and we were Jews, who didn't accept her Lord Jesus Christ as our Saviour. I guess Mrs. McGee needed the money, because she never said stuff like that in front of my mother.

"I'm telling you for your own good, Henry," she'd say to me, as she stood ironing sheets. "You're young. When you're older you can embrace the Lord Jesus Christ and you, too, can be saved."

"You mean convert?"

"Yes, son. That's right. Even Jews will be accepted into heaven if they convert."

"Oh. No thanks. Hell sounds better." I was a smart-ass.

Mrs. McGee never got angry at me for mouthing off. She said it wasn't my fault. I couldn't help being a bad kid since my father walked off and my mother was a divorcée. She didn't know where my father really was. I can imagine what she would have said about that. By the time I found out that my father had been in jail, Mrs. McGee wasn't around anymore.

I'm still thinking about my parents and Mrs. McGee, so I don't notice Albert until he is almost upon me. I sit up suddenly, horrified.

"Oh my god. Al. What happened?"

Albert leans on a cane. His bottom lip is swollen to twice its normal size. His right arm is in a cast. There are splints on all four fingers of his right hand. His eyes burn behind wire-framed glasses.

"Get up, Henry," Albert orders.

"What?"

"We've got to get you outta here." Albert's thick New York accent sounds more pronounced than usual. He looks around, sees the grey metal lockers against the far wall, limps over, swings one open. "Are these yours?" He holds up my clean blue jeans, the pair I came in with. They had been dirty and caked in blood, but Roger washed them for me.

"Yeah. What's going on?"

"I'm not kidding, Henry. I think you're in danger here. You've got to go home. Your boyfriend's a nurse, right? He can take care of you there." He limps over with my pants.

"Albert, what are you talking about?"

He perches on the end of my bed, leans in close. Whispers.

"Why do you think we both got beaten up? You live in Toronto. I live in New York. We were both jumped on the same day. Two different cities."

"Yeah?" I chew on my thumbnail.

"Yeah. Same day. I don't think it's a coincidence. Do you? Come on. Get dressed. I'll fill you in on the way."

"Albert, I don't know. I mean, I thought it was a bunch of kids."

Albert runs his good hand through thick grey hair. "Okay, Henry. You want to live in denial, go ahead. But how about you get dressed, we go to your place and I'll lay it all out on the line for you? Okay? Maybe then you'll believe me." Albert's fear radiates into the air. What if he's right? I feel hot, sweaty and uncomfortable. My chest constricts. I think back to the night it happened. I remember two men. A force against the back of my head and I'm down on the sidewalk. Boots, motorcycle boots, and two-toned cowboy boots. Brown and black. A trench coat. Men. Not kids. What did they say? What did they . . . ? "Serves you right, faggot." Arguing as I lay on the sidewalk. "Sure it's the right guy?" one asked. "Yeah, it's him," the other answered. What did they mean? Why didn't I remember that before? The room swirls. I feel faint. *The right guy.* Someone is after me. They followed me that night, tracked me down. It wasn't a random bashing. Roger was right.

"Oh god," I mutter. "Oh god." Albert waits as the recognition seeps onto my face. "Because of your work?" I ask.

"Who have you talked to, Henry? About it?"

I rack my brains. "People in ACTOUT, friends, a couple of reporters . . ."

"That's it. Reporters."

"What?"

"It must have been one of them."

"What?"

"Someone you talked to talked to someone else. Somebody very important knows what we're doing."

"You think?"

"I think someone's trying to scare us, is all. Please Henry, get dressed. We'll figure it out. But not here. Come on." He slips off the bed, using his cane for support.

I reach for my jeans, swing my legs out of the bed, slowly step into my pants. I'm still attached to the IV. I stare at it for a moment, unsure what to do, until I remember watching Roger undo IVs. I untape my arm, and quickly slide the needle out. There is only a drop of blood. I cover it with a bandage from the night-table drawer. Then I put my bare feet on the cold floor. I stand shakily. My muscles are weak, but I can stand. I hobble over to the locker and find my T-shirt. I slip my fractured arm out of the sling, slide my shirt over my head, then my sweater. My arm is throbbing when I replace the sling.

I feel Roger before he actually enters the room.

"Henry! What's going on? Get back in bed. Where's your IV? What are you doing?"

"Roger. Oh, I'm so glad you're here." I bury my face in his neck, choking on my tears. His arms are strong around me.

"Henry? What are you doing?"

I whisper in Roger's ear. "I have to get out of here, Roger. It's not safe."

"Henry, what are you talking about?" He spots Albert.

"I'll tell you at home, Roger. Please. Just help me get dressed."

"No, Henry, I won't. Not until you explain," he yells, a little loudly, considering my fragile state.

I take a deep breath, move a few inches back. "Roger, this is Albert. You know, from New York. Al, this is my lover, Roger."

Roger reaches over to shake Albert's hand. It's a little awkward for a moment, because Al's right arm is in a cast, but then they both figure out to use their other hand.

"See, Roger. Albert got beat up too. The same day as me."

"Henry, I told you. Dammit." Roger punches a fist into a palm.

"Please, Roger. I'll explain more at your place," Albert says. "I just think Henry would be safer away from . . . anywhere public."

"This is a hospital, Doctor. I work here. What can happen to him here?"

Albert shrugs. "The security isn't particularly tight around here, is it?"

"Well, it's not a prison, Doctor," Roger snaps, "it's a hospital. What do you expect?"

"Exactly. Please. Does Henry really need to be here still?"

Roger scratches the back of his head.

"Dammit." He goes over to the IV pole, takes down the bag, grabs the extra two from the night-table drawer, some spare IV needles, the cord, and drops it all into the empty brown paper bag in the waste basket. He lifts the bag out, folds the top over neatly, and tucks it under his arm. Silently, he fetches my socks, shoes and jacket. "Sit down on the bed, Henry." He hands me the socks and shoes. I start to put them on. Roger picks up the phone and dials three numbers.

"Shirley. Yeah. It's Roger. Listen, a family emergency has just come up. I have to leave early. Yeah. Right now in fact. I'm sorry. I'll explain later . . . Could you please? Really? . . . Oh great. Thanks. You're the best. Bye, Shirley."

Roger drapes my jacket over my shoulders. "All right," he says, "let's go." With my good hand, I take his arm and we shuffle out of my hospital room. Albert limps along behind us.

We are all silent the entire way home. Roger drives. I sit beside him. Albert's in the back. I'm amazed how beautiful everything looks. A new snow has fallen. It hangs on tree branches and piles up on car roofs. Even the red brick buildings, the big city buses, the grey sidewalks look pretty today. Colours are vivid, the diffused sunlight filtered through winter clouds is perfect. Wish I had my camera. I was only in the hospital six days, but it feels like I've been away for weeks. I'm so happy to be outside, I enjoy the sights on the short trip home, avoiding our horrifying situation most of the way. Roger parks the car in the underground parking garage of our building on Alexander, then helps me to the elevator.

Inside the apartment I collapse on the couch, exhausted. Our apartment looks gorgeous. Albert sits in Roger's big green arm-chair. Roger goes to the kitchen and returns with two bottles of beer and a can of ginger ale. He hands one beer to Albert, keeps the other. I get the ginger ale.

"So let me get this straight," Roger says. "You guys think you were both attacked by . . . who? The U.S. government? The FBI? Who?"

"I don't know which agency," Albert says. "But someone wants to keep us quiet. Someone has found out about our plans to expose the truth. They want to scare us off."

"How can you be so sure?"

"They thought I was unconscious. I was sprawled on the pavement in the parking lot outside my office building. I knew my arm was broken, and my fingers. My lip was split. I pretended to be out cold, thought it would make them stop. I heard them."

"What did they say?" Roger stands in the middle of the living room, agitated.

Albert winces. "They said, 'That ought to teach him to keep quiet.' They used my name. They know who I am."

"God." I cough, clear my throat.

"And Henry . . . ?" Albert looks really worried.

"Yeah." I cough again, rub my aching fractured arm.

"They know I'm working with ACTOUT Toronto."

"Shit." Roger throws up his arms. "Dammit, Henry. See? See? This is exactly what I was afraid of." He explodes out of the room. A minute later I hear the shower. I struggle to my feet weakly and with Albert's help, find a blanket and pillow for him in the linen closet. He wants to lie down. I go into the bedroom to wait for Roger.

"You're crazy, Henry. Crazy, crazy, crazy. If I didn't love you, I'd commit you," Roger says after we've eaten dinner. Wonton soup, chow mein and barbecue duck, ordered in from a local Szechuan restaurant. Finally, some real food. It's glorious. We are sitting up in bed, leaning on pillows.

"Roger, I know what I'm talking about. Albert has seven years of research. Facts, figures, documents, published articles. He can back this up."

Roger sighs deeply. "I know you're upset. It's understandable. After what you've been through."

"I'm right about this, Roger. It makes me sick, too. But I'm right, dammit."

"Henry, it's crazy. You sound like the 'Twilight Zone.' "

"This *is* the twilight zone, Roger. We *are* in the twilight zone. Think about it. All of a sudden in 1980, fags start getting sick. Why? How did this happen? Where did it come from? Men have been fucking each other forever. How come no one got sick before 1980 if it's because of the kind of sex we have? Huh? How come?"

"Henry, you've read the papers. You know where it comes from. The virus has been around for years, probably in Africa. Like the scientists say, someone brought it to New York."

"Yeah. They're saying some fag fucked a monkey. And everybody buys it. Some pathetic old fag from Manhattan who couldn't get laid, went cruising around in the wilds of Africa where he picked up a goddamned monkey and they had a torrid affair. Then the fag went home and had bathhouse sex with thousands of other perverted, disgusting, pathetic fags. That's the image. That's exactly the image the scientists are hoping to conjure up in the homophobic public mind, when they say that the virus started in green African monkeys and 'jumped species.' "

Roger starts scratching the back of his head again. "Well, so what, Henry? Maybe you're right. Maybe Albert is right. Maybe that's exactly what happened. Why do you have to be the hero? Why do *you* have to be the one to put your damn life on the line, Henry? I don't understand."

"My life is on the line anyway, Roger."

"Maybe not . . ."

"What are you talking about?"

"Well, you could start on anti-virals and protease inhibitors." Oh no. What is this? Tag-team nagging? Now Roger's going to bug me about drug cocktails too?

"Roger, we don't really know how well those drugs work. Don't you think I've checked into it? I've read all the literature, talked to the treatment advocate at the PWA Society. The drugs are new and experimental. We don't know if they'd work for me."

"But maybe they would."

"Roger, I don't want to talk about it."

Roger sighs. "Henry, no one's going to believe Albert's theory anyway. It's too crazy."

"I can't accept that. I have to think that someone will hear and do something, even if it's after I'm gone . . ."

"Oh Henry. I hate it when you say that."

"Why?"

"Why? Why do you think?"

"Say it, Roger."

But he doesn't. He leans over and kisses my bruised cheek. I wince. Smile weakly, and try not to give in to the panic rising in my belly.

Chapter *Fourteen*

I thought Roger would never leave. He was supposed to be on shift at 8:00 a.m. At 7:45 he was still here, asking what Albert and I intended to do.

"Nothing. Today, anyway. Relax, Roger. Look at us. We're both a mess. I promise, honey. We're staying in. All day. We'll be right here when you get home."

"Promise?"

"Yes, dear."

Roger rigged up a makeshift IV pole with one of our living room lamps. A trendy boom lamp. He taped the bag upside down to the chrome shade, then reinserted the IV needle in my arm and re-taped the tube. He wound the plug and cord around the base. I can pick up the lamp to move around the apartment.

"Anyway," I told Roger, "I'd look pretty silly wandering around town strapped to a lamp like this." A PWA in bondage.

"That wouldn't stop you, Henry."

Roger and I are so different, it's amazing we're together. You just can't explain love. We're a three-piece suit having lunch with denim and leather. A conservative gay white male and a Jewish commie pinko fag. Roger is a one-man guy. He was in a relationship for fifteen years before we got together. His boyfriend left him. I've never had a steady lover for long. My first boyfriend, Morris, lasted three months. After that I didn't have a boyfriend for years. All the time I lived in New York, I tricked. A steady stream of lovers and one-night stands. Guess that's how I got infected. I didn't volunteer for the hepatitis B experiment. I thought about it for a brief second, when I was reading the application with Joe, but all those questions about your job and your education made me feel inadequate. A high school drop-out from Canada who bussed tables at Diner Diner in the Village.

Albert says that's why I've been healthy until now. He thinks that everyone in the experiment got a major dose of HIV directly into their veins. Got sick quick and died. He figures those who acquired it second-hand, via sex, got a more diluted form, and it took longer for the virus to do its dirty work. The long incubation thing. The virus was watered down. Poor schmucks who volunteered for the vaccine trials got a pure one-hundred-percent= proof dosage of HI Fucking V. Same reason IV drug users go down faster than fags. Mainlining HIV right into their bloodstream.

I don't know how I got it, exactly. I had sex with hundreds of guys when I lived in New York. Why not? I was young, gay and free. Had my own little apartment, a job. No responsibilities except to myself. I practically lost my family over being gay. Pleasure was my only reward. In 1978, sex was love and freedom. Sex was how we knew we were okay. We could do anything we wanted with our bodies. Condoms? Are you kidding? For hets. What did we need them for? Sometimes I try to imagine exactly when I got infected. I think of some of the guys I was with. The tricks. Some of the men I dated. Most are probably dead by now. Or sick. Maybe I got it from all of them. Maybe I gave it to all of them. Maybe it doesn't matter.

Roger was with Steve from 1976 until 1991. Monogamous the whole time. Negative, of course. I didn't know guys like Roger existed. I'm continually afraid he's going to leave me. One day he'll wake up, look at me lying beside him and realize I am nothing but a thin, loud-mouthed, Jewish, nelly, HIV-infected fag, and he'll leave me. This I have never told Roger. Don't want to give him any ideas.

After Roger finally leaves for work, Julie phones. She's on her way over. Julie and I are still looking for a journalist who will write an article about Albert's theory. Most of the people we've talked to pass it off. To them, we are hysterical, paranoid AIDS activists. Those who believe us are terrified. We almost had a guy convinced, Michael Strong. He writes for the *Globe and Mail*, but he's not even out to his boss.

"It doesn't necessarily mean it'll out you," I pushed. "Lots of straight people write articles about AIDS."

"It's not that, Henry."

"So . . . what then?"

"The American government. If it's true, they're not going to take the exposure lightly."

That was the first inkling I had that I should be scared. Before that, I was just furious. Anger overrides fear, at least for me. I couldn't believe they used gay men as fucking human guinea pigs. That thousands of innocent guys were purposely infected with a lethal virus. Just to see if it works and how. I am so angry, I'm sick with fury.

The buzzer rings. I haul my lamp pole into the hallway.

"Hello?" I speak into the intercom.

"It's Julie."

"Come on up." I buzz her in. Albert is hunched at the dining room table. Notebooks, typewritten pages and textbooks are spread out all over the surface. He brought three huge boxes of research papers with him from New York. A lefty, Albert can still write. The attackers probably didn't know. They made a point of breaking all the fingers on his right hand. Albert says it's a good thing he's not a surgeon, or he might be finished. They got my right arm pretty good. I couldn't wield a pencil at the moment if my life depended on it.

When I open the apartment door, Julie strolls in, with a big red hickey on her neck. She is . . . je ne sais quoi . . . glowing?

"Julie, you look absolutely radiant."

She smiles. Her eyes dreamy. "It's Nomi."

"I thought so."

"I really like her."

I wag a finger at her. "I knew it. You lesbians are amazing. You're engaged, aren't you? Can I be the best man at your wedding? How about best fag?"

"Slow down, Henry. We only . . . kissed. Well, necked, really."

"I want to hear all about it." I steer her inside, schlepping my lamp. She frowns.

"What's with the lamp?"

"IV bag. Makeshift hospital. Roger did it. Isn't he a genius? Come on in. Do you want coffee?" I move us toward the kitchen.

"I'll make it. Just tell me where everything is," Julie insists. Normally I won't let anyone set foot in my kitchen. But my ribs hurt, my arm aches and I'm weak. It's hard to stand for long periods of time.

"Okay," I relent. "Beans are in the freezer. Grinder and coffee maker on the counter. I usually put in seven tablespoons for a full pot."

"Hi, Albert," Julie says on her way to the kitchen.

He looks up from his notes, in a daze, like he can't quite remember who we are or where he is. "Oh, hi."

Julie makes coffee and sets out chocolate chip cookies she finds in the cupboard. Albert gives her copies of some documents he recently discovered, to read. They sit across from each other at the dining room table, one reading, the other writing. I feel too tired to work and stretch out on the sofa to rest. I fall asleep. I wake up thinking about Morris Silverberg, my high school sweetheart.

Sometimes I blame Morris for my HIV status. Tall, dark, handsome, charming, and wouldn't you know it, he was even Jewish. My mother would have loved him for a son-in-law, if I'd been my sister. I fell in love with Morris the first time I met him. The new boy in class, grade ten. I was fifteen, Morris sixteen. Morris's folks were divorced, like mine, but Morris lived with his father. His father was in the movie business, an associate producer or something like that. He'd worked in TV and movies in New York City. He took a job with a Canadian film company in Toronto the year he and Morris moved to town. There were mysterious circumstances surrounding their move to Canada, the truth of which I did not learn until much later. Morris changed his story depending on who he was talking to. He told our homeroom teacher, Mrs. Birk, an older English widow, that his father had impregnated a young girl of fourteen and after paying for her abortion was obliged to leave New York. Mrs. Birk was shocked. He told some guys in our class that his father was mixed up with the Mob—you know, *the* Mob. Like in *The Godfather*. That he had come home from school one day to find three big men in his apartment, threatening his father over a drug deal. According to Morris, they didn't see him enter the apartment. He was able to sneak into his father's bedroom, find his father's handgun, load it, slink back into the living room and shoot all three thugs in the foot before they noticed he was there.

I didn't say anything, but Morris's story didn't add up. His father didn't seem like the type. He wasn't tough at all. He was no Solly, seemed kind of chicken to me.

But the guys were impressed.

"You should have seen them," Morris bragged. "They were clutching their feet with their hands, screaming and crying. My father scooped up all three guns and kept the thugs covered while I tied them up. We left them there to rot in our apartment in Manhattan, and split. We didn't even pack or nothing. Just called a cab, went straight to the airport and came here. For all I know, they're still there."

I looked Morris right in the eye to let him see I knew the truth. One teenage boy could not sneak up on Mafia guys and shoot all three before one of them stopped him.

Morris had an entirely different story for my mother. I invited him to my place for dinner one day shortly after we met. I was making spaghetti and meatballs that night. I sautéed mushrooms, garlic and onions, threw in fresh basil and oregano. I was cheating—using a jar of ready-made Heinz tomato sauce—although sometimes I used fresh tomatoes. My mother was still at work. The twins were outside in the park, throwing a baseball around. My sister Sherry was lying on her side on the living room floor, watching a "Flintstones" rerun. Morris was sitting up on the counter tossing sliced mushrooms into his mouth while we talked and I grated cheese.

"You do all the cooking?" Morris was shocked. He didn't know how to boil an egg. Got confused pouring cold cereal into a bowl. There was just him and his dad, Norman, and Norman didn't believe boys needed to know how to cook. They went out or ordered in, every single night, except if they were invited somewhere. Sometimes one of Norman's girlfriends would come over and cook dinner, but most of them were in show business too and only used their refrigerators to store cocktail onions, olives and champagne.

"My mother works late. And anyway, I'm a better cook than she is." I searched in the bottom of the vegetable bin for a red pepper.

Later, my mother asked Morris what brought him and his dad to Toronto. He told her it was because of the high crime rate in New York City. That his father was thinking of him. It wasn't a great place to raise a young son, and they both thought Canada would be a much better environment.

We were sneaking a cigarette in the boys' room, during Math class, when I confronted Morris on the fact that he had a different story for everyone who asked. He shrugged, inhaled and exhaled smoke, passed the cigarette to me.

"I tell people what they want to hear," he said.

I took a drag of the cigarette. "But what's the real reason you came here?"

He sighed, snatched the butt from my fingers. "To get away from my mother. She's crazy."

"She is?"

"Yeah. Been in the mental ward. Had a nervous breakdown when I was three. I hardly know her. She's been locked up ever since." He crushed the cigarette under his foot.

"Really?" I picked the butt up from the floor and tossed it into the trash can. Didn't want a teacher to find it.

He walked toward the door. "It's no big deal. I'm used to it.

They finally let her out last year. Ever since, she was calling my father every night and crying. My father couldn't stand it, so we came here." He tossed me a roll of Certs from his shirt pocket. We always chewed gum or sucked on mints after sneaking cigarettes in the boys', as if our clothes didn't reek of smoke.

Everything about Morris was exciting and glamorous. His father was in show business. He had a crazy mother. He grew up in Manhattan, right in Greenwich Village. He'd been to Shea Stadium, Broadway shows, Grand Central Station and the Museum of Modern Art. He knew sophisticated stuff. His father had a gun. He'd met famous people, like John Travolta, Al Pacino, Faye Dunaway. He'd even met John Wayne on a set once.

"He's no big deal," Morris said. "He's old. They use a lot of make-up in the movies, you know."

"He wears make-up?"

"Course. All movie stars do, Henry."

One day, just to impress Morris, I told him about my father.

"Really? In jail? What'd he do?"

We were walking around the hardware store, in the plaza near our school. Checking out the pocket knives, which, unfortunately, were kept in a glass case, near the cash register.

I shrugged, like it was no big deal, just as Morris always did. "He's involved with the local Mob. It's not the same Mob like in New York, but kind of the same." I didn't really know what I was talking about and hoped Morris wouldn't pick up on that.

"Well, what'd he do?"

I couldn't tell Morris my father got nailed for an insurance scam. Not after all the great stories he told about his father, so I did what came natural. I made something up. "He killed a guy," I said, surprising myself.

"What? Really?" Morris swivelled and looked me in the eye. I felt my face burn and realized I must be blushing, a dead giveaway. But I held my gaze and continued with my lie.

"Yeah. But you know," I peered around, dropped my voice to a whisper so Morris had to lean in real close to hear me, "the guy was real bad, you know, like he killed some people himself, you know, kids and old people."

"Why'd your dad kill the guy?" Morris whispered back. I shrugged and paused, drawing out the drama. "He had to. The guy was gonna rat on him."

"To the cops?"

"Worse. To the Mafia."

"Heavy." It was a shining moment. I had impressed Morris Silverberg, king of the tall tales, son of Mr. Showbiz. I beamed.

"Heavy," Morris repeated, nodding slowly.

I didn't learn the real reason Morris and his dad left New York until Morris and I had run away to Greenwich Village. We were living just a few blocks from where Morris had started out.

"Do you make a habit of getting caught by other guys' parents with your pants down?" I hollered when he told me. We were walking home to our bed-sitting room after several unsuccessful attempts to get into a bar. We were too young and it showed.

"Henry, I didn't do it on purpose. Shit happens."

"But Morris, the exact same thing? He was sucking you off?"

He sighed, and kept walking. "Yeah."

"What was his name?"

"Henry . . ."

"What was his name? I think I have a right to know."

Morris stopped in his tracks and faced me, with a look that said, "back off."

"Please." I tried a different tactic.

He sighed, and started walking away again. "Jeff," he said.

"What? Jeff? Jeff? Is that what you said?"

"Henry, what's the difference?"

"So what happened? When Jeff's mother walked in, I mean." I hurried up alongside him.

He laughed under his breath, remembering. "She was holding a stack of towels. We'd been outside playing baseball and told her we were taking showers because we were sweaty. She was bringing us towels."

"Yeah?"

"She dropped them. Her arms kind of went limp. Her eyes bugged. I thought she was gonna faint or something. She just kind of backed toward the door, keeping her eyes on us, then she left. Closed the door behind her."

"What'd you guys do?"

"We got dressed. I left. By the time I got home, she'd already called my father."

"What'd your father do?"

"He paced."

"He paced?"

"Back and forth. He told me to sit down in the living room, and he paced back and forth for a long time."

"Yeah? Then what?"

"Poured himself a large Scotch." Morris stopped at this point and started acting out his father, pacing back and forth on the sidewalk. We were in front of Ricky's, a sort-of-gay coffee shop where we hung out. "Shook his head, knocked back the whole drink in one gulp. Then he said, 'Go to your room and start packing.'"

"Yeah?"

"That's it. He didn't say another word. He went into his bedroom and closed the door. We left New York a week later."

"You just left?"

Morris pushed open the door to Ricky's. I followed. "Yep. I guess he thought it would help."

"Why?"

"Henry, where have you been? We lived right here in the Village. Look around. What do you see?"

"Oh." There were gay men everywhere. Lesbians, too. Norman thought if Morris was somewhere else, maybe he'd turn out straight.

Would Morris and I have lasted if we'd gone anywhere else but New York? There were too many choices in the Village. Like kids in a candy store. Why settle for one boy when the streets were filled with men? What did we know? We were kids. It was 1978, everything was opening up. Gay people were coming from all over to live in the Village. When Norman finally found us, Morris went back to Toronto with him. I stayed in New York. My mother didn't want me around anyway. She still had three young kids to take care of. Probably missed my cooking, but that's about it. Sherry took over my old room, the housework, moved right into my shoes.

That first year in New York, I couldn't get into the bars. But sometimes I could get into the bathhouses. And I could stand around outside and get picked up, taken home to some older guy's apartment. I was young and pretty. Lots of guys wanted me. Lots.

The way I figure it, if I hadn't fallen in love with Morris, my mother never would have caught me sucking his cock in my sister's bedroom. Morris and I would not have run away to New York City, the place where The Crisis began. If Morris hadn't gone back home after his father tracked us down, maybe we would have lived happily ever after, and neither of us would have ever fucked another guy. So, it's crystal clear. It is Morris Silverberg's fault that I am HIV positive.

"It wouldn't have made a difference," Albert insists. Julie is in the kitchen making an omelet for the three of us.

"Why not?" I've just finished telling him my Morris Silverberg theory.

"You would have come out anyway. Even if you'd stayed here, your chance of being positive would be high."

"How do you know?" I struggle up from the couch, drag my pole over to the table.

"No one knew about safe sex in Toronto until 1983 at the earliest. How old were you then?"

"Twenty-five." I pour coffee into my cup.

"Do you really think you wouldn't have been out by then, Henry, even if there was no Morris?"

I shrug. Who knows? "Maybe I would have married Marsha Slobodsky."

"Who?"

"A girl I knew in high school."

I knock back some tepid coffee. It's revolting.

"You guys want toast?" Julie calls out from the stove.

"That would be great," Al says.

"There's bagels in the freezer," I tell her.

Julie brings breakfast to the table. A large red pepper and mushroom omelet, split into three. It looks almost as good as one of mine. I'm impressed. I didn't know lesbians could cook.

"Al?" she says, sitting.

"Uh-huh?" He shovels eggs into his mouth.

"What if they followed you here? What if they know where you are?"

Albert stops eating, holds his empty fork up in the air. "I took precautions. I don't think it's likely."

"Precautions?"

He pops a piece of red pepper from his plate into his mouth. Chews.

"I phoned my secretary. Told her I needed time off and was going to Key West to lie in the sun. I had her book me a flight, make reservations at a hotel, rent a car, the whole bit. I left at the scheduled time, took a cab to the airport, checked in, went through the appropriate gate, waited until the plane left, took a train to Boston, and got on a charter flight from there to Toronto. I checked constantly. No one followed me. I'm sure of it."

"Oh," I reach for the butter.

"But we don't have much time."

My heart races. "Why not, Al?"

"If they've been monitoring you, they'll notice you've left the hospital. We can't stay here past tomorrow. We're going to have to move."

"Uh-oh."

"What?"

"Roger's not going to like this."

"I suppose not."

"Where're we gonna go?"

"You can stay at my place," Julie offers. "How's the omelet?"

"It's fabulous." Al's finished his and is well into his second bagel. I've barely begun. I don't feel hungry anymore.

"Julie, do you mean that? I mean, who knows how long we'll have to stay?" I've been to Julie's place. Just a small one-bedroom on Manning. Top floor of a house.

"You're the one who's taking all the heat on this, Henry. We've been using your name on all the correspondence. It's the least I can do," she says.

"I don't know." I don't want Julie in the same kind of danger Albert and I are in.

"I'm not so sure either. . ." Al says. "You could be under surveillance as well, Julie."

"But how could they know about me? My name hasn't been on anything. I haven't done anything much except research and photocopying."

"At this point, we just don't know. It could be dangerous for you," Albert insists.

Julie frowns. "I don't think so. You two were both attacked on the same day. If they knew about me, wouldn't someone have come after me also? Anyway, where else are you going to go, Henry?" She flips her long black hair over one shoulder, out of her food.

She's got a point.

"Uh-uh. No way. That's where I draw the line." Roger stabs the air with his fork. Julie left before Roger came home. Albert, of course, is still here. We are eating dinner, pasta with a light cream sauce I whipped up. I was feeling strong enough to sit at the table and chop veggies. The cream sauce takes five minutes to throw together. I used canned baby clams. Usually I use fresh, but it's not like I can dash out to the fish market at a time like this. Had to make do with what was in the cupboard.

Albert clasps his hands in front of his face, elbows on the table.

I grimace. "Roger, it's not that simple."

"Oh no? Why not, Henry? Why is it not that simple? Why is it that we can't stay in our own apartment?"

"They might have been watching me. When they find out I'm not still in the hospital, this is the first place they're going to look."

"They? Who's they, Henry?" Roger is still aiming his fork prongs right at me. I stare at them. He notices, and gently places the fork on his plate. He clasps his hands together in front of him, elbows on the table, thumbs against his forehead, almost exactly like Albert.

"We don't know, Roger. Could be the FBI. The CIA. We don't know," Albert answers.

"The FBI? The CIA?" Roger holds both hands out in front of him, palms up. "Why not? Maybe it's the Pentagon. Maybe it's double-o-seven, James Bond himself. Or Batman. Maybe Batman is after you, Albert? Huh?"

"Roger, please . . ."

"So, what are you saying, Henry? We have to leave? When? Tomorrow morning? I have to be at work at eight. What do you suggest I do? Where do you think we're going to go?"

"Julie said we can stay at her place. We could go there tonight, and hole up for a while," I suggest.

"Hole up? Hole up? Henry, who are we? Bonnie and Clyde? I have to go to work tomorrow. I can't hole up."

"That's the other thing, Roger." I take a deep breath, look at Albert, who wisely remains silent.

"What?" Roger looks worried.

"It would be best if you didn't," I say, biting the nail on my index finger.

"What? Go to work?"

I nod.

"Henry, I can't just not go to work."

"You could call in. Talk to Shirley. Tell her it's a family emergency and you have to fly home. Tell her it's your mother, and you have to go to Montreal."

"Henry, I don't like this. Not one bit."

"Yes!" Albert claps his hands together. "That's a marvellous idea."

I glare at Albert. For a moment I wish he wasn't here. I hate it when Roger and I fight. I want it to be over as quickly as possible. Roger doesn't like Albert. He's polite, but really he hates him. Roger holds Albert directly responsible for me getting beat up, for the KS, for the tension between us. Probably even for the inclement weather. It isn't fair of Roger. Albert didn't invent HIV. Albert didn't infect gay men. Albert's just the one who figured it out. Who desperately wants to blow the whistle.

"It's a marvellous idea, Roger, for you to go and see your mother," says Albert, the whistle blower. "I mean really go. It would be perfect. If we're being watched, it would confuse the hell out of them. And keep you safe."

"My mother. No, no, no. Let's just leave my mother out of this." Roger jabs the air with his finger.

"Just for a week," Albert promises.

"Forget it," Roger says firmly.

"We'll get the damn article printed by then, somehow." Albert sounds so determined I almost believe him myself. "We have to. We'll do it. Then there's nothing they can do to us. It will be out. They'll have to deal with the world then."

Roger stares at Albert like he's lost his mind. "You guys really believe that?"

"What?" I ask.

"Oh my god." Roger scratches his head. "If the CIA or the FBI is after you, why would they stop after you've exposed the government? Don't you think they'd really want to shut you up then? For good?"

We are silent.

"I'm right. Dammit, Henry. Aren't I?"

I look to Albert. I want him to say Roger is wrong. But Albert just looks troubled.

"Well," Albert stalls, "it's hard to say."

"Dammit, Henry."

"Roger . . ." I plead.

He marches into the bedroom.

Sometimes I worry that no one's going to believe Albert's theory anyway. Same old story. No one cares about dying fags. We'll get some reporter to write the article, but it'll be buried on page forty-seven in the human interest section. We'll come off sounding like crackpots. When did it all get so complicated? I used to be a simple AIDS activist, going on die-ins, organizing demos, protesting the health department. Now I'm in a John Grisham novel and my life is at stake. I'm Julia Roberts, a young law student who discovered a secret murder plan. Everyone is out to get me, I'm all alone and I can't trust a soul. Not that my life wasn't flashing before my very eyes anyway.

I follow Roger into the bedroom, my trusty lamp stand at my side. He's fuming by the window. Just for a change, it's snowing. We live on the third floor of a tall building on Alexander Street, two blocks from Church. Heart of the ghetto. Our building is 80 percent gay, and known as Vaseline Towers. The other tenants are little old ladies and the occasional fag hag. We have a balcony off the living room, facing south. Roger, he-man that he is, drilled holes right into the concrete and mounted planters for me on three levels of our balcony wall. In summer I have a spectacular garden. Fresh herbs, four kinds of lettuce, cherry tomatoes, hot chili peppers and jalapeños. I even grew corn last summer, in a five-gallon paint bucket. Usually I fill the remaining planters with petunias, snapdragons, carnations, daisies, anything pretty. Now everything is dead, covered in snow.

"Henry," Roger says, his back to me, "I don't like this whole thing."

"I know, Roger. Believe me, I had no idea things would get this complicated."

"When's it gonna stop, Henry?" He faces me.

"Well . . . you know. Like Al says . . . as soon as we get the story published . . ."

"Dammit, Henry," he cuts me off, "there's no guarantee of that at all. How do we know it's not gonna get worse?"

"Well . . ."

"Huh? We don't. Do we, Henry?"

"Roger . . ." I move closer, touch his arm lightly.

He pulls it away, abruptly. "No, Henry. Don't. I'm trying to think, dammit."

I wait.

He sighs. "Henry . . . I'm just an ordinary guy. I like my job. I like my friends. I like our home, our relationship. I don't want to fight with the government. I want to enjoy what we have together. All this political stuff, it's just not me."

I can see where he's going with this. My heart aches. I feel angry, though, more than hurt. "Well, it *is* me, Roger! You knew it when we first met. I've never lied to you. This is what I do."

"I know, Henry. And I respect that. But this time you're dragging me into it."

"Huh?"

"You are. We have to go into hiding. I can't go to work. I don't know what I'm going to tell Shirley. I'll have to take vacation days. I don't want to lie. And I'm worried about my job. You know, the government's talking about closing the hospital next year. It's not a good time, Henry."

"Roger . . . only for a few days. I'm sure this will all settle down in a few days."

"You don't know that, Henry. You don't know that at all."

He's right. I don't. I stand helplessly in the middle of the room.

"Henry, I just don't know if I can live like this. It's not me. We're so different. Sometimes I think we should just split up."

"Please, Roger, don't say that. I love you. I know you love me. We can work it out. We don't have to be the same to love each other."

"Henry . . ."

"Please, Roger, don't throw us away."

He pushes past me, suddenly, and heads for the door. He looks like he might cry at any moment.

"Roger! Where are you going?"

"I need to think. I'm going to Jim and Bruce's."

"What do you mean?"

"For a couple of days. To think."

"Roger, please don't . . ."

"Hey. Your friend out there said I should get out of the way. So, I'm getting out of the way. Isn't this what you wanted?"

"No," I say sadly.

He sighs. "I'll be over there. I'll call you in a few days."

"Roger . . ."

He stops in the doorway, his back to me.

"If Albert is right, about his theory and all," I'm struggling to keep my voice from cracking, "and I think he is, I want to be part of exposing the truth. If I'm infected because the U.S. military invented a new toy and they picked fags to try it out on, then I want the whole world to know. Somehow it . . ." My throat seizes. I'm going to cry or scream. Or both. I can't say what I really mean. We both know anyway. Makes dying easier. Sort of.

Roger walks out without looking back.

Chapter Fifteen

"This couch pulls out into a bed." Julie tosses cushions onto the floor, grasps a small handle poking out from the upholstery and yanks it. The sofa springs open. "And Al, I've got a foamy we can spread out, either here, or you can put it on the kitchen floor. Sorry. It'll be kind of cramped. But you know, it's not the Ritz."

"We really appreciate this, Julie," I say. "You're a lifesaver." Literally.

"It's no problem, Henry. I'm glad I could help. I wish I could do more."

"You're doing lots."

"What are you guys going to do?" Nomi asks. By the looks of things, Julie and Nomi were having a romantic evening before we arrived. There's a half-empty bottle of white wine on the coffee table. When Julie answered the door—in a robe—the lights were low and soft music was playing. Were we just a tad early?

"You know. In the long run. You can't hide out here forever." Nomi paces back and forth in the living room. She looks like Morris's father must have the day he found out his son was a homo.

"We won't have to," Albert reassures. "As soon as the story's printed everything changes. Think about it. Once this is public, if something happened to one of us, who would get the blame? It would be so obvious. They just want to prevent us from exposing it. Once we do, we'll be safe."

"You think?" Nomi stops.

Personally, I'm not so sure, but I say nothing.

I don't sleep well on Julie's couch, wake to the sound of kids playing outside. Albert, Julie and Nomi are all still asleep. I desperately want coffee, but Albert is sleeping on Julie's thin foam mattress on the kitchen floor. I don't want to wake him, so I lie here and think. I had a dream, earlier, about my mother. We were sitting side by side at her dressing table, putting on make-up.

"You should use a darker shade of red," she said, passing me a tube of lipstick, "see? It goes better with your complexion."

When I hit puberty, not long after my father's reappearance, I became fascinated with my mother's make-up. Belle used a red folding card table as her vanity. Four shoe boxes brimmed with lipstick, nail polish, eye shadow, liner, mascara, brushes and all the latest accessories, which my mother purchased wholesale at Eaton's. Her table was rich in shades and tones. When no one was around I tried out her make-up, doing my face up glamorously, imagining I was a Hollywood starlet getting ready to greet my public. I'd have loved to openly sit with my mother discussing fashions and hairstyles, but I didn't dare share this passion with Belle. I was a weird enough kid as it was. I knew to keep this longing to myself. When I moved to New York, I began buying my own make-up. I've never done drag for a living—I'm not that good—but I've been known to slide into a frock and wig and perform at the occasional benefit. I use my mother's name on stage, Belle. Just like a Hollywood starlet.

My mother hasn't exactly had her shit together this lifetime. Always dating a new man, embroiled in some drama or other. She drinks, takes Valium, has been in therapy for fifteen years and frets over everything. Solly, my father, is in even worse shape these days, from what I hear. I haven't seen him in over five years. The last time, he'd just flown in from Florida. Some kind of business dealings he had going on down there. He wouldn't say what and I didn't ask. I know he's in jail again. No one's heard from him in five years, and prison is the only thing that keeps Solly away that long. He adores his mother, my grandmother, and wouldn't willingly let so much time go by without seeing her. I haven't seen Bubbe that much lately myself. But if she thinks Nomi and I are cursed by God, maybe it's just as well. What would she say if she knew I have AIDS? Probably think she's right. Who knows? Maybe she is. Maybe I am cursed. Maybe we all are.

I can't wait much longer for my morning caffeine fix. If Albert doesn't wake up soon, I'll go into withdrawal. And it won't be pretty.

When the others finally wake, we sit around Julie's kitchen table sipping coffee and tea. Julie set out a plate of toast, peanut butter, a tiny jar of strawberry jam, some bananas and apples. Albert has already eaten three slices of toast. Nomi is forcing down her first. Julie munches on a banana. I'm on my third cup of coffee, too anxious about Roger to eat. Julie and Nomi exchange sultry glances. I'm sure they have finally consummated their, shall I say, relationship?

"I have to leave," Nomi grumbles. "My mother's expecting me. I promised to go to Aunt Rhoda's with her today, where the wedding's taking place. Apparently there are all kinds of preparations and they want me to help. Like, what do I know about weddings?" We laugh. "I wish I didn't have to go." Nomi gazes longingly at Julie. Heat sizzles. I fan myself with a napkin.

"Will I see you later?" Julie runs her fingers through Nomi's hair.

"I hope so." Nomi's eyes smoulder seductively. "Can I call you? I mean, I'd like to see you again."

"You'd better."

"See you guys," Nomi says to me and Albert.

"Say hi to your mother from me," I wave to Nomi with my good arm.

"Sure, Henry." Nomi and Julie walk hand in hand to the door. So romantic.

Albert gobbles another slice of toast. I reach for the coffee pot. Julie returns, moping.

I squeeze her hand. "You two look so cute together."

Julie sighs dreamily. "She's nice."

"So? Aren't you gonna tell me more?"

"Hmmm?"

"Details. I want details."

She smiles, glances at Albert. "Maybe later." She studies me.

"Are you going to call Roger today?"

I shrug. "Maybe I should wait. You know, let him cool down." Julie nods.

Albert eyes the last piece of toast. "Anyone want that?"

I shake my head, drink my coffee.

"I've been thinking," Albert says, chewing. "We need to get organized. Do you mind if I take the lead?"

"Please do." I'm glad someone will.

Julie's working with us today, not at the office. ACTOUT work is part of her job as the outreach co-ordinator of the Asian AIDS Network.

"Let's make a list. I mean, I'll write, and you two think of everyone you know in Toronto who's associated with the media. Okay? Then, let's systematically check off those who are distinct possibilities and cross off those who are merely dead ends. Okay?"

"Sure, Al," I say.

"Well, we already ruled out several people we originally thought were possibilities," Julie begins.

"Okay, good." Albert's pen is poised in his left hand over a blue, spiral-bound notebook. Pencils, erasers, extra notebooks, white-out and paper clips surround him. It looks like the first day of school around here.

"George Sanders, a very straight journalist, interviewed me a couple of times for the *Globe*," Julie continues.

"The *Globe and Mail*? That's your national paper, isn't it?" Albert asks, rubbing his neat, greying beard.

"That's right," Julie confirms.

"You've been interviewed often?" Al asks.

"I get called by the media all the time as a spokesperson for the Asian community—women and AIDS, Asian women and AIDS, you name it. I'm an official Asian dyke media rep," Julie says with irritation.

"That's wonderful." Albert completely misses Julie's annoyance, picks at some breadcrumbs on his plate with his fingertips, licks his fingers. "You must have some wonderful contacts."

Julie glances at me, shrugs. "A few, I guess. That's why I joined this committee of ACTOUT."

"Good." Albert is really pleased.

"We also thought of the gay papers," Julie continues. "There's *Xtra!*—we've contacted the editor, but he said they mostly focus on local news. We argued that this affects local gay men, but he won't budge. There's a small lesbian magazine, *Siren*, but their mandate is news about lesbians. I know a woman who writes book reviews for the *Toronto Star*, but she doesn't cover hard news. Jerry Somer is a freelancer, but his usual beat is entertainment. He said it's not too likely he'd get the story accepted. The only other possibility is Rick Jackson. I met him a year ago. He interviewed me about police relations with The Asian Community, as if there was only one. Very slick. The article wasn't bad. He only misquoted me twice."

"Forget him," I shake my head, "he doesn't write about AIDS at all." I've known Rick Jackson for years. A friend of a friend. Been to parties at his house. Only beautiful people allowed. Guppies, right out of *GQ*, sipping Absolut vodka, Perrier or imported beer. Six-digit salaries, expense accounts, luxury cars and tasteful condos. Rick is a career journalist. He writes for the *Star*, a mainstream daily. A typical mid-forties, middle-class, yuppie fag. Straight-laced. Trendy condo off Church Street, sports car, boat, the finest clothes, two pedigree poodles. His lover, Jason, was in real estate. Knocked down old houses and built luxury townhouses and condos. Filthy rich. Died a year ago. Rick kept him at home until he died. Jason left a fortune to Rick. More money than any one person could need in three lifetimes. Rick has spent his career entirely in the closet, even publicly denying his gayness. He has refused to write about AIDS, fearing it would brand him a fag. His field is political events, mainstream electoral politics.

"He's sick," Julie says.

"What?" I didn't know.

"I heard he's sick. He told his paper it's nothing to worry about, just stress. He asked for a month off, three months ago. He keeps extending it."

"Yeah?" Al nods, interested.

"That's what I heard." Julie leans back in her chair, taps her pencil in the palm of her right hand.

"So . . . ?" I prod.

"Maybe he's had a change of heart," Julie suggests.

"You think so?" I don't. Once a schmuck, always a schmuck.

"Who knows?" Julie keeps tapping. "It happened to Rock Hudson."

"You think old Rick might come through at the last second?" I'm skeptical.

"It could happen." She taps her palm one last time, then grips the pencil tightly.

The plan to go in disguise began in a fit of paranoia. We decided we couldn't leave Julie's place in our usual guise. What if the CIA had tracked us down? What if there were agents parked outside? I decided to go in drag. It's been a while, but this old girl can still waltz down the aisle when she wants to. Of course, I don't have my make-up and dresses here, but I'm not much bigger than Julie. After slipping into one of her skirts, I became utterly enchanted with the scheme.

I'm at Julie's dressing table, applying another layer of foundation to my face. She has enough make-up to choke a horse, as Solly would say. I should have no trouble. I've slipped my fractured right arm out of the sling for our mission. Roger would be furious. Without the support, it throbs, but that ratty old sling just doesn't go with the lovely skirt and sweater set Julie loaned me.

Albert is in the bathroom shaving off the beard he's had for twenty-five years. He grew it to protest a hospital policy in the seventies. Some bureaucrat decided that hospital personnel should not have any facial hair. Albert had always been clean-shaven, but if someone was saying he had to be, then he wouldn't. Big fuss for a couple of months. Doctors with beards threatened to sue. Nurses and orderlies shaved, in fear for their jobs. A lawyer from the ACLU was consulted. The media was alerted. With so much negative attention the hospital decided it wasn't a fight worth having. By then, Albert had grown used to not shaving. He preferred not to scrape a sharp razor across his face every morning.

Albert hobbles into the room, minus his beard, and strikes a pose, leaning on his cane. He looks fifteen years younger. Thinner, too.

"Wow," I say.

He seems shocked as well. "I haven't seen my chin in twenty-five years." He rubs his freshly shaven face.

"You look great." I add another layer of mascara.

"I think I'll cut my hair, too," he says.

"Why don't you colour it? If you get rid of the grey, you'll look like a whole different person."

"Not enough time."

"Ditch the glasses, then," I suggest.

"My glasses? I can't see a damn thing without them."

"You can hold my hand. I'll lead you."

"Henry, I can barely walk as it is."

"Don't worry. I won't let you fall." I roll on some fuchsia lipstick, exactly the colour my mother recommended in my dream last night. I'm starting to look rather lovely, if I do say so myself.

Albert disappears into the bathroom. I finish my face, sit back and check myself out in the mirror. I'm Belle, aged thirty-eight. Well, a touch more tasteful. She's more garish than I'd ever be, even for a show. Not bad, except my hair is short, and even I will admit my hairline is receding a tad. "Julie!" I yell across the apartment. "I need a scarf or a hat or something." I hear her rummage in a drawer.

"Here. How about this?" She strolls in with a large flowered scarf. "See? You can wrap it around your head like this." She winds it over her own head and looks divine.

"Let me see." Not quite as captivating on me. "I look like a cancer patient," I whine.

"You look great, Henry. Anyway, the point is to look different. You're not entering a beauty contest."

"Honey, Roger's on the verge of leaving me. I can't walk out this door unless I look fabulous."

"Henry, Roger's not here," Julie counters.

"I know." I force back tears and do a final make-up check.

Albert walks in, transformed. His hair is short. Without his thick glasses, he's gorgeous. Distinguished yet cute. Come to think of it, he also has a nice body. I hadn't noticed before.

"You guys look great," Julie says. "You both look completely different."

Albert squints and gropes for his professor-style tweed jacket.

"No," Julie says gently. "Don't wear that." She shuffles through her closet, pulls out a thickly lined denim jacket. "This was Peter's," Julie says, referring to Peter Lau of ACTOUT. He died last July, the day after Pride Day. "It's different from your usual look," she tells Albert. He slips into the jacket. If I saw him in the street I wouldn't recognize him. If the CIA is watching, I hope they don't have photographs of my mother. One look at me and our jig is up. I teeter slightly on Julie's heels, clutching my purse girlishly between my fingers.

"Well, I'm ready," I say.

Julie laughs. "I wish I had a camera."

The cab ride to Rick Jackson's apartment is utterly uneventful. I keep checking over my shoulder, expecting two men in rumpled suits to be following us in a dark sedan. I see nothing but Suzuki jeeps and other taxis. I cross my legs in a feminine way. It can't be helped. It just happens when you're wearing a dress and panty hose. I'm sitting by the window on the right side, Julie's heavy wool shawl draped over my shoulders. Albert is at the other window, cane propped against one knee. Julie's in the middle. Every so often she looks at me or Albert and giggles.

I know exactly where Rick Jackson lives. The last time I was there was about five years ago, for a party. I think it was Jason's birthday. I was with a man I was dating, also named Jason. What is it with the name Jason? Is it reserved for rich gay real estate tycoons? My Jason was a developer. I dated him for a couple of months. At the main doors, we scan the names listed on the inter-com system. There it is. Jackson-White. Jason's been dead over a year and no one has removed his name from the list.

"We should have flowers. So we look like friends visiting," I suggest.

"Oh, that's good," says the new and improved Al.

A grocery store across the street stocks a small, highly inade-quate selection of flowers. I choose a large bouquet, mostly carna-tions, plus two purple irises. "It'll have to do," I moan.

"Why? They're beautiful," Julie insists.

Clearly out of her element. The carnations are wilting, the colour selection is mediocre and the irises look as if they've been forced open by hand.

Back at Rick's building, we wait for someone to leave. As the door closes, I casually lunge for the handle.

We ride the elevator up to the eighteenth floor, walk down the hall to apartment 1803. My arm aches without the sling. I regret leaving it. Outside Rick's door, we take a deep breath. Julie knocks. A handsome man in a nurse's uniform answers. I recognize Philip Stone instantly. Roger knows him. I go to say hi, then remember I'm in drag, bite my lip, and wait. With any luck, he's never seen me perform.

"Hi," Julie says, "we came to see Rick?"

Philip smiles, surveys the flowers, Albert's broken arm and cane. He studies me a bit longer than necessary. "I'll have to check with Rick. Who should I say is calling?"

We hesitate for a brief second. "Julie Sakamoto," Julie answers. "He interviewed me . . . last year." She smiles. Philip swings the door open and steps back.

"Wait here. I'll be right back." Philip leaves us inside the marble front hall. I realize I've been holding my breath. My shoulders are almost at my ears. I breathe deeply to calm myself.

"I know him," I whisper.

"You do?" Albert shifts his weight.

"He's a friend of Roger's. We've met. Shit."

"What?"

"Maybe I should have told him it was me. Maybe he would have let us in."

"Not yet," Julie suggests. "If this doesn't work, tell him who you are."

"You think?"

"Yeah."

Philip returns, all smiles. "You can come in. Just for a bit though. He's very tired."

"Of course," Albert says diplomatically.

We follow Philip down a long hallway, past expensive oil paintings and framed black-and-white photographs, including an original Mapplethorpe. The hallway opens to a vast living room, with white carpets. On one side of the room is a majestic white couch. Lying across its length is Rick Jackson. He looks thin and tired. There are dark circles under his eyes, his grey-white hair is trimmed short. His mustache is impeccable. He is hooked up to an IV, real pole and all. Behind his head an end table holds a dozen prescription bottles. He wears blue silk pyjamas and a matching robe. The exceedingly warm room smells antiseptic. The air is stale. White carpets are so wrong for a sickroom. Rick scrutinizes us. We move tentatively closer. He checks out each one of us, as if trying to determine who we are. He fixes on Julie. He nods.

"Oh yes. Julie Sakamoto. I remember you. That piece about Chinatown," he says. He seems proud of himself. Maybe he's thrilled he can still remember people from his life before he got sick.

"Uh . . . it was police relations with the Asian community," Julie corrects.

Rick shakes his head. "Whatever." He glances at me, then at Albert. "It's nice to see you. I'm glad for the company. But why are you here?" This man gets right to the point, sick or not. Why should I be surprised, though? He's a journalist, trained to seek answers.

Julie smiles, bows her head slightly, looks him right in the eye.

"Rick, we need your help."

Forty minutes later, Rick leans back against his pillow, lets out a heavy sigh. We wait, having explained Albert's theory on the origin of HIV. The silence is long.

"So," Rick says finally. We all lean in close, holding our collective breath. "You want me to write the story, I suppose."

"Yes," says Julie.

"And submit it to my editor," Rick continues.

"Yes," she repeats.

Rick sighs. Then shakes his head. "He'll never buy it. Not in a million years. He'll want proof."

"I have proof." Albert practically falls over himself with excitement.

"You have proof?" Rick appears interested.

"I have seven years of research. Facts, figures, essays. Articles from medical journals, opinions of respected medical professionals, statistics and scientific data. Government documents. I've spent hundreds of hours at the Countway Medical Library at Harvard and the Boston and New York Public Libraries. I didn't bring my files with me today, but I have boxes filled with proof. They're yours if you want to see them."

Rick smiles, apparently amused with Albert. "Okay," he agrees. "Bring me your proof. I'd like to see it."

"Really?" Julie's excitement spills from wide eyes.

"Sure. I'll look at your research. I'm intrigued." With the theory or with Albert, I wonder.

"You are?" I ask.

"You're surprised." He chuckles. "I know, Henry . . ."

"Oh. You recognize me?"

"Yes. I've seen you in drag. I saw you perform at that benefit at Woody's. Was it last summer?"

"You were there?"

"Who wasn't?"

We all laugh. The tension in the room has been thick. Our relief is palpable.

"Why are you so surprised, Henry? That I might be willing to write the story."

I am afraid to say; maybe he'll be insulted and unwilling to help.

"Hmmmm?" Rick rests his hand under his chin, like an elderly relative.

I tread lightly. "I didn't think you were interested in writing about AIDS."

"Oh, that." He brushes me off. "Do me a favour, love," he says to Albert. "Fetch me some water from over there." He points to the jug of water and three long-stemmed glasses on the mahogany coffee table, behind Albert's chair. Albert turns in his seat and fumbles for the water pitcher. Without his glasses, I worry he might drop it, but he seems to do just fine, pouring water, bending forward and passing the elegant glass to Rick, whose hand brushes Albert's as he accepts it. Albert blushes. Rick drinks, then holds the glass in front of him. For a moment he is a man at a cocktail party, sipping on a dry martini. "Henry, I've been sick a long time. It's nothing new. I've just done well at hiding it. I've been HIV positive for nine years, at least. Believe me, even my best friends didn't know. I'm a private man. My lover, Jason, died last year. You knew Jason . . ."

I shrug. "A little. Not really. I dated Jason Steele."

Rick frowns. "He's dead too."

I nod. I actually hadn't known, but I'm not surprised. I'm used to mentioning some man I knew years ago in passing and hearing, "Oh, he's dead." Happens all the time. As common as hearing, "Oh, that store closed down last week," or "They've discontinued that flavour of ice cream." We're all just another flavour of ice cream. In a couple of years someone will mention my name and hear, "Oh, he's dead, you know. But he died at home like he wanted." I'm suddenly chilled. I miss Roger. I want to go home, to my lover's arms.

"I was here through it all," Rick continues, "while Jason was dying. I was also sick then, but not as sick as he was. Life changed after he died. I know, terribly cliché. All of this," he waves his hand at matching white furniture, state-of-the-art stereo equipment, original paintings and sculpture, crystal vases brimming with long-stemmed, pale yellow roses, "is not important. What's going to happen to it all after I die? I've spent my whole life accumulating things—apartments, cars, paintings, clothes, even men. What does it do for me? It didn't keep Jason from dying. And it won't save me." He shifts his body, looks directly at Albert.

"Dr. Maxwell . . ."

"Please. Call me Albert."

"Albert. I'm forty-nine years old. In 1980, I was thirty-three. Do you know how many lovers I'd had by 1980? I came out in 1974. Fucked my way through the rest of the seventies. Back rooms, the tubs, the park, Hanlan's Point, Fire Island, Provincetown. All kinds of sex. All kinds of men. We were all fine. Suddenly, in 1980, my ex's and friends began to fall ill. I remember the hepatitis B trials. I spent time in the Village back then, knew lots of men in New York. What hepatitis epidemic? I don't remember a single person talking about having hepatitis then." Rick sips his water. "I wondered about it at the time. The gay rights movement had only just begun. What would have prompted a federal health agency to conduct a special study aimed at preventing the spread of a disease sexually transmitted among homosexual men? There was no precedent. There was no obvious reason like winning votes in an upcoming election. The whole study seemed, shall we say, unusually progressive. It's been nagging me for sixteen years. Government does not institute expensive preventive health measures for special-interest groups unless it is politically expedient to do so. At the time, it would have been political suicide to vote for gay rights. Even now, look at how Clinton handled the military ban, or the same-sex marriage debates. I've always wondered what ulterior motive lay behind the hepatitis B trials. I believe you may be right, Albert." Rick finishes his water, hands the glass to Albert. "I would be quite interested in reviewing your data."

Albert thrusts the glass at me, grabs Rick's left hand, pumps it ecstatically. "Great. Wonderful. When? I could meet you anytime. Tomorrow?"

"Why not?" Rick smiles, laying his other hand over Albert's to slow him down. "I'm not going anywhere. Mornings are fine. Say ten o' clock?" He offers Albert a profile. I wonder if long ago someone told him it was his good side.

My chest fills with warmth. Tears roll. Sadness or relief? Rick Jackson, mainstream journalist, believes Al's theory enough to read the files. Julie was right. He is going to come through for us. I collapse into a big white armchair, suddenly exhausted.

Chapter Sixteen

he next day, Albert cabs it back to Rick's condo with his
three boxes of files. Rick hasn't promised anything, but Al
is convinced he'll write the article once he's seen the
research. I'm lying on Julie's living room floor with a pillow under
my belly, watching *The Life and Times of Harvey Milk* on the VCR.
San Francisco, late 1970s, the annual Castro Street Fair. A sea of
men watch Sylvester sing, "You Make Me Feel Mighty Real." Men
everywhere. In the heat of summer, stripped down to shorts,
bare-chested, crowded in the street, on balconies and fire escapes.
How many of those men are gone? I scan the crowd to see if I recognize anyone.

I hear laughter from Julie's bedroom. Nomi snuck away from
the wedding preparations. Julie's taking a long lunch break from
work. She and Nomi have been in the bedroom for over an hour.
Having sex, no doubt. I don't usually like to be in the same apartment while people are having sex in another room. It bugs me.
But the thought of Julie and my cousin making love feels like
apple pie. It doesn't bother me at all. I'm dying to call Roger at Jim
and Bruce's, but I want him to miss me. I've decided to play hard
to get, more attractive than begging.

The door to Julie's bedroom opens.

"Hi," Nomi says lazily, on her way to the kitchen, followed
closely by Julie. They smile at me. I wave. Nomi bends to avoid
hitting the blue-and-white cloth that hangs high in the doorway
to Julie's kitchen.

Julie giggles. "Nomi, you don't have to duck."

"Huh?"

"It's called a *noren*. It's supposed to touch the top of your head."

"It is?"

"Uh-huh." Julie is amused. "It's believed that it brushes evil spirits away."

Nomi runs a hand over her head. "Yeah?"

"Come here, you."

I turn my attention back to the video. News reporters are rushing down the halls of the law court. The jury has just reached the verdict. Dan White has been found guilty of voluntary manslaughter in the killings of both George Moscone and Harvey Milk.

Julie and Nomi wander into the living room, sit together on the couch behind me.

On the screen, hundreds of gay men and lesbians are rioting at City Hall, breaking windows, setting police cars on fire. Throwing rocks at the cops.

"I wish I could have been there then," Nomi says. "I was only twelve in '78."

I smile at her over my shoulder. "I was in New York when all this was going on."

We watch in silence for a few moments.

"Henry, want to go visit Bubbe with me?" Nomi asks.

I suck in a gulp of air. My grandmother. I haven't seen her in three months. She'll be mad. I look at Nomi.

"Do you?" she asks again.

Do I? I wouldn't dream of going on my own, now that I know she thinks I'm cursed by God. But Nomi might make the visit easier. And it may be the last time I see Bubbe. Either one of us might pop off at any moment. I shrug. "Sure," I hear myself say.

Julie has to go back to work. The thespians, as I've taken to calling the girls, are saying goodbye in Julie's tiny vestibule, while I replay *Harvey Milk* and try to make myself invisible.

"I wish I didn't have to go," Julie says.

"You really have to?" Nomi's voice sounds full of love.

Kissing noises. Silence.

"Yeah," Julie says, "I'm counting the last two days as ACTOUT work, but three days in one week would be pushing it."

"Yeah. I guess."

More kissing noises. I turn the volume up. 1978. The Briggs initiative, which would have banned gays from teaching school in California, has just been defeated. Harvey is at the height of his political career. He's making his famous "Come out" speech.

"And most importantly," Harvey stands on stage, behind a podium and microphone, right fist in the air above his head, "most importantly, every gay person *must* come out."

The crowd is jubilant. Hundreds of thousands of gay San Franciscans hang proudly on Harvey's every word.

"As difficult as it is, you must tell your relatives, you must tell your friends if indeed they are your friends, you must tell your neighbours, you must tell the people you work with, you must tell the people at the stores you shop in." The crowd cheers again.

"When are you leaving?" Julie asks Nomi.

Nomi sighs. "Tuesday."

"Five days," Julie says wistfully.

"Is that it? God."

"Call me later?"

"Love to."

Kissing sounds.

I turn the volume even higher.

"And once they realize we are indeed their children, we are indeed everywhere, every myth, every lie, every innuendo, will be destroyed, once and for all!" Harvey declares.

Julie and Nomi continue necking.

"And once you do, you will feel so much betta!" The crowd goes wild.

Nomi moans.

Harvey Fierstein picks up the narration. "Four days after the defeat of the Briggs initiative, Supervisor Dan White engineered his own defeat."

Kisses. Shuffling. Deadbolt clicks. More shuffling. Kisses. Door squeaks open.

"See you later, Henry. Help yourself to anything that's in the fridge," Julie calls.

"Thanks, Julie. You're an angel." I sit up to blow kisses. They smooch again. Julie leaves. I lower the volume.

Nomi lies down on the floor beside me, leans against my shoulder. "Oh god, Henry," she says, "I'm in love."

I kiss her on the cheek. "And it looks good on you, Cuz."

"What am I going to do?"

I shrug. "Enjoy it?"

Half an hour later, Nomi and I head north to Sholom Aleichem, to see Bubbe. I thought we should take a cab, but Nomi convinced me that her mother's car would not be recognizable. The main roads are ploughed. A brown streak of sand and salt runs the length of each lane. The pavement has a white, icy sheen. The wind is blowing. Barren tree branches sway. Mid-afternoon, traffic is light. We follow a streetcar up Bathurst for several blocks. With snow piled against the curbs there is no passing lane. The streetcar stops often. We wait behind it as people step on and off. At Bloor, the streetcar arcs into the station and we breeze past.

Near Sholom Aleichem we pass Jewish shops, Marky's Delicatessen, Goldsteins' Kosher Meats, The Negev Judaica Gifts and Books. A young Chassidic man, in a long black coat and sixteenth-century fur-brimmed hat, with a long beard and sidecurls that dangle in front of his ears, hurries along the sidewalk, holding the hand of a short-haired little boy, with keepah and sidecurls. We are almost at the old folks home. My breath quickens. I sigh.

Nomi turns, looks at me.

"Nervous?" she asks.

I nod.

"Yeah?"

"Well, you know how she feels about my father. Your father was the good son, the mensch."

"Well, sort of. Except she hated that he was an artist. She used to nag him to quit with the art and take a full-time job."

"Yeah, but she still saw him as a good son. A devoted father, good husband. My father is the bad guy. Been to jail, divorced.

Not particularly responsible. You know. Sometimes I think she's mad at me about him."

"It's because you look like him."

"I do not." I tilt the rear-view mirror in my direction. The last thing I want is to look like my father. He's big and burly. I'm small and thin. He's in his early sixties, dresses like Al Capone. Dark suits, white shirts, hand-painted ties. Suspenders, a fedora. Smokes big, thick, smelly cigars.

"I don't mean you *look* like him, Henry. You look different, but it's your eyes. You have the same eyes. You know, your father's a handsome man, suave, in a rough-and-tumble way. When Bubbe looks at you, she probably sees him."

"Oh boy."

"Anyway, she's crazy about your father. I mean, she doesn't approve of some of the things he's done. But she likes him. Everybody does. He's so full of life."

"That's what I'm worried about."

"Why?"

"She wants me to be like him, Nomi."

She grins. "Maybe you are."

Bubbe has lived at Sholom Aleichem for the last three years. Unlike most of the residents, Bubbe still has all her marbles. She moved in because her body started to go. She can barely walk. Cooking and cleaning are out of the question. She needs help getting in and out of the bath, dressing and walking. Basic functions. That's how I feel this week. Maybe I should see if there's a vacancy.

We tramp over hard-packed snow to the front of the building. In the tiny lobby between the outer and inner doors, two old men sit staring outside, and then at us as we approach. There is a security system. To open the outer door, you have to punch in a five-digit code.

I look over my shoulder at Nomi as I punch the numbers in. "It's 1, 2, 3, 4, 5, believe it or not. It's not because they're worried about break-ins; it's just so the old people can't leave the building

and wander off. A resident got out last July and started strolling
down the middle of Bathurst Street. Hit by a bus. Bam. After that,
they put this in."

"That's awful."

"Yeah. Tiny little man. Used to sit near Bubbe. Always had a
black derby on his head. 'Member him? He used to hum Yiddish
songs to himself, and laugh. Point his finger at us."

"Oh, yeah."

"There she is." Bubbe sits in her usual spot, on a plastic-cov-
ered chair in the small part of the large communal living room,
against the sliding glass doors. She looks tiny, older and more frail
than the last time I saw her. And it's only been three months. I
remember when she first moved in. She was really upset. All
through her life people thought she was younger than she was.
Moving into an old folks home changed all of that. People would
no longer think she looked young. People would know she was
old. An old woman who couldn't take care of herself. I think
about some of the guys my age who can't take care of themselves.
My chest tightens. One day I could be one of them.

Bubbe sits in her chair staring straight ahead, her black patent
leather purse tight in her lap. Last time I was here, I asked her to
show me what was inside. What would she need to carry around?
She seldom leaves the building. There was neatly folded Kleenex,
hard candies, a stale bagel wrapped in a napkin, bent photographs
of her grandchildren and her room key, on a long braided string.
There are five or six couches just like Bubbe's chair, all lined up,
blue, red and green plaid. Hideous. The walls are covered with
pale pink flowered paper, of the tackiest design. What I wouldn't
give to redecorate this room. The chairs are occupied with old
people, mostly women, a few men. Some are sleeping. Most sit
staring ahead, humming or muttering to themselves.

We walk over to Bubbe. She doesn't recognize me or Nomi
until we are inches away. Before we left Julie's I applied a layer of
foundation to cover the bruises on either side of my nose. The
dark purple marks fade somewhat behind the make-up, but not

completely. I'm back in the sling. I haven't figured out what I'll say when Bubbe asks about it.

She smiles. "Nomi, you came back." She sounds surprised, as if she's amazed to see her granddaughter again. We stand in front of her. She has to crane her neck way back to see us. She looks over at me, stares, smiles, then her face takes on a stern look. She shakes a finger at me. "Is that Herschel?"

I nod. Bubbe always calls me Herschel, my Hebrew name. She never liked English names. She takes my hand in hers. I sit beside her on the couch. Plastic crackles under me. "Where have you been? You haven't come to see me in a long time, Herschel. You're not turning out like your father, my no-good son, are you?"

I sigh. What can I say to that? Yes. Only worse, Bubbe. I'm cursed. Bubbe stares at me. "What happened to your nose, tatelah?" She puts both hands up to the sides of her face. "And your arm? Tatelah, it's broken? You were in a fight?"

"Oh no, I . . . I fell off a bus." Oh god. Fell off a bus? Where did that come from?

"You what?"

"A bus," I say again.

"I can't hear you, Herschel. Did you say a bus?"

I nod.

She shakes a finger at me. "You're too skinny. You should eat more."

Nomi sits on Bubbe's other side. Bubbe reaches for my hand, squeezes it, smiles, kisses me on the forehead. She turns and kisses Nomi's cheek. "You kids want a little something? Waiter!" she shouts. Bubbe calls the nurses waiters and waitresses. That way she can pretend she's in a Florida hotel or a Catskills resort. The staff let her get away with it. I guess it makes them laugh.

"Yes, Mrs. Rabinovitch?" A tall, dark and handsome orderly with an Israeli accent answers her call.

Bubbe looks up at him. "Oh, Dov. Can you do me a favour?"

"Of course."

"You'll bring us some tea, maybe? These are my grandchildren."

Dov nods at Nomi and flashes a suggestive smile at me. A member of the club. We *are* everywhere.

"Tea? For you, Mrs. Rabinovitch, anything." He winks and swishes away.

"He's from Israel," Bubbe tells us. "He's a folk dancer."

I'll bet.

Bubbe opens her purse, fiddles inside, pulls out a bran muffin wrapped in white napkins. With shaky hands she breaks it in two, hands half to me. "Have a piece of this, Herschel."

"Oh . . . uh, no thanks," I decline. "It's yours. You should have it." I try to pass it back.

"Tatelah, please. You're a growing boy. Eat something." She pushes my hand with the muffin back to me.

A growing boy? "Don't you want it?"

"Please, Herschel. Don't insult me. It's for you."

"Okay." I take a small bite to make her happy. Bubbe likes her visitors to eat or drink. It makes her feel like she can still offer a little something, even though she's not in her own apartment, with her own kitchen. It's not that bad. I take another bite. Bubbe breaks a piece from her half, hands it to Nomi, chews on some herself.

At the other end of the room, a tiny white-haired woman stands. She clears her throat and in a booming voice, surprisingly loud for someone under four-foot-six, begins to speak in Yiddish. I recognize words here and there. She smiles and continues speaking, peering around the room as she does so.

"Feh," my grandmothers says in disgust. "She's a communist."

"She is?" Nomi turns to look.

The woman is now using her arms and hands to punctuate a point. Everybody else, including the staff, ignores her.

"Every day it's the same story," Bubbe says. "She used to be a macher. A big shot with the Marxists. She used to make speeches. She's mishugenah. Every day after lunch it's the same thing. She stands up in the middle of the living room and makes a speech. A regular Ethel Rosenberg." Bubbe starts to laugh, then chokes on some crumbs. I pat her gently on the back.

In the nick of time, Dov arrives with our tea. He sets his tray down on the end table. With long slender fingers, he passes her a Styrofoam cup of lukewarm tea. She gulps some down. Stops choking. Gasps for breath.

"You okay?" Nomi asks.

She smiles and coughs.

"Bubbe, are you okay?" Nomi repeats.

She laughs. "Yeah, mamelah. I choke all the time. I eat a little something and then I choke. What can you do? I can't stop it. I choke." She smiles up at Dov.

"Okay now, Mrs. Rabinovitch?"

She nods. "Thanks, doll." She's right about that. He is a doll. I bat my eyelashes.

"Oh my," he says, floating over to take care of the communist, whose wild gesturing has caused her to topple backward into her chair.

We sit quietly for a moment, sipping tea, while Bubbe catches her breath. I look around at the other residents. On the couch beside me sits an elderly man in a black jacket, white dress shirt buttoned right up to the top, no tie and a simple black yarmulke.

"I don't live here," he says to a woman on his other side, who doesn't seem to notice him. She stares ahead blankly. "I live a few blocks away. My wife, Hilda, may she rest in peace, died a few years back. I'm a bachelor. I take my meals here for the company."

Bubbe notices I'm watching him. She leans in close to me, points at him. "He's a gigolo," she says.

We laugh.

"He is?" Nomi stares at the man.

"He wants to ask me out," Bubbe says.

"He does?" I'm impressed. Love in the nursing home.

"What do I need him for?"

"Did he ask you?"

"I know he wants to. He's a gigolo."

"Why don't you go out with him? Maybe he'll take you to the movies," I suggest.

"Feh." Bubbe waves the idea away with her hand. Then she turns to Nomi, takes her hand. "Mamelah, tell me. How long are you staying?"

"Just a few more days."

"So? Is it true? About your mother?" Bubbe leans right in until she's half an inch from Nomi's face.

"What, Bubbe?"

"She's going through with it?"

"You mean the wedding?"

"What, mamelah?" Suddenly, Bubbe is so hard of hearing Nomi has to yell.

"The wedding! Are you talking about the wedding?" Nomi shouts.

"What? Mamelah, speak up. I can't hear."

"The wedding! The wedding!" Nomi screams louder.

"Yeah, mamelah. The wedding. What about the wedding?"

Nomi laughs, her frustration collapsing. "The wedding is on."

"She's going ahead?"

Nomi nods.

Bubbe leans in even closer to her granddaughter. Their faces are practically touching. "Tell me, mamelah," Bubbe says, "do you think it's right? Don't you think it's too soon?"

I can see Nomi struggling. If she agrees with Bubbe, it will be all the ammunition our grandmother needs to keep giving Auntie Faygie a hard time. For all her sweetness, Bubbe can be very judgmental. Nomi does think it's too soon, but she can't say so to Bubbe.

Nomi shrugs. "I don't know."

"It's too soon," Bubbe agrees with herself. "It's not right."

She turns to me. "What you think, Herschel? Do you think it's right?"

Why is she asking me?

"Herschel? It's too soon. Am I right?"

"Well . . ." I struggle.

"What's everyone gonna say? It's not right." Bubbe answers her own question.

"So, if you're so sure, why ask me?" I say, not sure if she can hear me.

"Am I right, Herschel?"

"What do I know, Bubbe? I'm cursed by God," I blurt out. Then I'm sorry I said it. She's an old woman. From a different era.

Silence. I don't know if she heard me or not. Nomi looks frightened. Her mouth is tight. She pulls her head back, as if waiting for a blow. Bubbe stares straight ahead, face closed, the lines in her forehead set in a deep frown.

"It's not right," she repeats. I don't know if she's talking about Aunt Faygie, or me and Nomi.

An old woman in another chair waves her hand in the air. She pushes herself to standing, then struggles across the room, leaning on a chrome walker. She wheels right up to Nomi and stares. Bubbe looks at the woman in disgust, raises a hand, tries to wave her away. Bubbe doesn't like any of the other people who live here. She wants them to leave her alone, especially when she has visitors. The woman drags her walker closer to Nomi, metal clanging on tile floor. Reaches out a hand and touches Nomi's arm.

"Tell me something, dear," she says to my cousin in a thick Yiddish accent. "Can I ask you a que-vestion?"

Nomi nods.

"Because I just vant to know."

"Sure . . . what?"

"I've been trying to figure it out." The woman pauses for a breath. "Are you a boy . . . or are you a goil?"

Nomi stares back at her, stunned. I fail to stifle a laugh. A loud guffaw of my nerves erupting. Bubbe swats at the woman again. "It's my granddaughter. Leave her alone. What's the matter with you? She's a girl. She's a lovely girl. Go away!"

"It's a goil?" The woman is surprised. "I thought it vas your grandson."

"Feh." Bubbe waves the woman away. The woman shuffles

slowly back across the room. "Looks like a boy," she tells the gigolo. He nods and smiles.

Bubbe giggles nervously, pats Nomi's hand.

"So, mamelah. What do you think about your mother?" Our grandmother returns to Aunt Faygie's marriage plans.

Who cares? I want to scream. We came here to tell you we're not cursed by God and all you want to do is talk about Nomi's mother and her damn wedding.

"Do you think she's doing the right thing?" Bubbe persists.

Nomi looks at me, the sadness clear on her face. "She's doing her best."

"But do you think it's right?" Bubbe is fishing for something. "Your father, may he rest in peace, has only been gone a year."

"It's almost two years, Bubbe," Nomi corrects.

Bubbe ignores her. "Do you think it's right, that she's already seeing another man?"

"Bubbe . . ." Nomi takes both her hands. "Pa's been dead a while now. I know it's hard for you to see . . ."

The tears roll down the creases on Bubbe's lined cheeks. "You don't know what it's like, mamelah. To lose a son. Why? How did this happen? He was a young man. It isn't right, mamelah, for a mother to outlive her son. You don't know."

"No," Nomi agrees.

"It's not right," Bubbe says.

"No."

"Herschel." Bubbe turns to me. "Tell me the truth, tatelah. Are you sick?"

Uh-oh.

"Don't think I don't know what's what. I watch the news. Young men your age, sick as dogs." She shakes her head.

My throat constricts. It's hard to draw a breath. I had no idea she knew so much.

"The truth, Herschel. Are you sick, too?"

I swallow, clear my throat. How can I tell her? "Not yet," I say.

"You don't have it?"

"Not yet," I repeat.

"You're not sick?" She moves her face closer, peers right into my eyes.

How can I lie to her now? I nod yes, slowly.

"Herschel? You have it?"

I nod again. Eyes fixed on hers.

She takes my hand. Squeezes hard. Says nothing.

Part

Changing Room

Chapter Seventeen

y mother's car won't start. Three tries, the engine turns over, but won't catch. Probably too cold. The temperature's dropped. I can barely feel my own frozen fingers. The fourth time, the motor starts, and I gun it.

"Careful, Cuz," Henry laughs, "twelve people will have simultaneous heart attacks over the racket." He gestures toward the nursing home.

This old car is starting to die. Maybe after Ma marries Murray, she'll be able to buy a new one. We sit shivering in the parking lot and wait for it to warm up. There is condensation on the windshield and back window. I switch on the defrosters. I don't know how much more of this icy weather I can take. I'm so frozen, I'm afraid I'll never thaw out.

"She heard me. Didn't she?" Henry wipes his foggy side-window with a gloved hand.

"I think so. And you heard what she said to that woman. About me."

"Yeah. So maybe we're not so cursed." His eyes are sad and hopeful at the same time.

"Yeah. Maybe. Henry, you sure floored me when you confronted her."

"Yeah. Sorry. I didn't mean to. It just came out."

"I'm glad you did. I didn't have the guts."

Henry laughs.

"What's so funny?"

"We'll have to get Josh to find out what she really thinks. You know how she talks about everyone behind their backs."

"Yeah. Josh'll find out." I pull the car out and turn right on Bathurst Street. I'm picking up Ma at the Wilson subway station.

Henry's going to grab a train south, go back downtown on his own.

"Are you sure you can handle the subway?"

"Yeah. Slowly. I'll take a cab from the Spadina station back to Julie's."

"Cause I can take you right downtown . . . if you want."

"Are you kidding? And sit in a car with Faygie for a half an hour? No offence, Cuz, but I can't handle the grilling."

I laugh. "Gotcha."

Henry sighs. "Boy, I'm sure glad that's over."

"Yeah. Thanks for coming."

"Don't mention it, Cuz."

As I turn the car into the Kiss 'n' Ride parking lot I see Faygie on a plastic bench inside the passenger waiting area. When she spots the car, she stands and waves.

Henry holds the car door open for her on his way out.

"Henry, is that you?" She swoops in to kiss him once on each cheek, leaving bright red lipstick marks in her wake. "Henry, it's been too long. Oh my god! What happened to your arm?"

"Fell," he lies.

"Is it broken?"

"Fractured."

She eyes him suspiciously. "You're too skinny. But then, you've always been skinny. I should be so lucky. Me, I put on the pounds just by looking at food. So you heard?"

Henry looks more amused than overwhelmed, although he definitely looks a bit of both. "Heard what?"

"My wedding," my mother says, as if everyone in the entire western hemisphere should know about it. "I'm getting remarried on Sunday. You'll come of course? I didn't have your number or I would have invited you sooner. What about your mother? How is she?"

"She's fine. Pretty good."

"Oy, can you believe this weather? I must have been crazy to plan a wedding in December. It's so cold. And the crowds, with all their Christmas shopping, are killing me." She sits in the front seat. Henry closes her door, walks around to my side of the car.

"Thanks for the ride, Nomi."

"No problem."

"Henry!" My mother leans across the seat so she can see him. "You're not coming shopping with us?"

"No thanks." He grins. "I've got to get back downtown."

"Okay. But I'll see you Sunday for my wedding?"

"I'll try, Aunt Faygie."

"You'll come. You'll come. Take care of that arm, Henry. And eat something. You're too skinny." She sits back.

"Talk to you later," I say to Henry.

He smiles, waves and climbs the stairs into the station.

Faygie and I are about to visit Yorkdale, a delightfully suburban mall. I despise malls. In my real life I'd never set foot in one. Never. Suburban malls are not exactly havens for butch dykes. It's not like I'm going to blend in or anything. My mother is oblivious to this. She doesn't realize that I flaunt it just by breathing. I am obviously and blatantly a dyke when I walk down the street. It's in the length of my hair, the clothes that I wear, the way I walk, the way I talk. The nightmare begins after we park. The closer we get to the doors of the mall the more dread I feel. My mother throws an arm over my shoulder. She's in a fine mood.

"We'll start with Edith Hampton's, then we'll check out Fairfashions, then of course we'll go to Beacons. Rhoda tells me there's some nice dresses just in at Miss Victoria's, although they're usually a little expensive for my taste. Oh, and I want to look in Linstins and Stellers. And Nomi . . ."

"Yeah?"

"I want you to be honest with me. If something doesn't look good, I want you to say, okay?"

"Sure." I am not qualified for this job. I know nothing about dresses. I'm not even sure I can fake it.

My mother plunges through the glass doors to the mall and we are in. Muzak floods my ears. Recycled air assaults my lungs and nose. Gaudy Christmas decorations are strung everywhere. All around us heterosexuals are shopping, drinking coffee, pushing wire buggies, buying holiday gifts. I half expect an alarm to sound and flashing lights to sweep over me. An announcement will come over the PA. "Attention shoppers, Jewish lesbian entering through the south doors." But my mother seems at ease, so I let her carry me along. Edith Hampton's is our first stop.

Ma skilfully swooshes dresses on their plastic hangers along circular steel rods.

"This is cute." She holds a flower print dress in front of her, tucking the hanger under her chin. "Oh, isn't this elegant?" She slings dresses into my arms. My job is to hold her stash. When I'm completely laden, she leads us to the fitting rooms. She sashays right past the attendant. I follow. The woman grabs my arm.

"Excuse me. Only three items at a time in the fitting rooms."

"Okay," I say. My mother swivels around.

"Three? That's ridiculous. So we have a few extras. Can't you just mark it down? Do you think we're here to steal? Do I look like a criminal to you?"

"No ma'am, store policy."

My mother puts her hands on her hips. No store policy is going to stop Faygie Rabinovitch. "Well, it's a stupid policy. What am I supposed to do? Go back and forth, and back and forth? Maybe I just won't try anything on at all. Maybe I just won't buy anything here," she informs the clerk.

"Sorry, ma'am, store policy." The poor woman looks distressed.

"Ma," I plead. "It's no big deal. I can stand here with the extras."

My mother glares at me. "It's the principle, Nomi. I'm a good customer. Last month alone I bought two outfits here. Where's the manager? I want to speak to him." She bellows so loudly that people all over the store stop and stare.

"Please, ma'am. Let's not get excited here. I'd call the manager, but she's on coffee break." The clerk nervously looks around.

I feel sorry for her. "Ma. It's not her fault."

"Nomi, stay out of this."

"Ma'am, if you'll just wait here, I'll get the assistant manager."

"Fine."

The clerk leaves her post, desperately looking around. The second she's gone, my mother grabs my arm. "Come on!" She leads me into the first cubicle.

"Ma . . ."

We dash inside. My mother shuts the door. I stand against the wall of the cramped stall as my mother strips down to her bra and girdle. The girdle is long-line, and tight. She thinks it improves her figure. Faygie slips a dress over her head.

"Zip me up," she orders. I oblige.

"Well, she was right here." We hear the clerk outside. "I guess she changed her mind. Thank god she left. She was so obnoxious."

We giggle. My mother puts a finger to her lips. She tries on all seven dresses, decides she doesn't like any. We drape them all back on their hangers and leave them on the hook in the fitting room. My mother opens the door a crack, peers out.

"She's still there." Faygie is a ten-year-old, playing hide-and-seek. I haven't seen this side of her since before my father died. She's in better spirits than she's been in for two years. Maybe Murray is good for her.

"What are we going to do?"

"You go first," my mother says.

"Me?"

"Yeah. Go distract her."

"Distract her?"

"Go ask her to show you something, then I'll make a break for it."

"Ma, we didn't rob a bank."

"Go," she nudges me out the door. The clerk spins around, sees me. A look of confusion crosses her face.

"Oh," she says.

"Hi," I say. "Listen, can you show me something in size, uh, fourteen?"

She leans forward, peering past me. "What happened to your mother?"

"My mother? Oh, she wasn't feeling well. She left."

The clerk does not look convinced. She marches to the cubicle where my mother is hiding, throws the door open abruptly to reveal Faygie Rabinovitch, shopper extraordinaire, who sweeps past her, talking loudly as she goes.

"All the dresses in here are last year's fashions. I wouldn't shop here if it was the last store on earth."

"Ma'am!" The clerk yells. My mother ignores her and leads me out of the store.

"Ma." I stop her after we are safely several stores down in the mall. "I'm a nervous wreck. Why did we do that?"

"Nomi, calm down. I was just having a little fun. Where's your sense of adventure?" She shakes her head and continues down the mall, heading for our next stop.

In Fairfashions, my mother has no choice but to stick to the three-items-only policy in the dressing rooms. High-tech sensors in the cubicles detect electronic tags on each piece of clothing and go off when someone has more than three items inside. My mother knows this. I don't ask her how she knows. I can only guess. I wait on a chair outside the dressing room area while she tries on each dress. She emerges every couple of minutes in a different one and preens before the mirror.

"So? What do you think?" she asks.

What do I know about dresses, Ma? I want to say. But I'm trying hard to be the daughter she's always dreamed of. "Well," I begin, "turn around." I wish we could have brought Julie along. Julie could actually help her pick a nice dress. Me? I'd rather be with Murray, picking out ties or suspenders. That, at least, I know about.

"So?" My mother is impatient.

"Well, it's not quite right," I decide, though I am not sure exactly why.

"Do I look fat?" she frowns.

I stand and walk around her, studying the sparkly silver dress that clings badly. "No, Ma. You look great. I just don't like . . . the colour of that one." I am grasping at straws. Does she know I'm trying so hard?

"Okay. I'll try the next one. You're not getting tired?"

I shake my head. Faygie disappears inside the tiny room. I collapse on the cracked orange vinyl chair. Will this torture end soon? Moments later I am called upon again to be a fashion consultant. Maybe Henry should have come. He'd do better at this than me. Even Josh is good with fabrics. Maybe I should have offered to wash my mother's floors or the windows, or to shovel the driveway. When I was a teenager, it was my job to cut the lawn, a position that did not come to me easily. I remember watching my father mow the lawn when I was little. I'd beg him to let me help.

"You're a girl," he'd say. "Go inside and help your mother. Izzy'll help me here." Only Izzy never wanted to. Izzy was always taking things apart and putting them back together or mixing strange potions with his chemistry set. And Josh liked to help my mother cook. I was the only one interested in outdoor chores. I'd watch as my father moved back and forth with the lawnmower. Each time, I'd beg, he'd say no. Then one day when I was eleven, he called me over, told me to stand in front of him. He put my hands on the handlebars and let me push with him. We finished the whole lawn like that. The next time, he let me do it by myself while he watched. After that it was my job. I loved it so much he never had to ask. Our lawn was always impeccably cut.

My mother was deeply troubled by her daughter's entrance into such male territory. "Do you think it's all right, Harry?" she'd ask.

"She loves it. What's the difference? She's happy. That's all that matters. Anyway, the boys won't do it. Izzy would rather fix the mower than use it and Josh is in here with you. Now *that* I'm a little more worried about, Faygie. I don't want my youngest son to turn out queer, you know what I mean?"

"So?" My mother pops out of the changing room, this time in a tight purple cocktail dress. "How about this one?"

I shake my head. Too tight. Too purple. "Nah. Not a nice cut," I say, with no idea where that came from.

My mother nods in agreement. I guess I scored points.

Miss Victoria's, the next store, is a real scream. Caters to the rich.

What they are doing in Yorkdale shopping mall, situated in a lower-middle-class neighbourhood, I don't know. From the second we grace their entrance, we are assigned a personal attendant, Francine, and a fancy private dressing room, large enough for four or five ladies, with plush carpeting, three-way mirrors, soft music, and a dressing table with an antique chair. Francine grills my mother for details.

"What's the occasion?" Francine's large red plastic glasses hang across her breasts on a black string.

"My wedding. I'm getting remarried."

Francine claps her hands together in glee. "Wonderful. Widowed or divorced?"

I think this is pretty fucking personal, but Faygie doesn't seem to mind. Stoically she answers, "Widowed."

The attendant simply nods. "Now, where is the affair taking place?"

"My sister's house."

"I see." From Francine's response I think she has just placed us somewhere below middle on the class meter. "So . . . what did you have in mind?"

"Well, off-white, not full-length, but not short. Below the knee. Some lace, but not too much. A spring chicken I'm not," my mother says, as if no one had guessed her age until that moment.

Francine giggles. She flips her hand in that limp-wristed motion usually used to put down fags, as if my mother is the most witty person she has ever met. "I think I have a sense of what we're look-ing for, dear," she tells Faygie, then winks at me, places her glasses on her nose and flounces out of the dressing room. A few moments later she is back with one dress. Francine waits as my mother tries it on. I try not to look bored. The dress is a size too big for my mother, pink and much too frilly. It looks awful. I try to catch my mother's eye. The attendant claps her hands together.

"Now that. Is perfect," she says. "That. Is you." She pauses between words as if it will give her opinion more weight.

"It is?" My mother does not seem convinced.

"This creation is an original design by Marco. Imported from France. There is no other dress like it in Canada." Thank god. Hopefully there is no other dress like it in the world.

"Well, I don't know," my mother hesitates.

"Oh dear. It. Is. You. I don't think I even need to bring out any others. This one. Works. So beautifully." A better con job. I haven't heard. In a long time. I figure my mother can see right through this phony.

"Well, how much is this one?" she asks.

Francine shows all thirty-two of her white polished teeth. "My dear. You only get married once. Oh well, twice perhaps," Francine laughs at her own blunder. "Now, money should not be of concern on the most important day of your life."

"Well . . ." my mother admires herself in the mirror, "you are. Right. About that." She adopts Francine's manner of speaking.

She is? I desperately try to catch Ma's eye. The dress is terrible. Even I can see that. And the clerk is so full of shit, I don't know how she can stand up and walk around.

"Well . . ." my mother says again. "Maybe you can hold it for me. You know, I'd like to take it, but I promised my daughter some lunch first."

The clerk's eyes fill with glee. She swoops down for the kill. "Why don't I get the paperwork started. You know, get that part out of the way." She opens a dainty drawer in the dressing table and extracts a pad of paper. "Now, can I have your name, please?"

"Certainly." I look at Faygie in horror. Has she lost her mind? I'm thankful we'll be having lunch soon. I vow not to let her put a cent down on this dress. "Mrs. Jack Kennedy," my mother says.

It takes every ounce of discipline to keep my jaw from dropping to the floor.

The clerk looks at my mother skeptically. Faygie responds, "I know, it's a funny coincidence. You know, before Kennedy was the president my late husband's name wasn't any more interesting than John Smith. But now, well, I can't even make a dinner reservation without someone commenting."

"Of course. Now, Mrs. Kennedy, if I can just get your address and phone number."

"Certainly." My mother rattles off an address in a rich area and an equally fictitious phone number.

"Now, Mrs. Kennedy, how will you be paying?"

"Well, with my gold card of course."

"Of course. May I take an imprint now and save us the bother later?" Like, may I clean your toilet now so you won't have to think of such messy low-life affairs later?

"Naturally," I hear Faygie answer. I must stop her. She doesn't have a gold card.

"Ma . . . mother . . ." I stammer, trying to sound sophisticated. "I really am famished. Can't we finish this . . . business," I spit out the word like ca-ca from my mouth, "after luncheon? Please, Mother?"

Faygie gives me a condescending look, then turns to our clerk and shrugs. "Of course, dear. How thoughtless of me." She stands, takes my hand. "We'll be back within the hour. And please," she clutches one of Francine's bony arms, "whatever you do, don't sell that dress to anyone else."

"No. Of course not, Mrs. Kennedy. Enjoy your lunch."

My mother and I trip over each other on the way out, we're laughing so hard.

Just when I thought we were about to stop for a snack, my mother hauls us into Stellers, which is a relief after Miss Victoria's. This low-end department store feels somewhat familiar, the kind of place I might venture into for bedsheets, small appliances or rubber boots. Tables are piled haphazardly with shirts, pants, underwear. Bright signs on chrome stands declare "Clearance. 50% off." Every few minutes, the PA system crackles and a manager announces another sale.

Even Faygie is beginning to tire, because this time she doesn't actually try anything on, just browses through the dresses hanging on the racks, holding some up against her body and asking for my educated comments.

"I don't know," I say about a particularly ugly print flower number.

My mother drops the dress to thigh level, sighs. "Well, Nomi. The whole idea is you're supposed to be helping me."

"I'm trying Ma. It's just not . . ."

"What?"

"My . . . specialty. I don't even wear dresses."

"But Nomi. You *are* a woman. You're my only daughter. I need you."

"I know, Ma. I'm here and I'm trying. But I'm just not that good at this."

She sighs, as if the world's greatest tragedy has just befallen her.

"Ma, come on, give me a break."

"Is it so much to ask?" She doesn't look at me as she speaks. She flips through dresses frantically.

"No."

"I only have one daughter, and she can't even help me on the biggest occasion of my life," she says to I don't know who. God, maybe?

Now I'm starting to feel like a failure. I pout.

"Nomi? Can't you just try a little?"

"I am, Ma. Believe me. It's hard enough to just . . . be in here."

She looks around and then back at me like I'm crazy. "What's so hard? Nomi? It's a store."

"Oh boy."

"Nomi." Her hands fly to her hips. The dress she is holding dangles alongside her legs. "I'm trying to understand, but you're not helping me."

I sigh.

"Well?"

"Ma, I told you. I know nothing about dresses. Nothing. I can't breathe in here." I feel stifled. Hot. The recycled air seems devoid of oxygen. An Alvin and the Chipmunks version of "Have a Holly Jolly Christmas" plays over the loudspeaker.

Ma hurls the dress back onto the rack. Hangers squeak. "I don't know," she mutters to herself. "You used to like dresses. When you were little."

"Ma, that's ridiculous. I never liked dresses." A woman in the next aisle has stopped to eavesdrop. I glare at her. She pretends to study a skirt and top.

"When you were little you used to wear dresses all the time."

"That's because you forced me to."

"You're a girl."

"I'm a dyke," I yell, perhaps a little loudly, considering we're in the ladies' wear department.

"Shah." She waves me down. Looks around, sees the woman, gives her a fake smile.

"Why? You think I'm cursed by God, too?" I sputter. Cartoon steam could be blowing in buckets out of my ears right about now.

My mother stops everything. Stares at me.

I flee the store. I'd go further, except the thought of being lost and alone among hordes of crazed Christmas shoppers in Yorkdale Mall is too horrifying to imagine. So I stand, sulk and wait.

Moments later my mother appears. "Who said you're cursed?"

I look away.

"Nomi . . . "

"Bubbe."

"She said that to you?"

"No. To Josh."

"Oy, Nomi. I'm sorry."

I sigh.

A pregnant woman walks by, with three small children in tow. We watch her weary face pass.

"How about an ice cream?" Ma says.

I shrug.

She flings an arm around my shoulder and squeezes me to her. "Come on, Nomi. The Ice Palace has seventy-five different flavours. You're gonna love it." She steers me down the mall.

We sit and eat ice cream at a small round table in the food fair. A giant Christmas tree in the middle of the mall is held upright by wires that run up to the ceiling. The branches are covered in candy canes and coloured balls. There is a huge line-up of kids waiting to sit on Santa's knee. I have a blackberry and kiwi frozen yogurt. My mother has ordered a double scoop of coffee crunch ice cream. She spoons a large glob of coffee crunch into her mouth, waves the pink plastic spoon in the air. "You know, Nomi . . . I mean no offence."

I shovel frozen yogurt into my mouth and grunt.

"I just thought . . . my daughter could help me pick out a nice dress."

"Ma . . . I'm just not used to . . . malls." I say the word mall like it's the most disgusting thing imaginable.

"Nomi, don't you ever go shopping?"

"Not really."

We slurp ice cream. A little boy on the store-Santa's knee begins to wail.

My mother sighs. "Okay. I'm sorry. I just thought it would be nice. You're my only daughter."

"Yeah, Ma. I want to spend time with you, too, but how about we do something I'm good at?"

"All right. I thought maybe you'd enjoy this . . ."

"Ma . . ."

"Okay, I wasn't thinking."

"It's all right," I relent, "it's not so bad."

"No?"

"Sure."

The frozen yogurt is soothing on my throat. A young mother scoops up her frightened child and eyes Mr. Claus suspiciously.

"Ma? How are you doing now? You know? With your decision to marry Murray?"

She smiles. "Better."

"Yeah?"

"I think I was just scared. You know, I was married to your father for twenty-eight years. The idea of marrying another man is frightening."

"Yeah."

"Anyway, Murray's nice."

"Yeah?"

"A real gentleman." She waves a spoonful of coffee crunch to punctuate her point. "You probably wouldn't believe it, but we've never . . . you know."

"Never?"

"I don't mind saying . . ." She lowers her voice. "I know you kids jump into bed with the first person you see, but Murray has been a perfect gentleman the whole time we've been dating."

"Oh." I don't know what to say. The thought of my mother having sex with anyone is more than I can bear.

"We're waiting until we're married. Don't you think we should?"

"Sure." Why ask me? What do I know about straight relationships among the fifty-something set?

"Anyhow, between you and me, Nomi, Murray's very romantic."

"He is?"

She nods. "And I don't mind admitting to you, I've been lonely."

"Well, good, Ma. It sounds like you're making the right decision."

"I'm a little nervous about Murray moving in, though."

"You are?"

"He agreed right away when I told him I wouldn't leave my house. My kitchen. I'm used to my kitchen, Nomi. I can't go and cook in another woman's kitchen."

"No, Ma. What are you worried about?"

She tips her head from side to side. "Well . . . you know how men are . . ."

I smile. "Not really, Ma."

"Oh. Well, so far he's been a perfect gentleman."

"Yeah . . ."

"He's been very sweet, charming. But . . ."

"But?"

"That's courtship, Nomi."

"It is?"

"Sure. He's on his best behaviour. Who knows what he really lives like. What if he throws his dirty socks on the floor and expects me to pick them up?"

"Oh."

"What if he's in the habit . . . ," she looks around to see if anyone is listening, ". . . of leaving the toilet seat up?"

I shrug.

"I hate that. Tell you the truth, Nomi, it's the biggest pleasure of living alone. Not once in the last two years did I worry maybe the seat was up when I went to the bathroom in the night. With your father and your brothers, I could never get them to do that one thing."

"I know."

"I thought with your brothers if I taught them right away, they'd get the hang of it. Joshua was always a little better, but even he forgot half the time."

"Ma, why don't you insist on it? Maybe on your honeymoon, before he actually moves in."

She looks shocked. "I can't do that."

"Why not?"

"He's a man, Nomi."

"We've established that fact, Ma."

We eat in silence for a moment.

"You think I can really do that?"

"Sure, Ma, it's the nineties. You can do anything you want."

She raises her eyebrows. "You think?"

"Don't let him push you around, Ma. He wants to be with you, just as much as you want to be with him. Don't forget that."

She smiles. Likes my advice.

"It was nice to see your cousin Henry. I don't know when the last time I saw him was. Must have been at your father's, may he rest in peace, unveiling. He's so skinny."

"Yeah."

Faygie leans right in and delivers her next line in a stage whisper. "He's not sick, is he?"

I pitch my plastic spoon into my empty cup. "Of course he's sick, Ma."

"Oh my god. Is it . . ." She stops before she says the dreaded "A" word.

"Of course, Ma."

"Oh my god. Does Belle know?"

"No. Not yet."

Her hands fly up to both sides of her face. "Nomi. He has to tell her. A mother has the right to know."

"Ma, you know Belle. She can barely take care of herself. Henry's just . . . waiting for a good time."

"Is he . . . ?"

"Is he okay?"

She nods.

"Well . . . he's been HIV positive for a long time." I hesitate, not sure how much Henry would want me to say. "His system is . . . weak. He could get sick anytime."

"Oh my god."

"Yeah . . . but you know, Henry's like his father. Full of life. I think he's going to be okay for a long time yet."

"What happened to his arm and his face?"

I wince. "Well, he was attacked, by two men. In the street."

"Oh my god. Why didn't you tell me? Is that why you've been visiting him so much?"

"Sort of."

"This whole . . . AIDS thing." She says the word AIDS as quietly as death.

"What?"

"Well, in my day, we didn't just jump into bed with every Tom, Dick and Harry. We courted. We waited. When we got married, we slept together. People didn't run around the way they do today. Maybe . . ."

"Ma . . ."

"Maybe Henry should have been more careful . . ."

"Ma, it's not that simple."

"Why not?"

"Why not? Because no one knew it was there. Henry probably got infected a long time ago, before any of us knew."

She shakes her head. "It's terrible. Poor Belle."

"Poor Belle?"

"That woman has had nothing but tzuris. Her whole life. Look at her jailbird husband."

"Uncle Solly? Aren't they divorced?"

"Yeah. Yeah. *Ex*-husband. That's what I mean. Look what she's had to put up with in her life. Your Uncle Solly, raising four kids on her own, and now this . . ."

"Ma, this is happening to Henry, not his mother."

"Well, it's her problem too." My mother shakes her head, sighs, and digs her plastic spoon into coffee crunch, finishing it.

Part

Some Like It Hot

Chapter Eighteen

*J*ust before afternoon rush hour, the subway car begins to fill up. I slump into a seat at the far end and rest my sore arm on my knee, careful not to look directly at anyone. My body rocks with the rumbling car. Tires squeal on steel tracks each time we slow for a station. The rhythmic motion lulls me into a daydream.

My father was sentenced to six years in prison when my mother was five months pregnant. When my twin brothers were born, Belle was in a cynical mood. Her husband was in jail. She had suddenly become a single mother with not two, but three small boys. The doctors didn't know she was carrying twins until the second baby started to emerge. What a shock that must have been. Hard enough coping with one new baby as your husband is carted off to jail, but two? I've always blamed the strain of her life situation for her naming my younger brothers Larry and Moe, after two of the Three Stooges. I used to tease my sister Sherry that if Ma had stayed in that mood, she would have been named Curly. She was called Curly half the time anyway, coming after Larry and Moe.

I don't see Larry and Moe much. They live here in town, but their Toronto and mine aren't on the same planet. Though I'm six years older, most people mistake them for older. They're politically conservative, culturally xenophobic and straight as two thick planks. Worse yet, you could hang a vacant sign on them. Absolutely. I don't know what happened. Maybe it's their response to our family troubles. Early childhood was different for me. Before my father went away, I had five good years as the only child, first son, with a mother and father passionately in love.

Every night for my first five years, Solly tucked me in. Every night, he told me his famous bank robbery story, with slight variations. I remember the stories. How he'd laugh. The tickle of his mustache when he kissed me goodnight. His Aqua Velva scent. "There's something about an Aqua Velva Man," my mother used to sing, imitating the TV commercial. My brothers never had the pleasure. When Larry and Moe were born, Solly was gone. Belle was depressed. I was jealous of the time and attention my brothers took. They never slept more than three hours at a time that first year. And they often slept in shifts, so just when my mother would lull Moe to sleep, Larry would wake up screaming. I don't know how Belle managed. She was sleepless in the suburbs that entire year.

Larry and Moe walk a straight and narrow path, sort of. Larry sells life insurance, which is a joke since it was an insurance scam that sent our father to jail. And Moe is the assistant manager of a sleazy video arcade on Yonge Street, a little more in keeping with our family style. They live two blocks from each other and make the exact same choices. At thirty-two, neither is married yet. They go on double dates, often with much younger women. They hang around with their group of high school guys. Play poker every Thursday night. Drop by each other's places, work on their cars together, go to football games, watch the World Series, the hockey playoffs, bet on the fights. I see them once in a while. Big occasions, like our grandfather's funeral, or when Nomi's dad died. Long ago I stopped going to family weddings and bar mitzvahs. People can be vicious on happy occasions.

"So? Nu, Henry? When you getting married?"

"Henry. Not married yet? What's the matter? Something wrong with you? Don't you like girls?"

"Henry? How's your old man? Still busting rocks in Kingston?"

At funerals, people are kinder.

"Henry . . . Nice to see you. It's been too long."

"Henry . . . You look good. Nice suit. Is it wool?"

"Henry . . . How's your father? Been a while since we've seen him."

Funerals are a bubble in time, a small window of opportunity.

A moment after death when the whole universe shifts. At Uncle Harry's funeral, even Larry and Moe were nice. They hugged me, looked me right in the eye.

"Hey, bro," Larry punched me in the bicep.

Not to be outdone, Moe threw an arm around my shoulder and squeezed, if only for a second. "Good to see you, guy."

Caught up in the macho mood, I rapped Moe playfully on the chin, and gave Larry a brotherly tap in the stomach. Guess I did the right thing—they both beamed. For once I was acting like the older brother they dreamed of. Someone who knocked them around a little. Maybe I reminded them of Solly and they were suddenly nostalgic for the father they never really knew.

I haven't told my brothers about my HIV status. Coming out was hard enough.

"I got nothing against fags," Larry said. I'd asked them to meet me at a bar, the lounge at the Carlton Inn, off Yonge Street. Straight enough to make them feel comfortable and just three blocks from Woody's, my favourite gay bar, where I knew I'd want to go after. For a couple hundred drinks and to be with my people.

"Yeah," agreed Moe. "Just spare us the details. Okay, Henry?"

"Aw gee, Moe," I replied. "I was all set to give you the play by play of my last visit to the baths."

They had no idea I was kidding. The look on their faces could only be described as horror.

Sherry was a little more mature when I broke the news to her. I invited her over to my place for dinner, told her over chocolate almond coffee and Grand Marnier. Only the best for my baby sister.

"I thought so," she said, taking a big bite of a strawberry tart.

"What?"

"Henry!" Her tone was reproachful. "I have gay friends, you know."

"No, I didn't know."

"Of course." She dipped her finger into the centre of her tart, scooped out the glob of pale yellow custard.

After two more Grand Marniers I told Sherry the rest. I wasn't planning to. I guess I needed someone in my family to know. She cried.

"I'm sorry, Sherry," I brought a box of Kleenex to the table, "maybe I shouldn't have told you."

"No, Henry. Oh god, I'm sorry." She grabbed a handful of Kleenex and wiped her tears. "But you're not sick yet, right?" Her eyes so full of hope.

"No, kiddo. I feel fine. Just positive. Who knows? They're discovering more treatments every day. You know. I could be fine for years. Maybe I'll die of old age or be hit by a truck one day."

"Yeah, or maybe the world'll end. I heard there's gonna be another ice age. Maybe in our lifetimes." She blew her nose loudly.

"Oh yeah, where'd you read that? The *National Enquirer*?" I playfully threw a crumpled-up napkin at her.

As for my mother, I've been dropping little hints about my HIV status for the last year. So far, she hasn't picked up on it. If she has, she's too afraid to ask, I guess. Soon I'll have to tell her. I don't want to be one of those guys who waits until he's on his deathbed before breaking the news. I've tried a few times; it's just so damned hard. At the moment, Belle is happy. And given her track record, I don't expect it to last. As soon as she breaks up with Bernie, I keep telling myself. I'll wait until she's miserable again. Why spoil her happiness?

Albert is back at Julie's place when I arrive. I collapse on the couch beside him. He's balancing a cardboard pizza box on his lap, munching a slice.

"Everything's going great," Albert beams. There's a little smear of tomato sauce on his chin. He is positively glowing. I try to interpret what I'm seeing.

"You got laid," I announce, helping myself to a wedge.

He smiles. Broadly. Takes a big bite of pizza.

I slap my thigh. "I knew it. I knew that would happen."

"Well . . ." he says.

"What?"

"I wouldn't say exactly laid. You know. Rick's pretty sick . . ."

"Yeah . . . ?" I prod.

"But we . . . were sexual," Albert says coquettishly.

Something in the way he announces this strikes me as odd and familiar at the same time. "You sound like a lesbian. That's exactly how lesbians talk."

"So?" he says defensively.

I shrug. "Nothing."

"Oh."

"So how about the article?"

"Well. We spent most of the morning going over the research. I left it all over there. Rick's going to keep reading it himself."

I pick a piece of pepperoni off the top of my slice, pop it into my mouth. "So what do you think?"

Albert smiles, winks. "I think Rick's going to come through for us."

"Yeah?" It's the first good news in a long time.

"But let's not get our hopes up too high. Not yet. He said he wants to read my documents and verify the sources himself before he makes a commitment."

Sounds like a long process. I'm bone-tired. Completely drained. I want to go home. I want to be in my own apartment. I want the damn article written and published. I want Roger to come home. I'm scared I'll never see him again. "How much longer do you think it's going to take, Albert?"

"It's really hard to say . . . I'm thinking of moving over to Rick's place."

"You are?"

"That way I can help him verify my research faster. Plus, he asked me."

"Isn't it kind of soon?"

"Henry." A serious look in his eye haunts me. "You know as well as I do. We don't have all the time in the world."

"Right." I suddenly feel stupid. "Well, if you're going, I'm going. I want to go home. I miss Roger."

Albert frowns. "I don't think that's wise, Henry. They're probably watching your place."

"Al, I have to. Roger might leave me. I have to go home and call him from there."

"Henry, it may not be safe."

"Al. I don't care. I don't want to lose Roger. If Roger leaves me, the FBI can't hurt me. They can torture me and I won't notice a thing."

"Henry . . ."

"Well, it's true. I know what you're thinking—drama queen— but it's true, Al. I don't want to live without Roger."

"Henry, I'm sorry. Maybe it's my fault. If you hadn't got mixed up with me, you and Roger . . ."

"Al, quit it. Roger and I would have had this fight one way or the other. I just need to go home and deal with it from there."

"Henry?"

"Yeah?"

"Be careful."

"Always." I flash Albert the most reassuring smile I can muster. It seems to work. He nods, and continues eating.

At 1:00 a.m., I stand before Julie's bathroom mirror applying a final layer of lipstick. Two hours ago I decided that if I'm going to sneak over to my apartment, I should do it in drag. Albert left earlier for Rick's. Julie is asleep in her room. I creep around her apartment, trying not to wake her. She has to work in the morning.

When I'm ready, I call a cab and wait on the front porch. Julie's shawl is wrapped around my shoulders. Large, thick snowflakes stick to tree branches and pile up on rooftops. Already three or four inches. When the taxi arrives, I step outside. My feet are covered in snow within seconds. Julie's black pumps offer little protection. I scoot into the back seat of the cab, slam the door behind me.

"Fifty Alexander Street. It's near Church," I say in my normal voice.

The driver turns right around to stare at me, laughs, nods his head. "Of course it is, buddy."

"Well, don't get your tits in a knot, honey," I say. "I'm sure in your line of business I can't be the first man you've seen in a dress." For emphasis I dab at the corners of my mouth with my forefinger.

"First one tonight," he mutters, turning around. He slips the car into gear and begins to drive me home. Casually, I glance around for the FBI. Everything is still. Parked cars up and down Julie's street appear empty. We drive on. The city sleeps under a blanket of fresh snow.

Outside my apartment building, fifteen minutes later, the driver smiles as I give him an extra-large tip. I'm thrilled to be home, alive and in one piece.

"Have a nice night, miss," he says sarcastically.

"Same to you, honey." Like a drunken saloon girl, I boot the door shut with my foot.

The lobby of my apartment building is the most gorgeous sight in the world. Even the overdone Christmas decorations don't annoy me. Exhausted, I punch the elevator button and wait. My heart hangs heavy. Standing in the lobby of our building, I miss Roger. I miss him so much. How nice to sink into the sheets of our queen-sized bed. Sheets that still carry Roger's scent. A room with all our things.

I sense something as I slide my key in the lock. I prod the front door of our apartment open silently. My heart begins to race. The TV in the living room is on. An old Greta Garbo movie is playing. I recognize it immediately. *Grand Hotel.* Greta utters her famous line, "I vant to be alone." Couldn't have said it better myself, Greta. There is nothing I vant more right now than to be at home, alone. The lights are on. I smell cigarette smoke. No, a cigar. I'm terrified and furious at the same time. An agent is in my apartment, in our private space, polluting our air with a cheap cigar. I know I should just leave. He hasn't heard me. I could sneak out and away, but I'm enraged. I vant to sleep in my own bed. I've had it with sneaking around, constantly looking over my shoulder. The thrill has worn thin. I vant the intruder out.

Recklessly, I reach for Roger's tacky, miniature imitation-marble David statue, grateful for the first time ever for its presence. I creep toward the living room. At the doorway, I peer in. I can't believe it. He's lounging in my easy chair, his back to me. Feet up on Roger's antique pine coffee table. A half-empty bottle of Jack Daniel's sits by his feet, beside an ashtray overflowing with cigarette butts, and a greasy cardboard Kentucky fried chicken bucket.

Slowly, I lower my arm.

"Hi, son," my father calls over his shoulder, not bothering to look. "I took the liberty of letting myself in. You really should get better locks on this joint."

I say nothing. Solly turns in his chair to look at me.

"Jesus Christ." Jack Daniel's spills down the front of his shirt.

Chapter Nineteen

"Jesus, Henry. You look just like your mother did twenty years ago. Scared the shit right out of me. Thought I was hallucinating for a second there. Jesus." Solly pours himself another shot of Jack Daniel's and knocks it back. He wipes his mouth with the back of his hand.

I'm lying on Roger's black leather couch opposite him, leaning against a pillow with my feet up. My skirt is hiked up above my knees. Julie's scarf, which I removed earlier, lies on the coffee table, soaked. I have gratefully accepted Solly's offer of a drink and am nursing my second glass of whiskey. The amber liquid slides easily down my throat, its warmth spreads throughout my belly, relaxing me. It feels good to be home. My initial shock at seeing my father after so long, and his at seeing me in drag, have worn off. Sitting here with Solly the gangster, I feel safe and protected for the first time since this whole thing began. My daddy's here. No one can touch me now. He's probably got a gun. Or at least a switchblade. He's had to watch his own back for years, it's second nature to him. The sorry sucker who makes his way this far will have to deal with Solly Rabinovitch, two-time convict, con-man, ex-member of the local Mob. My apartment is a Brink's armoured truck.

Solly pours himself another shot, sets his glass down on the end table beside the big easy chair he sits in. He squints and half closes one eye. There is a five o' clock shadow on his face. He is stripped down to his white undershirt, muscles bulging, black pants, a real he-man. Probably wonders what he did to deserve a son like me.

"So let me get this straight, Henry . . ." He laughs at his own joke. "Straight. Get it? Let me get this straight." He laughs some more. "Uh . . . you're in hiding."

I nod, take a sip of the burning liquid. "That's right."

He picks up his glass, drains half of its contents. "You could be under surveillance, even?"

I nod again. "Yep. It's possible."

"The FBI you say?"

"Yep. Or maybe the CIA."

"Maybe the CIA," he repeats, his head nodding up and down like one of those little white fuzzy dogs people put in the back windows of cars.

"That's right."

"The CIA." He purses his lips, still nodding. He seems kind of impressed. Like he never thought his son, the fag, would be into something so heavy.

"I mean, we don't know for sure, you know."

"Right."

"But we can't be too careful."

"No. So," he gestures at my outfit, "so this is kind of *Some Like It Hot*. Right, Henry?"

Some Like It Hot. Jack Lemmon and Tony Curtis as two jazz musicians who witness the St. Valentine's Day Massacre. To hide from the gangsters who want to kill them, they go into drag, and join a touring all-girls swing band. "Yeah, Pop. *Some Like It Hot.*"

"So, you're not one of those, uh, whatcha call it . . . female impersonators or anything like that, are you?"

"No, Pop." I smile, bat my eyelashes innocently. That my specialty is the Jewish divas—Barbra singing "People," Bette as she was in *The Rose*—is more than Solly needs to know.

He nods, happy with my answer. It's one thing to have a fag for a son, but one who dresses like a woman, that he doesn't want to know about. "I'll tell you, Henry. When you walked in that door, I almost had a stroke. I swear, dressed like that you're the spitting image of Belle. You know that?"

"I noticed."

"Jeez. For a second I thought somehow she knew I was here and came to harass me."

"What?"

He pops his unlit cigar into his mouth, rolls it around from side to side.

"Why would she harass you?"

"You know. Let's just say I'm a little behind in my payments."

"Payments?"

"You know. Whatcha call it. Alimony."

"You still pay alimony?"

"Yeah. Sort of."

"I didn't know you still saw her."

"Henry, your mother's crazy about me."

"She is?"

"Always has been. She just can't handle . . . my lifestyle."

This time, I break into laughter over Solly's choice of words. "Just like you've never been able to handle my lifestyle."

"Touché," he concedes, holding his almost-empty glass up high in a toast, then polishes off its contents. "And your arm. What the hell happened to you, son? You were in a fight maybe?" He asks this in a hopeful way, like maybe I'm not a complete sissy after all.

"You could say that." It's not a total lie.

"The other guy looks bad, right Henry? I mean you got in a few yourself, huh?" He punches the air with each fist like a heavy-weight champ.

"Oh, sure." I give my father exactly what he wants. "Guy ended up in the next bed over. Probably still there."

"Attaboy, Henry." I don't know if he's humouring himself or me.

I finish my drink and place the empty glass on the coffee table. I'm starting to feel drunk. I don't usually drink anything stronger than a beer, maybe a cocktail at a dinner party, with a slight fondness for Grand Marnier. Solly's always had a taste for Jack Daniel's. True to his tough guy image, he can drink any dude under the table and back again. He stands up, refills my glass, then his own. I rub one eye. When I bring my hand down it's covered in mascara. Forgot I had it on. I don't say anything. I act like it's no big deal that I'm lying on the couch in a rumpled dress, torn stockings, make-up smeared all over my tired face. Solly looks over at me, shakes his head, says nothing.

We sip our drinks in silence. Outside, the rapid spin of tires, a car skidding in heavy snow.

"Let me ask you something . . ." Solly says.

"Sure, Pa."

"How did you know? I mean, when did you know? How did you know . . . how did you know . . . about yourself, I mean?"

"How did I know I was gay?"

"Yeah."

We really are playing truth or dare. The father and son heart-to-heart talk I've always dreamed about. I pinch myself to make sure I'm not dreaming. Then I eye him suspiciously. This kind of honesty rarely happens between a father and a son. Is somebody dying here or what? Well, I am, but I'm not on my deathbed yet. Is there something wrong with Solly that's bringing on this sudden bout of truth?

"I guess I always knew," I tell him.

"Was it my fault? Something I did?"

I laugh. "No, Pop. It wasn't you."

"Was it because I wasn't around? You didn't have a father around. You didn't have a man's influence. A boy needs that, you know." He points at me with his cigar.

"Pop, look at Moe and Larry. Straight as arrows and I had more time with you than they did."

"Yeah. That's right. So, why, then, Henry?"

"I don't know, Pop. Some people just are gay. It's not bad. I'm happy. I really am."

He shrugs. "So, you're okay?"

"Yeah. Maybe you'll meet Roger. He's great, you know. Best thing that ever happened to me. Takes care of me. If you stay a few days, maybe you'll meet him."

"Sure. Maybe," he says, looking horribly uncomfortable with

the idea. Like he can deal with me because I'm his son, but some fag he doesn't know, well, that's pushing it.

Solly gets up, pulls the drapes apart just a crack. The glare from streetlights reflects off the balcony snow.

"I still don't get it, Henry." He replaces the curtain, returns to his chair. "The part about the FBI or CIA, whoever."

"Pop, don't you see? If the article gets printed . . . we're saying the U.S. government created AIDS on purpose, back in the seventies, as a weapon for germ warfare, and purposely injected the virus into people as an experiment. Hidden inside vaccines. To see if it would work. And now we have a worldwide epidemic. We're saying that the president himself ordered the experiment. Don't you see, Pop? If we're right, don't you think the U.S. government's gonna want to squelch that? Squelch us?"

"I don't know, Henry. The whole thing sounds mishugenah to me." He holds the cigar between his thumb and forefinger, jabs at the air as he speaks.

"I know. That's what I thought at first. But Albert's got proof."

"He's got proof?"

"Yeah."

"He's got proof . . ." Solly repeats, skeptically, as if I'd just declared that I could fly, or I'm from Mars.

"I'm telling you, Pop. I didn't believe Albert at first either, but when I started reading the documents, it all adds up."

"Jesus Christ, Henry." Solly goes over to the window again, peeks out. He pops the cigar into a corner of his mouth, leans back against the wall. "Why are you wrapped up in this?"

I take as deep a breath as I can and blow it out heavily. I wish he could read my mind. This is so fucking hard. "Pop, I came out in '78. I was living in New York then, remember?" Solly chews on his cigar. "No one knew how it was spread then. We didn't know until later." I wait. Let it sink in.

He fumbles in his shirt pocket for his silver lighter, lights his cigar. Stares at me. "I kind of figured."

"I'm sorry, Pop. If I'd known . . ."

"Oh boy." He puffs on his cigar.

"If any of us had known, we'd have been careful . . ."

"All right." He holds up one hand. "Enough said. What's done is done. Henry . . ."

"Yeah?"

"I mean . . . You don't look so bad . . . a little thin, but you've always been skinny . . ."

"Yeah, Pop. Other than this . . ." I hold up my fractured arm. "I'm doing pretty good." I don't mention the KS. One step at a time. I haven't seen my father in five years.

"Good," he peeks through the curtains.

"Pop?"

"Yeah? What?"

"Why do you keep looking out the window?"

"Why?" He rolls his cigar around in his mouth. "Let's just say, you got your troubles—I got mine. And don't ask me about it again. All right? Don't worry about it."

I want to know more, but don't ask. Probably he owes someone money. That could be why he's here. Hiding out. I shudder to think how long he might plan on staying.

"So how about your Aunt Faygie, huh?" he says, unnaturally cheerful. "I hear she's getting married again. You going?"

"I don't know, Pop. Depends on what happens next. Anyway, she doesn't really like me."

"Nah. She don't like me too much either." He smiles. "I figure I'll go."

"Really?"

"Sure. For sport, you know. And for the food. Plus, I haven't seen your Bubbe in a long time, you know."

"Yeah, I know. I just saw her." I sigh. "She thinks I'm cursed by God."

He takes the cigar out of his mouth and laughs, full-bellied and loud.

"What's so funny?"

"She said the same thing about me once."

"She did?"

"About thirty years ago."

"I didn't know that." I sit up.

"It's her favourite expression, like, for whatcha call it, anything she don't understand, I guess."

The laughter pours out of me, pressure releasing, like a boiling kettle screaming on the stove.

"Yeah, so don't pay attention to it, Henry. It don't mean a thing. Anyway, if I go to Faygie's wedding, I'll see the relatives all at once. Save me the trouble of paying each one a visit."

"Pop, were you actually invited?"

"Invited? This is my dead brother's wife. Who needs an invite? You want another drink?" He refills my glass, with a flourish.

Part 7

I Left My Heart

Chapter *Twenty*

his is it. The big day. Faygie Rabinovitch gives herself in holy matrimony to Murray Feinstein. This morning, I reluctantly tore myself from Julie's exquisite arms to be uptown for the festivities. With Albert and Henry gone, we had Julie's apartment to ourselves. My mother wasn't thrilled when I told her I had a date, and would be out all night. I went to Julie's anyway. I couldn't help it.

"Oy, I'm so nervous," my mother says when I walk into her house. On the bed, she has laid out the tastefully off-white wedding dress she finally purchased yesterday afternoon with Aunt Rhoda's help. She's wearing her bright green and orange flowered housecoat. Ma can't sit still for a second.

"Your Aunt Rhoda was already here this morning, can you believe it?" she says.

"Ma, that I believe. How are you doing?"

"How should I be doing? I'm as nervous as a bride." She giggles.

"What can I do to help?"

"Well, I wish you could help with my make-up, but don't worry, I know it's not your specialty. Rhoda's coming back. Just sit and talk to me while I fix my hair. There's coffee on. Be a doll and bring me a cup while you're going."

An hour later Rhoda appears. "Nomi," she says, letting herself in. "So the big day is here already. Can you believe it? I've come to help your mother. Where is she? Faygie!" She shouts.

"I'm back here, Rhoda. Am I ever glad to see you."

"Don't worry, Faygie." Rhoda marches purposefully down the hall toward my mother's bedroom. "We'll start with your foundation. Did I ever tell you? A good foundation's the most important thing."

"Yes, Rhoda. One more time and I'll strangle you."

"All right, already. I'm just trying to help."

I retreat into the kitchen for a cup of coffee.

A few hours later, Rhoda screams, "Oh my god. Don't come in yet," at my mother and I as we push at the front door to Rhoda's house. Guests are milling about in the front hall.

"Rhoda," my mother barks back as Rhoda shoves the door closed on us, "have you lost your mind?"

"Faygie," Rhoda whispers through a crack, "Murray just got here. He's right behind me."

"So?"

"So? It's bad luck for the groom to see the bride before the wedding. Wait a second. I'll get rid of him, then you can come in." Rhoda gives the door a final heave and shuts us out.

My mother giggles. In spite of her fears for this marriage, Faygie looks radiant.

The wedding party is small. Me, my brothers, Cheryl, Sheldon, Irma Kushner and her family, Murray's best friend, Sidney Posner, a widower in his late fifties. He is balding and overweight, a butcher. My Aunt Shel has shown up, with that husband of hers and her kids. Great Aunt Bessie flew in from Miami yesterday and has been driving Aunt Rhoda crazy ever since with suggestions. Sonia Greenblatt hovers in the hall, presumably hoping to nab an eligible bachelor. Izzy arrived early with Bubbe. Josh has brought Maria. I wish Julie was here, but it's way too soon for me to bring her to family events.

There are rented folding chairs lined up in rows in Rhoda's living room, about thirty seats in all. Rhoda shuffles everyone in. The ceremony is about to begin. The rabbi takes his position under the chupa at one end of the room. I sit beside Bubbe. Izzy's on her other side. Between the two of us, we hope to keep our grandmother quiet. Sidney, the Best Man, and Rhoda, as my mother's Matron of Honour, walk down the aisle together. Then Murray. Finally, my mother.

"Doesn't she look beautiful?" Sonia whispers.

"Where's the groom?" Aunt Bessie asks.

"He's there already. Beside Faygie," Sonia tells her.

"He's there? I didn't see him walk," Bessie says.

"He walked. He walked."

"Shhh."

The rabbi begins to recite the blessings in Hebrew. I watch my mother's face. She looks nervous, yet happy. My mother, and then Murray, sip from a cup of wine. The rabbi reads the marriage contract. Murray slides the ring on Ma's finger. Sidney slips the napkin-wrapped glass under Murray's foot. He breaks the glass. The bride and groom kiss.

Everyone shouts, "Mazel Tov!"

"Did he break the glass?" Bubbe asks.

"He broke it," Izzy tells her.

"He broke it?"

"Yeah."

"It's over?"

"The ceremony, you mean?"

"Did they get married?"

"Yeah, Bubbe. They got married."

"Is the rabbi here?"

Izzy looks at me. Shakes his head. "Come on, Bubbe." He stands, holds out his hand to help her up.

After the ceremony, the folding chairs are stacked in a corner. Murray brings out a case of champagne. Drinks are served. Rhoda's teenage son Mark is in charge of music. His father has instructed him to stick to Frank Sinatra, Connie Francis and Benny Goodman. Nirvana, Guns and Roses and Bare Naked Ladies are strictly forbidden.

Rhoda's dining room table is loaded. Noodle kugel, a chopped liver mould in the shape of a heart, crackers, potato knishes, latkes, fancy individual quiches, chicken fingers, zucchini sticks, a vegetable platter, salami, corned beef and pastrami, rye bread, pickles and olives.

"Everybody grab a plate. Eat. There's plenty," Rhoda yells as she flutters around the kitchen and dining room, filling plates, serving more.

Bubbe walks from person to person, looking a little lost. I take her by the arm.

I smile. "Bubbe, you want help? Let's get a plate and get you some food."

She looks up at me. "What does the rabbi say?" she asks. "Does he think it's okay? It's not too soon?"

Ignoring her, I say, "How about a knish? They're fresh."

"What, mamelah?"

Cheryl joins the line behind me. "It's not even catered," she complains to Sheldon.

"Sure it is," I face her. "Are you kidding? The pâté was flown in from France just an hour before you arrived. It's been marinating for days in twenty-year-old cognac."

"Really?" says Sheldon, reaching beyond me for a big scoop of Aunt Rhoda's home-made chopped liver.

"Okay. That," says Josh to Maria, "is called kugel. It's . . . kind of like spaghetti, only with apples and cinnamon."

"Doesn't look like spaghetti."

"Okay, maybe more like macaroni."

Bubbe tries again. "Nomi, mamelah, what if your mother is making a big mistake?"

"Cake?" I say, as if I didn't hear her. "You want some cake?"

Josh rolls his eyes at me, smiles. "Bubbe, how's the gigolo?" he asks.

"What, tatelah?"

"The gigolo!" he screams at the top of his lungs, "the gigolo!"

"Oh." She has heard him. "The gigolo. He wants to ask me out."

"The what?" asks Cheryl.

"I know he wants to ask you out, Bubbe. You should go," says Josh.

Sidney Posner sidles up to Sonia Greenblatt. "So, I hear you work in the gift shop with Faygie." He plops an olive into his mouth.

Sonia's eyes brighten. "Has my friend Faygie been telling you things about me?"

Sidney puffs out his large chest. "Only good things. Did you try the gefilte fish? It's incredible." He reaches over Sonia for another piece.

Great Aunt Bessie teeters behind Aunt Rhoda "helping," white leather purse over her arm, in the same lime-green dress she's worn to the last five family weddings, hair curled and sprayed, wearing her signature bright red lipstick, and rouge.

"Rhoda," she screeches, thickly accented, "you should have a pot holder under that kugel. It's gonna boin dat lovely tablecloth."

"It's on a trivet, Aunt Bessie. Oy," Rhoda looks up at the ceiling, exasperated.

Aunt Bessie looks at Rhoda, confused. "A vat?"

Rhoda's door bursts open dramatically, and who should be standing in the doorway but Uncle Solly, in a blue pin-striped suit, white shirt and a wide blue tie, hand-painted with two palm trees blowing in the breeze. In his arms he carries a huge bouquet of flowers. Beside him, Henry in black jeans, a blue shirt, rainbow-striped tie and black blazer. The whole party stops dead and turns to face the door.

"Oh my god," someone says.

"Who is it?" asks Bubbe.

"Solly, you made it," says Aunt Shel, happy to see her big brother.

"Is it Solly?" Bubbe asks.

"What the hell is this?" Solly booms. "A funeral? Maybe I got the wrong address. I thought this was a wedding. Where's the party?"

"Solly." Bubbe shuffles toward her first-born son, whom she hasn't seen in five years. "Solly? Is it you?"

"Ma! You look terrific. I think you're shrinking, though. You're looking kind of short."

My uncle bends to embrace his mother. "Ma? How ya doing?"

She pulls back, shakes a finger at him. There are tears in her eyes. "Solly, you no-goodnik. Where have you been? I haven't seen you in so long. I thought you'd never come back."

"And stay away from you? How could I do that? I'm nuts about you. Everyone knows that."

Bubbe pulls Solly downs to her height by his lapel. Shouts in his ear, "Don't think I don't know where you've been."

"What, Ma?"

"You've been a guest of the government again, haven't you, Solly? The government's been paying your room and board behind bars."

For once in his life, my uncle is speechless. He holds his mother's gaze. She shakes a finger at him. "Okay. Enough said. Next time, you'll at least write me a letter."

She shifts her feet two inches over to Henry. "Herschel? You came too? Good. You're too skinny. You gotta fatten up. Eat something, tatelah. There's lots of food. Your aunt's sister made a spread. It's included," she adds, as if we were in a hotel or restaurant and without this information, Henry might think he had to pay for a plate of food.

"Okay, Bubbe." Henry leans down, kisses our grandmother on the cheek, catches my eye, smiles.

I wave.

"Uncle Solly!" Josh yells from the kitchen doorway.

"Is that Josh? Look at you. You're a man. Last time I saw you, you were still a pisher. Come here, you." Solly holds out his arms.

Josh goes over. They hug, like men, slapping each other hard on the back.

"Where's your mother? Where's the bride? These are for her." He holds out the flowers.

My mother makes her way to the door, with Murray in tow. "Solly!" she says. "Glad you could make it." She reaches out to hug him.

"Well, you know, I happened to be in town. And who is this? Must be the lucky guy."

"This is Murray. Murray, this is my late husband's older brother, Solly." The two men shake hands.

"Come in. Come in. Grab a plate. There's plenty of food," says Murray.

Aunt Bessie abandons Rhoda's side and drags her feet along the carpet to the door. Through thick horn-rimmed glasses she peers at Solly and Henry.

"I know you," she announces to Henry, "you're Solly's son. Give me a kiss."

Henry bends down. She grabs his face in both hands, plants a sloppy kiss right on his mouth, smearing red lipstick on him.

"Where's your wife?" She looks behind Henry.

"I'm not married."

"What? A nice young man like you? You should be married by now."

"Not yet."

"When I was your age, we were married already. Ach." She waves one hand down. "You young kids . . . he should be married," she says to the room.

"He's not married?" Sonia asks, looking Henry up and down.

"My son Danny's not married either," Sidney tells Sonia, shovelling a heaping spoonful of potato salad into his mouth. "And he's almost forty."

Sonia eyes him suspiciously.

Henry frees himself from Aunt Bessie, makes his way over to me.

"I didn't think you'd come," I say.

He shrugs. "Pop wanted to."

"I didn't know he was in town."

"Neither did I, until I found him in my apartment."

"Really?"

"We had the most amazing talk. About everything."

"That's great. Does he know about Roger?"

He nods. "They haven't met yet. I'm not sure how long Solly is staying . . ."

"Henry. Tatelah," Bubbe shouts, "come and get a plate. Eat something." She tells everyone around her, "He's too skinny."

"There's lots. Look, I'm putting more out," Rhoda informs everyone.

"Rhoda, the table's full," my mother points out.

"Never mind. There's always room for a little more." Rhoda schleps a tray of meat into the dining room.

Mark keeps the Frank Sinatra flowing and soon people are dancing out into the hall. Murray asks me to dance. He takes me around the waist. I have to concentrate really hard to let him lead. I'm used to leading. I can tell that Murray has been dipping quite heavily into the champagne. He wavers a bit on his feet and his smile is sloppy.

"Nomi, you look beautiful tonight," he says.

"Thanks, Murray." I'm wearing black dress pants, a white shirt and, to make my mother happy, I had Josh help me tie her red sheer scarf around my collar.

"You know, I have a nephew around your age. Yossi. He's an accountant. Maybe you want I should introduce you?" He winks at me.

I purposely step on his toe.

"Ow."

"Oops," I smile sweetly.

Uncle Solly saunters over. "What kind of music is this, Nomi?" he bellows at the top of his lungs. Murray stops swaying. I pry my hand from his, giggle.

"I mean, shit, Murray. Taped music! What is this? Connie Francis? Whattsa matter? You cheap or something? This is your wedding, for Christ's sake. You should have hired a band."

"You think?" Murray blushes.

"Aw, what the heck. Don't have a stroke or anything, Murray. The food's great. How are you, Nomi? Long time no see." He turns suddenly, grabs me in a bear hug, picks me up off my feet. "Don't she look great?" he asks Murray.

"Yeah. I was just telling Nomi she should meet my nephew, Yossi," Murray says.

Solly laughs. Guffaws, really. He punches Murray on the shoulder, playfully. "That's a good one, Murray. Meet your nephew. Whattsa matter with you? She don't want to meet your nephew. Your niece, maybe . . ." He winks at me. "Ain't that right, Nomi?"

"Huh?" says Murray.

"Open your eyes, Murray. Whattsa matter with you? Don't you get around once in a while?" Solly sweeps me away from Murray. "What a putz," he says. "Should we dance?"

I let Solly carry me away with the music. He really is quite a dancer, easy to follow. Aunt Bessie has roped Henry into a dance. They sway back and forth beside us, Bessie's purse, slung firmly over her arm, banging into Henry's side rhythmically in time with the music. My mother has joined Murray. Over Solly's shoulder I watch her dance with her new husband. Murray whispers in her ear. She tips her head back and laughs. Pure joy. It occurs to me that finally I'm happy too. I imagine what it would be like to be here dancing with Julie, instead of my uncle. At just that moment, Aunt Bessie cuts in, to dance with me. Uncle Solly graciously bows, relinquishes me into the arms of my seventy-five-year-old great aunt. She smells of moth balls, raw onions and cheap perfume. Uncle Solly and Henry stand looking at each other for a moment. Solly laughs mischievously, grabs his son, and leads him off the dance floor in a dramatic tango. You can practically see a red rose in Henry's teeth.

"So what about you, Nomi?" Aunt Bessie shouts in my ear. "You're not married either?"

"No, Aunt Bessie," I say. "You?"

"Me? What do I need a man for? So I can pick up his dirty socks? I already had the pleasure with your Uncle Sam, may he rest in peace. Men," she snorts.

The music changes. My cousin Mark slips on an old Chubby

Checker version of "The Twist." Aunt Bessie lifts up her skirt, exposing her white long-line girdle, and twists for all she's worth. Not to be shown up, I twist along. Everyone cuts very loose.

Chapter *Twenty-One*

"*L*ove ruins everything," I explain to Julie. It's our last day together. My family duties are over. Last night, after the wedding reception, my mother and Murray left for the airport. They've gone to Miami Beach for their honeymoon. Julie and I are having a drink at The Rose. Monday afternoon, not many women here.

"Don't you mean love *rules* everything?" Julie twirls the mini-umbrella in her Bloody Mary between her fingers.

"No. *Ruins*."

"Why?" She runs her stocking foot up my leg.

"It does. Think about it." I raise her foot to my lap.

"Tell me." She teases her toes against my crotch. "Tell me," she repeats, running her tongue along the rim of her glass.

If I don't kiss her soon, I will faint. I struggle to regain my thoughts. "Well . . ."

"Uh-huh?" She licks her lips, intent on torturing me.

"Well," I swallow hard, focus on her lovely almond eyes. Dancing with life, burning with fire. I could sink into them and die happy. "Like," I clear my throat. "Say you're single. You're a single dyke about town. You have an apartment, you have a job. You have friends. Maybe you're thinking about going back to school, taking a few courses, joining a group or something. You get it all in place, maybe even buy a dog and house-train it. You get used to sleeping with your dog at your feet. Everything's going smoothly. Your life is on track. You can take care of yourself. This is the nineties. You are a nineties babe. Maybe you'll pierce your eyebrow or your tongue, spice life up a little, and then bang! You meet someone, fall in love and everything falls apart."

"What?" Julie laughs, slides her foot from my lap, leans forward and takes my hand. "What do you mean, 'falls apart'? Wouldn't love enhance everything?"

"Well, yeah. Except now you start to feel again." I squeeze her hand, play with it. Her skin is fine silk.

"So? What's wrong with that?" She kisses my fingers lightly.

"Well, before, you were living. The bills were paid. The kitchen was clean. You had time on Sundays to do your laundry. Walk your dog twice a day. Your career was on track. Your friends were happy with you. Then, you fall in love and everything changes. Your apartment is a mess, you quit school or flunk out. Your bills rack up, unpaid. Your friends are mad at you for not spending time with them. Your family gets upset too. Your boss notices how happy you are and starts to crack down on personal phone calls. Even your dog is disturbed. Your garden, if you had one, falls into disarray. Your house plants wither and die. Everything is ruined."

Julie laughs. She laughs and laughs, her silken hand stroking my arm. "Come on," she says, standing, "let's go to my place. Let me ruin you."

The phone rings, just as we enter Julie's apartment. "The machine'll get it," she says, pushing me up against the living room wall. She nestles her face in my neck, kisses me softly. I'm vaguely aware of the phone ringing, answering machine beeping, while Julie runs her tongue up my neck to my ear.

"Hey Julie, it's Albert. Fabulous news. Rick's writing the article."

Julie stops kissing. We listen to Albert.

"He's at the computer this very second, finishing what we hope is the final draft. And here's the best part—he's already talked to his editor, who's practically wetting his pants over this. His editor needs to see copies of my documents for verification. And for the record, they have to phone the president's office. I can't wait. Rick's editor is coming over to pick up the story personally. He wants to meet me. A dream come true. The story might run in the morning paper, maybe even on the front page. No guarantees, yet. But I think we did it! Break out the champagne. I just spoke to Henry and he . . ." Beep. Long-winded as usual, Albert is cut off.

"That's great," I say to Julie.

"So are you."

"Julie . . . I want you so bad."

"Then take me."

Her desire breaks through to my battered heart, healing me. Our eyes lock in a feverish embrace. We move slowly forward, kiss. Her hands in my hair. Hungry, impetuous. I tear my mouth from hers and kiss her face, lick her neck. She whispers my name. The rhythm of her voice cries out to a place inside that opens just for her. Skin and spirits meld, secret messages pass between us. She draws me into a fiery gust of passion, cunts burning, skin tingling, a fury of feelings, until our bodies take over and there is nothing to be said that has more than one syllable. Turbulent, unrestrained need pulls at us both and we give in to it, give over our power, our everyday control, swept up in desire's current. White-water rapids hurtle us downstream to the edge of the falls. Over the brink we plunge, tight in each others arms. Waves of orgasm rip through us both, bedsheets tangled, bodies entwined. Love and lust tumble together, pierce the surface to open vulnerability. Drenched in sweat, we kiss and stroke each other tenderly. In one short week, Julie has brought me back to life. I am in love with her simple, honest way. A brave woman, with a beautiful heart. I know this about her without a doubt. I hold her tight in my arms.

Julie sleeps beside me, one leg wrapped around mine, clutching me. I'm awake, enjoying this precious time. Sadness creeps up. Tomorrow morning I'm on a plane back home, leaving this wonderful woman. I miss San Francisco, palm trees, warm weather, my friends. Can't wait to get away from the snow. But I'll miss Julie too.

The phone rings.

The answering machine does its little click dance. Then I hear Henry's voice.

"Hi. It's Henry. Listen, just called to say . . ."

I slip my arm out from under Julie and reach for the phone on her bedside table.

"Henry!"

"Hey, Cuz."

"We heard about the article. That's great, Henry." Julie stirs. Her eyes open. She looks up at me, love all over her face. Or is it lust?

"Yeah. I can't believe it."

"Henry . . . It's all over. Right? I mean, you guys should be safe now, right?" I sink down, take Julie back in my arms. She traces circles on my naked belly with her fingers.

"I don't know. I mean, Albert says we won't know until tomorrow or the next day whether the story's going to run. But as long as Solly's here, I have my own personal bodyguard. And I think he plans to stick around for a while."

"Good timing, huh?" I glide my open palm up and down the length of Julie's back.

"Yeah." Henry sounds sad.

"No word from Roger?"

"Well, I left another message with Jim and Bruce. They said they'd pass it along."

"Henry?"

"Yeah?"

"Roger loves you."

"Does he?"

"Is there anything I can do?"

"Nah. Thanks, though. I'll be okay."

"Yeah?"

"You know," he says, resigned, "that's life."

"That's love," I correct. Julie sucks on my neck. I stifle a moan. Clutch her tighter.

"Listen, Cuz. It's been great spending time with you. Have a great trip back. And Nomi, don't be a stranger."

"You got it. Why don't you come to San Francisco for a visit soon? You and Roger, I mean."

"Real soon. After all this, do I need a vacation."

"Henry, keep phoning Roger. He's gotta talk to you soon." My hands slink down Julie's back to her ass.

"I hope you're right. Anyway, if he comes home I hope he's ready to meet his father-in-law."

"Oh boy."

"You can say that again. Hey, give Julie a big fat kiss from me."

"You can count on that."

"Love you, Cuz."

"Same."

The phone slips from my fingers, to the floor. Julie and I kiss hard and furious, as if we've been apart forever. Naked chest against soft breasts. Nipples harden. Her hands are everywhere. Soft hands, touching, searching, feeling.

"Oh god," I whisper, cupping her ass. We rock on the bed. I want to taste every part of her. She feels so right, made just for me. I lick her neck to her collarbone, take her hard nipple in my mouth. She writhes under me. The rarest rose, sweet and luxurious, I want her so much. With every inch of my body, I give my love to Julie, take her in my heart. She pours her love over me slowly, like honey from a jar. We make long slow love, that lingers and smoulders like the red-hot embers deep in the belly of a fire. The ice surrounding my heavy heart melts away. I lie in her beautiful arms. There is no doubt about it. I am ruined. Absolutely ruined.

Chapter Twenty-Two

My first night back in San Francisco, I hide underneath the quilt, on Betty's couch, crying the Julie blues. Betty thinks I'm crazier than ever.

"Nomi, you're taking this too seriously." She sits beside me on the sofa, channel surfing with the mute on. "You barely know the woman. Sounds like a great vacation romance. But, if I were you, I'd forget about her."

"Don't be ridiculous, Betty. I'm in love."

Betty switches the television off. "Tell me again about the AIDS conspiracy thing. *That* sounds incredible."

After Betty goes to bed, Julie phones. We talk 'til three in the morning. With that and the time change, I don't hear my alarm clock go off. I'm late for work.

"What the hell happened to you?" Patty snaps when I rush into the pub an hour late.

"Sorry, Patty. Jet-lagged I guess. Here." At least I remembered to bring Patty her six-pack of Ex. I place it on the bar.

She stares at me.

"No," she says. "Something happened. And I can't wait to hear all about it."

"I'm telling you this for your own good, Nomi. You should just forget about her," Betty lectures over breakfast the following day. Well, Betty's eating breakfast. Two slices of sourdough toast with peanut butter and a bowl of Shreddies. I'm drinking coffee. Black, with lots of sugar, my third cup. And moping.

"Believe me, Nomi. It's for the best. Look, you live three thousand miles apart."

"Thirty-five hundred."

"Oh my god. Thirty-five hundred miles. That's two lifetimes away."

"I know."

Betty peers at me. "Oh my god."

"What?"

"You're not thinking of moving back there, are you?"

I sigh. "It's crossed my mind. But I love San Francisco, and I hate Toronto. Winter. Yuck. Anyhow . . ."

"What?"

"Well . . . I moved here to be with Sapphire and look what happened."

"Exactly." Betty eats and I sulk. "Anyway, I know someone who has a crush on you." She thrusts a huge spoonful of Shreddies into her mouth and chews loudly.

"Who cares?"

Betty practically chokes. "Who cares?" Her mouth is full. I can see little pieces of chewed Shreddies. "Nomi. You really have gone around the bend this time. No kidding. Who cares? Hah. That's the craziest thing I ever heard you say."

"No it's not." I dip my spoon into the bowl, add more sugar to my coffee. I've already put three spoonfuls in. I'm hoping a sugar high will help my mood.

Betty chews silently. "No. You're right. It's not the craziest thing you've ever said. But it's right up there." She points her empty spoon at me. A drop of milk falls to the table. "Nomi, listen. When I tell you who has a crush on you, you're gonna flip."

"No I'm not. I already told you I don't care. I don't even want to know. So, don't tell me."

"Girl, you *are* in love."

"That's what I've been trying to tell you." I add two more spoons of sugar. Betty continues eating.

"I've been thinking . . ." I say.

Betty looks up from her cereal.

"I want to get the rest of my stuff out of Sapphire's. I don't have lots . . . but is it okay with you if I bring it here, I mean for now?"

Betty grins. "No sweat, babe. I got a storage locker in the base- ment. Practically empty. Want me to go with you to pick it up?"

"Yeah." I don't want to be alone with Sapphire and I definitely don't want to run into Rambo, who might very well be there. "I'm going to ask Patty if I can borrow her jeep."

"Good idea, Nom." Betty reaches for the Shreddies box. Refills her bowl. "Time to move on."

The phone rings. I glance at my watch. Ten in the morning. It can't be Julie. She'd be at work. Just in case, I leap up and race for the phone.

"Hello?"

"Nomi. How's the weather there?"

"Oh, hi, Ma. I don't know. I haven't been outside yet. Why?"

"Guess where I am?"

"You're in Florida. Miami Beach."

"Yeah doll, but guess where?"

"I don't know. In your hotel room?"

"No, doll. I'm at the pool. Murray rented a cell phone. Isn't that incredible?"

"Yeah, Ma. It's fascinating."

"What's the matter Nomi? You sound depressed."

"I am."

"What's the matter? You lose your job?"

"No, I still have my job."

"A fight with your roommate?"

"No, Ma. We're fine."

"Nomi, it isn't Sapphire, is it?" She sounds horrified.

"No, Ma."

"Then what?"

I hesitate. Can I tell my mother what tears my heart in two? Will she say the right thing? Or will she say something insensitive, then we'll have a big fight, which she'll remember for the rest of her life as "Nomi ruined my honeymoon." The official story. Rela- tives will repeat it to each other for years, shaking their heads.

"It's nothing, Ma. I'm just . . . premenstrual."

"Oh. Well, it happens. Did you take some aspirin?"

"Yeah, Ma. I'm just waiting for them to take effect." If they don't, maybe I'll try heroin.

"Oh. Here comes Murray with our drinks. I gotta go. Just wanted to say hi, doll. You take care. Love you. Bye."

"Bye, Ma."

I hang up, lean against the back of the couch and stare into space.

At noon, the phone rings again. I know it will not be Julie. It'll probably be for Betty. I answer anyway.

"Betty's place."

"He's back."

"Henry!"

"Did you hear me?"

"Roger's back?"

"Yeah. I'm so happy I had to call you."

"He's there now?"

"In the shower, the hunk."

"Is your father still there?"

"Pop's officially installed himself in the den. Temporarily, he says."

"What does Roger say about that?"

"Well . . . they're not getting along so good."

"What happened?"

"Roger insisted that Solly smoke on the balcony, but you know Solly."

"Oh god."

"He called Roger a communist, which is, of course, ridiculous. I told Pop he means Roger's a fascist, and anyway, I'm the resident communist. 'Get outta here, Henry,' he said. 'You don't care if I smoke.' Which actually isn't true. I'm just kind of scared to insist and Roger's not."

"Oh god."

"As soon as Roger's out, or asleep, or even in the other room,

Solly lights up. He's got a family-sized can of Lysol. He sprays whenever he's been smoking. Of course Roger loves that."

"What happened?"

"Solly claims to be smoking on the balcony and the smell somehow drifts in. Also, he gets in little digs about it."

"Yeah? Like what?"

"You know. We'll be eating dinner and he'll say, 'There's no proof, you know, that cigarette smoke is bad for you. Look at George Burns. The man lived to be ninety-nine fucking years old, smoked like a goddamned chimney.' "

I laugh. "What are you going to do?"

"Nothing. Stay out of it, let them fight it out. Anyway, Roger's been so sweet to me since he's been back. Said he loves me, and couldn't stand life without me. Also, he says he understands more about me now that he's met Solly."

"Well, keep me posted. It sounds . . . interesting."

"Yep, it's definitely that. And did you hear about the article?"

"Yeah, Julie told me. The story's finally going to appear in the *Star* . . . this Friday, right?"

"Yeah. Or maybe even Saturday. Circulation's higher for the *Saturday Star.*"

"I'll cross my fingers."

"You'd better. Rick says you can never count on an article being published until the ink hits the paper."

"Tense."

"I'll say. But he says it looks good. His editor's behind him, which he says is half the battle."

"Call me the second you know for sure. Okay?"

"You got it . . . Cuz?"

"Yeah?"

"You don't sound so good. You're sad, huh?"

I sigh. "Miserable. I miss Julie."

"Well, if it's any consolation, she's pining over you too. She looks like she lost her best friend."

"Oh, Henry, what are we going to do?"

"You'll think of something. Have you talked to her?"

"Yeah, but it almost hurts more to talk. Who knows when we'll see each other again? I don't know what's going to happen."

"Nomi, no one ever does."

"I don't know if I can do this, Nomi." Julie's gorgeous voice tears me apart.

I am under the covers, with the lights off, the receiver pressed tightly to my ear. I spend all my time on the phone. I'm going to have to beg Patty for more shifts to pay my long-distance bills. My heart thuds uncontrollably in my chest. Julie doesn't know if she can do this. Damn. This is it. I know exactly what she's going to say. She can't do this, she's going to break up with me. "Oh," I say, falling from a high-wire. Plummeting to my death.

"It hurts too much."

"Oh." Hitting bottom.

"Doesn't it hurt you?"

"Yes." It hurts so much I can't stand it. If she breaks up with me, I'm going to throw myself off the Golden Gate Bridge.

"I want to come out there for a visit," Julie says.

"You do?"

"I want to see you."

"Oh god, Julie."

"What is it?"

"Oh god."

"Nomi, what is it?"

"I thought you were going to break up with me."

"Break up with you? No." She sounds frantic. "Is that what you want?"

"No. I want to be with you. Julie, I want to marry you." Oh my god. Did I just say that? Oh god. What a stupid move. Now I'll probably scare her right off. What a putz I am. Too serious, too fast.

"You do?"

"Yeah," I muster, holding my breath.

"Nomi, are you asking me to marry you?"

"Yeah. No. Well, maybe." Shit. I'm not sure what to say now.

"Oh, Nomi. You're crazy. I miss you so much."

"When do you want to come out here?"

"Right now."

We both laugh. "Yeah, but when really?"

"I don't know. As soon as possible. I'll have to ask for time off work. I could take a week, plus two weekends, before and after . . . that's nine days altogether."

"Julie, that would be so great."

"Yeah?"

"Yeah. Oh, except . . ."

"What?"

"Well, uh . . . I'm still crashing on Betty's couch. Uh, I'd have to ask her if it's okay with her . . . or maybe I can find somewhere else for us to stay. Somewhere with more . . . privacy."

"We could stay at a B & B or something."

"Well . . . Patty, my boss, has a two-bedroom. She uses the second room as kind of a den. I could ask if we can stay there while you're here. What do you think?"

"That sounds all right . . ."

"She'll say yes. She's so thrilled that I met someone. She's dying to meet you. All my friends are. Except when you come, I want to keep you indoors and all to myself."

"Oh yeah?"

"Yeah."

"Nomi?"

"Yeah?"

"Is your Uncle Solly really in the Mob?"

"Oh." I laugh. "Well, yeah. But not like the Mafia. Not the Italian Mob. The Jewish Mob."

"There's a Jewish Mob?"

"Sure. You didn't know?"

"No."

"Sure. Well, I think he used to be. I don't know if he's still in.

It's not like I walked up and asked him. Solly's full of stories, some are true, some aren't. Who knows what he's really up to. I heard once, though, that in the forties . . ."

"Nomi," she cuts me off.

"Yeah?"

"Shut up and kiss me."

"Oh god, Julie, I wish I could."

"You will."

"When?"

"Soon."

Yiddish Glossary

BALEBOOSTEH: An excellent and praiseworthy homemaker, a good wife.

BAR MITZVAH: The ceremony held in the synagogue when a boy reaches thirteen. The boy learns and recites a passage from the Torah, which signifies that he is becoming a man, an adult. Usually followed by a celebration.

BUBBE: Grandmother.

CHALLAH: A braided loaf of egg bread.

CHASSIDIC: Refers to a sect of Jewish mystics founded in Poland during the eighteenth century. Groups of their descendants live in several large North American cities and maintain their traditional ways of dressing and following Jewish law.

CHUPA: A special canopy held over the bride and groom during the wedding ceremony.

FEH: Exclamatory expression of disgust: "Phew!" "Ugh!" "Phooey!"

GEFILTE FISH: Ground fish cakes.

GONIFF: Thief, crook, dishonest businessman; a shady, tricky character it would be wise not to trust.

KEEPAH: Skullcap. Small head covering, worn by men, to remind them that God is always above. Observant Jewish men wear a keepah always, less observant men wear one only in synagogue.

KLUTZ: Clumsy person.

KNISHES: Dumplings filled with groats, grated potatoes, onions, chopped liver, chopped beef or cheese.

KUGEL: Egg noodle casserole.

LATKES: Potato pancakes.

L'CHAIM: Literally, "To Life." A toast when drinking wine.

MACHER: Big shot. A real operator. Someone who arranges, fixes, has connections, a big wheel. Someone who is active in an organization, like the zealous president of the Sisterhood or the PTA.

MAMELAH: Term of endearment for a girl.

MANISCHEWITZ: Brand name. Manufacturers of kosher products, such as sweet red wine, matzah meal, instant soup mix.

MATZAH: Unleavened bread, like a large cracker.

MATZAH BALLS: Balls formed from a dough of matzah meal and eggs, then boiled and added to chicken soup.

MATZAH MEAL: Crumbs made from matzah, used in place of bread crumbs.

MAZEL TOV: Good luck, congratulations.

MENSCH: A good person. Someone who is honest, fair and kind.

MISHUGENAH: Crazy.

MOMZER: Bastard.

NU?: An expression approximating "So?" "Well?"

OY: A cry, used to express anything from ecstasy to horror.

OY VEY: Literally means "oh pain," but is used as an all-purpose expression to mean anything from trivial delight to abysmal woe.

OY YOY YOY: Same as oy, only more so.

PISHER: Little kid.

PUTZ: Stupid, ignorant person; a fool, a jerk, an easy mark.

SCHLEMIEL: A foolish person, a simpleton, a born loser, a social misfit.

SCHLEP: To drag.

SCHMUCK: Literally, slang for penis; an idiot, a jerk.

SHAH: An order to be quiet; a command to "shut up."

SHIKSA: Non-Jewish woman.

SHOLOM ALEICHEM: "Peace unto you."

TATELAH: Term of endearment for a boy.

TZURIS: Troubles, woes, suffering.

YARMULKE: Skullcap (*see also* keepah).

YUTZ: A loser.

ZAYDE: Grandfather.

Acknowledgements

There are many people who helped in the creation of this book.

A huge appreciation to Della McCreary, Barbara Kuhne, Andrea Imada and Mary Watt of Press Gang Publishers for editing, support, promotion and the million and one other things publishers do every day.

Thanks to Ann Decter for insightful editing, Sheila Norgate for the gorgeous cover art, Val Speidel for her design, and Daniel Collins for the author photo.

Thanks to Dr. Alan Cantwell for answering questions about AIDS and explaining his theory on the origin of AIDS, as outlined in his books *AIDS and the Doctors of Death* and *Queer Blood*, both published by Aries Rising Press, from which I gathered information and paraphrased sections. And to Dr. Leonard Horowitz, author of *Emerging Viruses: AIDS and Ebola—Nature, Accident or Genocide?*, which was also valuable to my background research. *And the Band Played On*, by Randy Shilts, gave me additional insight into the politics of the AIDS crisis.

Thanks to Janice Linton, librarian at the Pacific AIDS Resource Centre library, a program of AIDS Vancouver, and to Jeff Gray, Treatment Information Counsellor at the British Columbia Persons with AIDS Society, for assisting me with information on current HIV treatments.

Nisa Donnelly, Jess Wells, Bruce Hillier, Keith Stuart and James Johnstone read early drafts of this book and offered editorial suggestions. My parents, Jack and Marion, helped with Yiddish words and information on Jewish weddings. Lucy Jane Bledsoe published the original short story "Love Ruins Everything" in her anthology *Heatwave: Women in Love and Lust*.

Lisa McArthur, Maike Engelbrecht, Lois Fine, Tova Fox, Arlene Tully, Chea Villanueva, David Maelzer, Shirl Reynolds, Trigger and Dianne Whelan provided support, encouragement and friendship.

Dix, Rachel Pepper, Nisa Donnelly, Jess Wells, Matt Bernstein

Sycamore, Robert Thomson and Wayne Fitton assisted with research. Richard Banner and Victoria Chan bailed me out of countless computer nightmares.

Arigatō to my fiancée, Terrie Akemi Hamazaki, who continues to offer inspiration, love and encouragement. I thank her for her patience when I had deadlines to meet and had to work long and late, sometimes even on a Saturday night when we were supposed to be having a romantic date.

Oh, and thanks to Charlie Tulchinsky-Hamazaki for being a cat.

About the Author

KAREN X. TULCHINSKY is the award-winning author of *In Her Nature*, a collection of short stories. She is co-editor of *Queer View Mirror 1 & 2: Lesbian & Gay Short Short Fiction*, and *Tangled Sheets*, and is the editor of *Hot & Bothered: Short Short Fiction of Lesbian Desire*. She also co-authored "Across the Lines," published in the Lambda Award-winning *Sister & Brother: Lesbians and Gay Men Talk About Their Lives Together*. She has written for numerous magazines including *Curve, Diva, The Georgia Straight, Look West* and the *Lambda Book Report*. Karen lives, writes and teaches creative writing in Vancouver, Canada. *Love Ruins Everything* is her first novel.

PRESS GANG PUBLISHERS has been producing vital and provocative books by women since 1975. For a complete catalogue, write to Press Gang Publishers, #101-225 East 17th Avenue, Vancouver, B.C. V5V 1A6 Canada or visit us online at http://www.pressgang.bc.ca